Enjoy This Title

The Nashua Public Library is free to all
cardholders. If you live, work, pay taxes,
or are a full-time student in Nashua you
qualify for a library card.

Increase the library's usefulness by returning
material on or before the 'date due.'

If you've enjoyed your experience with
the library and its many resources and
services, please tell others.

Nashua Public Library
2 Court Street, Nashua, NH 03060
603-589-4600, www.nashua.lib.nh.us

GAYLORD RG

Vineyard Stalker

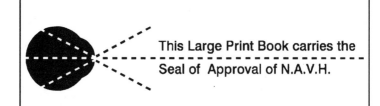

This Large Print Book carries the
Seal of Approval of N.A.V.H.

A MARTHA'S VINEYARD MYSTERY

VINEYARD STALKER

PHILIP R. CRAIG

THORNDIKE PRESS

An imprint of Thomson Gale, a part of The Thomson Corporation

Detroit • New York • San Francisco • New Haven, Conn. • Waterville, Maine • London

LIBRARY OF CONGRESS CATALOGING-IN-PUBLICATION DATA

Craig, Philip R., 1933–
    Vineyard stalker : a Martha's Vineyard mystery / by Philip R. Craig.
        p. cm. — (Thorndike Press large print mystery)
    ISBN-13: 978-0-7862-9511-1 (alk. paper)
    ISBN-10: 0-7862-9511-2 (alk. paper)
    1. Jackson, Jeff (Fictitious character) — Fiction. 2. Private investigators — Massachusetts — Martha's Vineyard — Fiction. 3. Martha's Vineyard (Mass.) — Fiction. 4. Recluses — Fiction. 5. Large type books. I. Title.
PS3553.R23V535 2007b
813'.54—dc22   2007019798

Published in 2007 by arrangement with Scribner,
an imprint of Simon & Schuster, Inc.

Printed in the United States of America on permanent paper
10 9 8 7 6 5 4 3 2 1

For my grandchildren:
Jessica Harmon, Peter Harmon,
Riley Craig, Amelia Craig,
and Bailey Lynch

. . . There in the starless dark, the poise,
the hover
There with vast wings across the
canceled skies,
There in the sudden blackness,
the black pall
Of nothing, nothing, nothing —
nothing at all.

— ARCHIBALD MACLEISH

The End of the World

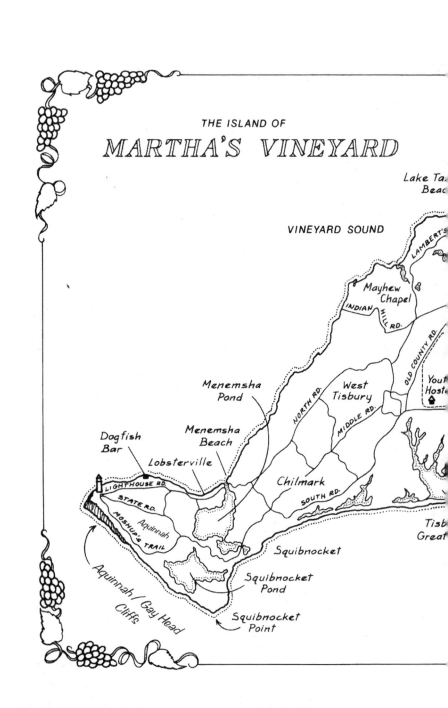

THE ISLAND OF

MARTHA'S VINEYARD

Lake Ta...
Beac...

VINEYARD SOUND

LAMBERT'S

Mayhew Chapel

INDIAN HILL RD.

OLD COUNTY RD.

Menemsha Pond

NORTH RD.

West Tisbury

MIDDLE RD.

You...
Host...

Menemsha Beach

Dogfish Bar

Lobsterville

Chilmark

SOUTH RD.

LIGHTHOUSE RD.

STATE RD.

Aquinnah

MOSHUP'S TRAIL

Squibnocket

Tisb...
Great

Squibnocket Pond

Aquinnah / Gay Head Cliffs

Squibnocket Point

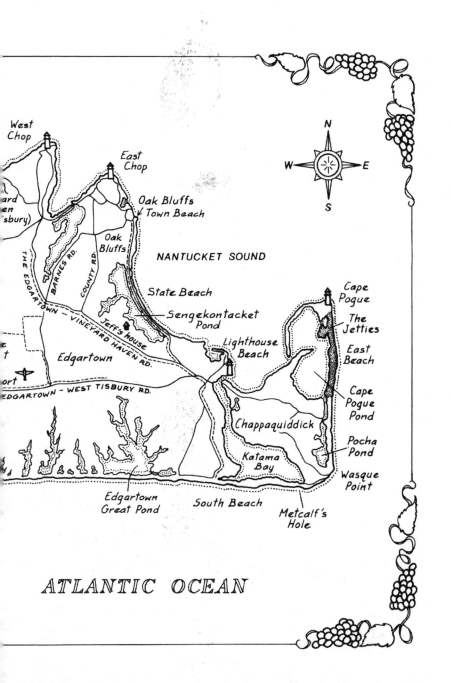

1

Zee and the kids had gone to America to visit Zee's parents in Fall River, so I was having breakfast in the Dock Street Coffee Shop listening to Chad Martin trying to decide just which of Martha's Vineyard's public institutions was the most maddening. "You could make an argument for the Registry of Motor Vehicles," said Chad between bites of sausage and eggs, "but lately the Registry seems a bit more rational than it was in the old days. Remember when we used to say that in order to work there you had to take an IQ test and fail it?"

"Yep." I nodded and kept eating.

"Well, nowadays you can say the same thing about those saps at the PO and the Steamship Authority."

"Oh, I don't know," I said. "The people I deal with at the counters seem pretty nice."

"Sure," said Chad, "but the bigwigs you never see are either dumb as sticks or they've dedicated their lives to ineptitude."

I gave him an admiring look. "Ineptitude, eh? That's a pretty impressive word for you to be throwing around this early in the morning."

Chad waved his fork. "You take the PO, now. You can start with the parking lot. The parking places are laid out so crazy that you have to park every which way and, when you try to leave, the poor damned pedestrians never know where a car's coming from and have to look every direction at once to keep from being run over. It's a miracle nobody's been killed yet."

"I'm not sure the PO owns the parking lot," I said.

"And because of that rotten drainage system," Chad went on, "whenever we get a good rain, half the lot turns into a pond a foot deep."

Lake Po was the popular name for it. It eliminated half the parking spaces in a lot that was already too small.

"And it's worse inside the building," said Chad, wiping his plate with the last of his toast. "You get other people's mail, they get yours; you get your packages back, sometimes two or three times, because somebody thinks the 'from' addresses are the 'to' addresses; you get yellow slips and after you stand in line for a half hour you find out there's no packages; or there's packages and no yellow slips; you get letters months after they were mailed, and some poor bastards have to pay penalties on overdue bills because they never got their bills at all!"

He looked at his own breakfast bill, dug out his wallet, and put money on the counter. "The lines are so long that people cheer when they don't get a yellow slip in their boxes. The poor bastards in the line talk about bringing somebody in there to sell coffee and doughnuts in the morning and martinis in the afternoon, and how somebody could make good money being a substitute line stander. They say they're going to have a contest about how to improve the service at the Edgartown post office, and the winner will get a PO box in West Tisbury. You want me to go on, J.W.?"

"I think that's enough for now."

"Next time we can talk about the Steamship Authority," said Chad. "Now there's a beast without a head. See ya later."

He walked out.

"The trouble is," said the waitress, as she took away his dishes and silverware, "that he's right."

"It's an imperfect world."

I glanced after the departing Chad and

saw a woman sitting at the far end of the counter looking at me. She was eating a bagel and an egg. I didn't know her and was surprised to see her pick up her cup and plate and come and sit beside me on what had been Chad's stool. I guessed her to be about fifty, although it's hard for me to tell women's ages these days when mothers sometimes look younger than their daughters. She was wearing a skirt and a summer shirt, and was a good-looking woman.

"You're J. W. Jackson," she said. "I'm Carole Cohen. I'm a friend of Zee's."

She put out her hand and I took it.

"She has a lot of friends," I said.

She got right to the point. "I have to be in the office later this morning, so I went by your house early. Nobody was there, but then I remembered Zee saying you came here for breakfast now and then. The waitress pointed you out and I've been waiting for your friend to leave. I need some help."

I was surprised. "What kind of help?"

"Zee's told me that you were in Vietnam," she said, "so I assume you must have gotten some combat training. She also said you were a policeman before you came to the island. She said that you can be trusted and I asked around and other people agree. I'd like to hire you to go up to my brother's place and keep an eye on things when he's sleeping. He's had some troubles. He needs to sleep sometime, but when he does he can't keep a watch himself."

"Who's your brother?"

"Roland Nunes. Maybe you know him. They call him the Monk."

I didn't know him but I had heard of him. He'd gone off to war full of the stuff that makes heroes but had come back so changed that his friends hardly knew him. He lived somewhere up in West Tisbury, I'd been told, and had gotten religion, although nobody seemed to know just what kind.

"I wasn't in 'Nam very long," I said. "I got hit on my first patrol and never went back."

"My brother was there a lot longer," she said. "Here's my problem: Somebody is coming around his place causing trouble and I'd like to know who it is. Whoever it is is sharp enough to stay out of sight until Roland's asleep. I want Roland to have some extra eyes and I'd like you to provide them. I can pay you a little money and I don't think the job should take too long. Just long enough for me to learn who the guy is. Once I know that I can handle things alone."

"What kind of trouble?" I asked.

"Somebody threw a dead skunk into Roland's water barrel, then sneaked into his garden and pulled up a lot of his vegetables. Then he set fire to Roland's shed. My brother smelled the smoke and put it out, but that was just luck. Whoever's doing all this seems to be getting more serious each time."

"You should call the cops."

"I don't want to involve the police. I don't want to hurt anybody, either. I just want Roland to be left alone."

I felt much the same way about not wanting to hurt anybody, but as for being alone I had had enough of that. I liked living with Zee, Joshua, and Diana and would be glad when they were home again.

"Like you said, I was a cop myself, once," I said. "Most of the cops I know are all right."

She nodded. "Zee told me you were on the Boston PD a few years back, but that you quit and came down here to live. She said it was because you were tired of saving the world. I can understand that. It's why I'd like to have you take this job. I don't want to hire somebody who takes pleasure in roughing people up. I just want a pair of eyes."

Carole Cohen's timing was good. I had a few days to myself and my house seemed too empty to live in, in spite of the two cats, Oliver Underfoot and Velcro, who also missed having Zee and the kids around.

"You have any idea who the guy is or why he's doing what he's doing?" I asked.

"It could be any one of several people," she said. "You know much about the so-called ancient ways here on the island?"

"Not much. I know they're old roads and paths that people used a long time back to get from here to there. And I know a lot of them have been closed off by new people who've bought land and don't want anybody crossing their expensive property."

She nodded. "When I was growing up here as a kid you could get to almost any beach to fish and you could hunt lots of places, but now more and more of the gates are locked. Did you know that there are 251 POSTED and NO TRESPASSING signs on that five-mile stretch of North Road between North Tisbury and Menemsha?"

"I know there are a lot, but I never counted them."

"I did, one day when I was going up to Menemsha. Some places there are two on the same tree. The point is that those signs and the locked gates and the closed ancient

17

ways are all part of the same big change on the Vineyard: people with money wanting to close off spaces that used to be open." She finished her bagel, and added, with a touch of irony, "I should know. I'm in real estate."

It's an island joke that there are fifteen thousand year-round residents of Martha's Vineyard and fourteen thousand of them are in real estate.

Zee and I don't like NO TRESPASSING signs and have none on our property, and my least favorite land preservation group, the Marshall Lea Foundation, is known to me as the No Foundation because it puts signs up on many of its properties announcing no picnicking, no hunting, no fishing, no hiking or biking or trespassing of any kind. A pox upon the No Foundation.

I thought those signs on that stretch of North Road were about the ugliest sights on Martha's Vineyard, but on the other hand, I don't like it when people tell me how to live my life, so I had to accept the right of the North Road property owners and the No Foundation to post as many signs as they saw fit. Of course it wasn't the signs themselves that most offended me; it was the people who put them up. I imagined I felt the way old-time free-range cattle and sheep men felt when people began to put

18

up fences.

"You think the guy who's bothering your brother is one of those people who put up the signs and fences?" I asked.

"Maybe." She watched while the waitress refilled our coffee cups, then said, "My brother has an ancient way running through his property and on into the state forest. He didn't know it was there when he built his house, but he likes the idea of it and he plans to keep it open. Sometimes people come by, following it, and they're usually surprised to find him living there.

"The thing is, we've got a cousin, Sally Oliver. You may have read about her. She's the family athlete."

"No."

"A triathloner. You know: bikes, swims, then runs a marathon, or something like that. Anyway, her mother, who was my aunt, and my brother were very close, and she had opposed the Vietnam War from the beginning. She bought that land when he finally came home from the war and created a trust with a covenant that he could live there as long as he wanted.

"But when my aunt died Sally became the trustee, and now Sally wants to sell the land but Roland doesn't want to move. When he dies, she'll get the land, but she doesn't want to wait. I've offered to buy her out, but she's gotten better offers from other people who want to build another McMansion right where he lives."

"People who'll close off the ancient way."

"That's what usually happens."

"And you think this prowler is an agent for one of those buyers?"

"A couple of people interested in the land are abutters, but there are others."

"Maybe your cousin Sally is behind the vandalizers."

"Whoever it is is getting nervier. Roland has to be away from the house during working hours, and lately I half expect to hear that his house has been burned down while he's been gone."

"Maybe your brother should go the charitable route and sell to the Land Bank with the stipulation that he has life residency rights and that the ancient way stays open."

"He can't sell the land because he doesn't own it. The trust does. Besides, other people have a lot more money than the Land Bank and Sally isn't going to sell to the Land Bank when she can make a lot more money elsewhere."

I finished my coffee, looked at my bill, and put some money on the counter. "I think you should definitely get the police in on this," I said. "If nothing else, they can ask your brother's neighbors and your cousin some questions and let them know that they're interested in what's going on. That could be enough to scare off this vandal, because nobody likes to have the cops keeping an eye on him."

Carole Cohen put money beside mine, finished her coffee, and said, "Let's step outside."

We went out onto Dock Street and crossed to the parking lot. The lot was already beginning to fill even though it was early morning, because parking spaces in Edgartown are hard to find in the summer. In the channel beyond the yacht club, on the south end of the lot, sailboats were riding a following wind out into Nantucket Sound. On the Reading Room side of the lot, boats were being loaded with people and gear in preparation for trips to the fishing grounds. Beyond them, on her stake, bobbed our own catboat, the *Shirley J.*

We stopped where nobody was near.

"You're right about people not liking cops keeping an eye on them," said the woman, "and that includes my brother."

"Nobody likes it," I said. "Not even innocent people like it."

"My brother isn't exactly innocent," said

Carole Cohen in a quiet voice. "He went AWOL in Vietnam almost forty years ago and he never went back. As far as the army is concerned, he's still missing in action and legally dead, but what he really is is a deserter. I don't think anybody's looking for him and I don't want them to. That's why I don't want the police involved."

She had surprised me for a second time in half an hour, because the gossip about the Monk was that he'd been a Green Beret, a warrior who'd done tour after tour, a sniper with a trunk full of medals who had returned home a hero.

"Do you tell this to a lot of people?" I asked.

"Not many. The only other person who knows about it is Jed Mullins. He was with Roland in Vietnam and now he lives in Vineyard Haven. They were pals over there. I think Roland saved his life once. He won't be telling anybody anything that would hurt Roland."

"Don't you think you're taking a chance telling me? You don't even know me."

"I know Zee and I've talked with people. And now I've seen you and I think I can trust you." She gave me a thin smile. "Besides, if you go to work for me, we need to be honest with one another."

22

"If the army can't account for him, how come they haven't come here looking for him?"

"Because he apparently disappeared in combat and then he stayed away for almost ten years before he came home. By the time he got here the army had decided he was probably dead and had other things to do than look for him. If anybody asked him, Roland told people he'd never been missing at all; that there'd been one of those paperwork mix-ups and that he'd been honorably discharged. The people he told believed him and the people they told believed them. After a while, it was common knowledge." She smiled again. "Like George Washington and the cherry tree."

"You'd better not enlighten your cousin Sally or those other people who want his land," I said. "I doubt if his secret will be safe with them."

"I agree. Sally doesn't know anything about it. The thing is that both Ford and Carter offered clemency to deserters in the mid-seventies and since then, until lately, the army just filed its old cases. But now they've got this new war and soldiers are heading for Canada every day, so some of the old cases are being activated to discourage more desertions. I'd like to settle this matter before anybody starts digging around in Roland's past, looking for leverage to make him sell. Well, what do you say? Can I hire you? I figure it shouldn't take more than a few days to catch this guy in the act and ID him. After that you'll be out of a job again."

Zee and the children would be gone for another week, and I was bored. Very bored.

"All right," I said, making yet another of the many mistakes in my life.

2

Roland Nunes lived in West Tisbury, in a tiny one-room house in a meadow reached by a narrow path. I parked my old Land Cruiser on the side of the paved road behind Carole Cohen's Volvo, and we walked to the house together.

"Where's your brother now?" I asked.

"He works as a carpenter. He needs money, but not much."

"If he's working days, the prowler must know it. Why doesn't he come by when your brother's away?"

"As I told you, I'm afraid he may do just that, but so far he hasn't. Maybe because I stop by now and then and he's afraid I'll see him. Or maybe he's afraid someone else will see him. Up till now he's only come at night after Roland's gone to sleep."

A night visitor, but not one of Amahl's.

"This trail isn't wide enough for a car," I said.

"You could probably get one of those old VW bugs in here if you didn't mind scratching it up a bit. My brother rides a moped. He used to use a bike, but he's modernized."

Roland Nunes, the modernized Monk.

The path, she said, was part of the ancient way she'd mentioned. It led across her brother's meadow, past his house and shed and garden, across a lovely little stream, and on into the state forest. On either side of his land were the private holdings owned by people who had offered to buy out him and his cousin. There were fences not of Nunes's making marking the boundaries.

When we reached the meadow, she gave me a tour. Roland Nunes's one-room cabin was made of mud and wattle and was roofed with thatch, and when I saw it I thought of Innisfree, although there was no lake near, only the stream on the far side of the meadow, flowing south as most streams do on Martha's Vineyard. As far as I knew, it was the only cabin of its kind on the island. It had a packed dirt floor covered with woven rushes and sporting a large, much worn, oriental rug, along with other possessions Nunes had probably salvaged from the Dumptique, the tiny "store" at the West Tisbury dump.

I was also fond of the Dumptique, where good, usable stuff was saved instead of being buried in the West Tisbury landfill by the ardent environmentalists who believed that dump picking was unhealthy and immoral. Once, every island village had a dump like Edgartown's Big D, a store where everything was free and you could return your purchases, no questions asked, if not satisfied, and where a lot of people got materials to build and furnish their houses. Then the antilandfill people had put an end to that golden age, and dump picking had stopped everywhere but in West Tisbury where a few hearty women had created and still maintained the Dumptique, one of the island's glories.

There was a double cot against one wall of Nunes's little house, from which I thought I detected the faint scent of lavender. Hmmmm. On another wall, above a small table and a single wooden chair there was a shelf with a half dozen books, and there was a counter on a third wall that held a small propane stove, a washbasin, and a bucket. On the wall above the counter were shelves holding mouse-proof containers, a few pieces of china, some silverware and ceramic cups, a few pots and pans, and some glass jars of food. On the fourth wall were pegs holding a winter coat and shirts and a shelf holding other clothing, towels, and a pair of heavy boots. Against the wall was a small wooden chest. In one corner of the room was a coal- and wood-burning heater, the only defense against the cold of winter.

The one window and the door of the cabin had no doubt also been salvaged from the West Tisbury dump.

There was no electricity or telephone. There were no kerosene lamps, only a half dozen thick candles for light.

Pretty austere. No wonder they called him the Monk.

Behind the house was a fire-blackened mud and wattle shed that held his ax, a shovel, and a rake, and also served as a garage for his moped. On a shelf were mouse-and-squirrel-proof plastic containers of seeds and a small collection of hand and garden tools. Beyond the shed was an outhouse.

Nunes got his water from an outside hand pump attached to a pipe driven down to the water table, and he stored a supply in a barrel where the dead skunk had been deposited.

According to his sister, he had hand-dug his well down through the sandy soil almost to the water table using a borrowed rotary posthole digger with a handle that could be lengthened by attaching additional lengths of pipe to it. When the sides of the hole began to collapse as fast as he dug, he put a well point on the end of a pipe and drove the pipe on down to the water table using a pipe driver borrowed from the same man who'd loaned him the posthole digger, an aging ex-employee of the Edgartown Water Company, who had taken the tools with him when he retired. It pays to know oldtimers.

Nunes's garden was neat but showed the damage of which his sister had spoken, since some rows of vegetables held only a few plants where clearly there had been many others. Nunes had replanted the rows, but not much was coming up yet.

"How does he keep the deer away?" I asked.

Carole Cohen pointed as the answer came around a corner of the house in the form of a large, black cat. "Mr. Mephistopheles gets credit for that. Deer don't seem to like the smell of a cat, and Mr. Mephistopheles marks his territory every day."

"Our cats do the same, and we don't have deer problems either."

Mr. Mephistopheles yawned hello and lay down in a sunny spot.

Beside the garden, mounted on a short pole, was what looked something like a large birdhouse. I recognized it immediately.

"I saw these in 'Nam," I said. "I haven't seen one since."

"Yes," she said. "A spirit house. Roland told me he liked them when he saw them there and in Thailand, and he thought it would be good to have one here." She walked with me to the miniature house and indicated its contents. Inside the single room were a tiny stone Buddha and another small stone carving of a god I didn't recognize.

"Vishnu in the form of an elephant," she said. "He told me he got the Buddha in Vietnam and the Vishnu in India. And because it couldn't hurt, I put my mother's rosary in there, too. See it?"

"Yes."

In front of the little house was a narrow porch upon which were a small vase of wildflowers and a burner holding smoking incense.

"I don't know much about these houses," I said.

She shrugged. "I think the idea is to give a home to the spirits. Roland says he's not very religious, but he likes the notion of spirits and brings them flowers and incense for their pleasure. In return, he says, they keep an eye on his garden."

"They didn't stop the guy from tearing it up."

"No, but Roland says that may be his fault because he's lived a very imperfect life."

"Most of us have."

I looked around and could understand why someone would like to buy the place. The meadow was gently rolling, the trees around it moved gently in the wind. The sound of the stream dancing over rocks was like the distant laughter of women.

At the foot of the meadow where the stream passed beyond Nunes's land and flowed on into the forest there was a small pond that had once powered a mill of some kind. A hundred and fifty years before, there had been small mills on many of the island's streams, but none I knew of remained operational, although the West Tisbury mill, across the road from its millpond, looked like it could be put back into working order if you wanted to spend a bit of money.

On the far side of Nunes's millpond was a low hillside consisting of a deposit of clay that Nunes had mined for the walls of his house and shed.

I studied the house.

"Where'd he learn to build like this?" I asked.

"He says anyone can do it," she said with a small smile.

I doubted that, but many people who can do things well wrongly think that everybody could do it, if only they decided to. They seem to feel that it's only a matter of desire and the learning of the craft, when in fact it's also a matter of talent. As my professorial friend John Skye says, "You can teach someone how to paint, but you can't teach him how to be Rembrandt." I suggested this to Carole Cohen and she made a small acquiescent gesture.

"I think your friend is probably right. When Roland left Vietnam he traveled west through Asia and Europe, and he saw houses made like this. He talked with people who built them and then, when he got here and was living in a pup tent, he found this clay deposit and realized that he had the materials available to build one for himself for almost nothing.

"He told me he went to the library and read more about mud and wattle, then went over to Plymouth and found a man — an old Scot — who taught him how to thatch, then came back here and found grasses and reeds he could use for that. He knew he had to have a good, overhanging roof, because mud and wattle walls won't stand up to rain. Have you ever seen the ruins of the abbeys in England?"

"I've never been to England."

"You'll go someday. When you get there, visit Glastonbury or Tintern or any of the other ruins and you'll see that there are only broken walls left. When Henry VIII broke with the Catholic Church, the abbeys were rich and powerful institutions and he wanted them under his control, so he removed the lead roofs of those that resisted him, and without the roofs, the buildings very rapidly became ruins." She gestured at her brother's house. "A mud and wattle building is susceptible to the same forces, only more so; Roland worked hard to become a good thatcher."

"And he succeeded."

"He said there was a lot of trial and error at first, but he had time and he still had the pup tent to live in and he liked the work. He built the shed first and moved in there while he worked on the house. When he got a wall built he'd cover it with sheets of plastic or canvas that he got from the sites where he worked before it got toted off to the dump. Then he'd build another wall and do the same again until the place was ready to roof. He cut and dried straight young trees for beams and trimmed them with a broad ax, and when he had them in place he thatched the roof. He says that a good thatched roof should last fifty or sixty years, and that's longer than he'll need one."

"He did everything by hand. Why?"

"He says he wanted to simplify his life. But he's not a purist and he didn't try to go back to the Stone Age. He uses metal tools and he has a propane stove, and he had that bicycle for transportation before he got his moped." She made a gesture that took in the whole of his land. "He says this is almost all he wants or needs."

I thought of the double cot, but only said, "He must not have a lot of guests. There's only one chair in the cabin."

"No, he likes being alone. He says he listens a lot."

I became aware of the wind's sigh and the faint laughter of the stream. "Modern house building can be a noisy business," I said. "I can understand how he'd like these sounds when he comes home."

She looked at me. "I don't think he minds the sounds of work. I think he's still escaping the sound of war. Does that make any sense? He left Vietnam over thirty years ago."

I still sometimes dream of the mortar attack on my first and only patrol. The incredible noise of it and the flying dirt and leaves and broken branches and body parts shock me out of sleep and I wake sweating and making some sort of sound and find Zee holding me and saying, "It's all right, it's only a dream, we're here in our bed and I have you in my arms."

"It's possible," I said. "He must confide in you quite a bit."

"I'm his sister. I make him talk to me. I'm a bully." She smiled and her whole face became younger.

"Does he have any friends?"

"He's a very friendly person."

"That's not quite the same thing."

"I don't know much about his friends, but he must have them."

"Tell me about his life."

"I don't know what you mean."

"What does he do when he's not working or gardening? Does he go to places where there's music? Does he have a beer now and then? I didn't see a radio in the cabin, so I don't think he listens to the Sox games. What does he do? Tell me about that."

"I guess I don't know much about his life. I always think of him as being right here, living very quietly. Why do you ask?"

"Because this person who's bothering him may be from that life and have nothing to do with your cousin or the people who want his land."

She frowned. "I didn't think of that. I suppose it's possible. But I'm willing to bet that Sally or some would-be buyer is behind the trouble."

"You don't care for Sally, I take it."

There was iron in her voice. "Would you care for someone who was working hard to take away your brother's home?"

"Probably not. How does Roland feel about her?"

She sighed. "Roland doesn't criticize anybody. Never. That's one reason they call him the Monk. He's too gentle for his own good. Did you ever hear the story about the angel who had his eyes put out by an evil creature, then later risked his life to save the creature from some horrible fate? When he was asked why he did that, he replied that angels have no memories. Roland is like that. It's as though he can't imagine evil intent."

"Do you think your cousin Sally is evil?"

"Oh, I don't know. Maybe that's too strong a word. I know she got in trouble once for beating up another triathlon contender, but if she's behind this guy who's

36

stalking my brother she's doing an evil thing!"

I had been running my eyes around the perimeter of Nunes's property.

"What is it you want me to do here?"

"I want you to spend a few nights keeping watch. If you see the man who's been doing these things, I want you to find out who he is. That's all you have to do. I'll take it from there."

"I may be able to spot him, but unless I apprehend him it'll be hard to identify him."

"I have some things that should make your job easier. They're in my car. Have you seen all you need to here? I wanted you to know the terrain before it got dark."

"I've seen enough for now," I said.

We walked back out to her car, and she pointed across the paved road at a narrow opening in the scrub oak. "There's where the ancient way continues on a little way. There's a gate across it about thirty yards in. Another sign of modern times." She got a pair of binoculars and a camera out of her car and handed them to me.

"These are both for night work," she said. "They belong to Jordan, my husband. Some infrared principle, don't ask me what. You can spot him with the glasses and then get his picture without him even knowing it.

After you get his picture you can scream and yell at him and scare him away before he does any damage. The next day I'll know what he looks like and a little later my lawyer will be having a talk with him, and that will be that."

"Simple," I said. "Does your brother know what you're having me do?"

"I'll tell him this morning before I go on to the office."

"Maybe you should ask him, not tell him."

"No," she said, firmly. "I'll tell him. I want this business to stop. Now. Before it really turns ugly."

3

I went home and spent the rest of my day with the cats, who, between rests in the summer sun, followed me about wondering when the rest of the family would be home. I worked in the garden for a while, then got on the roof of the house and tried yet again to find and repair the pesky leak that happened every time we had a heavy rain driven by a northeast wind. I had been fighting that leak for years and had never found it. One reason for this failure was, of course, that the leak only leaked when it was raining and my chances of locating it during a storm were almost as low as finding it between storms. I tarred a few places I hadn't tarred before, and hoped I was right this time. Maybe I should hire Roland Nunes to thatch us a roof. The kids would like that.

Back on the ground I sat in a lawn chair with the night glasses and camera and read the printed matter that came with them.

The glasses were easy but all cameras are a challenge to me, so I studied its papers seriously. Both items apparently had come from one of those spy supply places that will sell you whatever you need to pry into other people's lives and avoid the long arm of the law. In this case, the camera promised you a good black-and-white night photo at up to a hundred feet, with the subject never being aware that his picture was being taken. It had a portable power source that allowed you to take it with you wherever you went.

I diddled with it until I thought I knew how to turn it on and off and how to focus it. Then, since it was a warm and sunny day, I had a Sam Adams and some crackers with bluefish pâté and thought about the night to come. Carole Cohen's plan was so simple that it might actually work; however, many a simple plan has turned to dust when put into action and I didn't want to become dust.

Oliver Underwood and Velcro trailed me out into the yard and, after a few leg rubs, lay down in the shade of the yard table, sharing and increasing my loneliness for my family. My children were changing so fast that I didn't like missing even a week of their lives. I thought of the Monk living alone for more than thirty years and wondered how he'd managed it. Even during the years when I'd been between wives and was living here in the woods, I'd not been bereft of friends of both genders. The Monk was apparently made of sterner stuff. Or, I thought, remembering the fragrance of lavender, perhaps not.

After an early supper, I put the glasses and camera into a small backpack, along with a sweater, some dried fruit, a water bottle, and a flashlight, then I got into dark clothes and drove to West Tisbury. I parked a hundred yards down the road from the ancient way so the prowler, if he came by that way, wouldn't associate my truck with the Monk, and walked back to the path. The sun was low in the west and my shadow was cast before me as I went down the path into the meadow.

As I reached the house, a man emerged from the ancient way coming out of the woods beyond the stream. He crossed the water on the granite stepping-stones laid down there decades before and came to meet me.

He was about sixty-five years old, I guessed, and was very sun-bronzed and lean. He wore khaki clothing and sandals and a floppy-brimmed hat. No saffron robe. He walked with a comfortable stride, neither fast nor slow. He was carrying a hatchet and there was a canvas bag hung from his shoulder.

"You must be J. W. Jackson," he said, with a smile. "I'm Roland Nunes."

We shook hands. His was thin and strong, the hand of a worker.

"Your sister has given me a job," I said.

"Yes, so she tells me. I hope her plan works, but even if nobody shows up tonight I'll be able to get some sleep that I need."

"I'll try to keep the peace."

"Have you eaten? I have bread and fresh vegetables." He gestured back toward the woods. "And I've just found mushrooms enough for two."

His voice was gentle but rich and his bottomless eyes were impossible for me to read. He seemed totally at ease.

"I've eaten," I said, "but you go on with your meal. I'll try not to intrude on you while I'm here."

"It's no intrusion," he replied. "I rarely have guests but I'm glad to have one when it happens. I don't have much here in the way of creature comforts, I'm afraid, but you're welcome to what there is."

"What I'd like to do is walk the circumference of your property to get a better notion of where this prowler might be coming from. Then I want to find the best spot to wait for him."

He made a slight bow. "Very good. It would please me to talk with you when you return from your explorations." He pointed a hand to the east. "There's an old stone wall just inside the woods there beyond the stream. It leads down yonder around the mill pond and it marks the end of my land in that direction." He pointed north and south. "There are new fences there and there, built by my neighbors, and the paved road is my western border. It's almost seven acres, all told." He gave me an amused, crooked smile. "It was cheap when my aunt got it, but it's valuable real estate these days. No wonder people covet it."

"I have a few acres of my own. My father bought them when nobody wanted to live in that part of the woods. Now I pay a lot of taxes just for owning it."

"Yes, taxes," he said with no resentment in his voice. "I'm fortunate in that my land is in trust and the trust pays the taxes. If I had to pay them, I might have to move and let my cousin sell the place."

"I can't do anything about my taxes," I said, "but maybe I can help out with your prowler."

Another small bow. "I hope you'll have

tea with me when you finish your reconnaissance."

I could feel his eyes on my back as I walked back toward the paved road.

There was an old stone wall paralleling the road. It was low and gray and covered with lichen, and it was greatly fallen down, unlike many of the island's other walls which were now being built and rebuilt at great cost by the many stone workers whose craft had become fashionable among the wealthier islanders. When I was a boy, a good stone wall builder was rare, but now there were dozens of them, some working for the same rich employer for years as his stone fences stretched farther and farther around his land and between his fields.

There was so much stone work being done on the Vineyard that they had to import the rock. I knew because I'd talked with a local guy who also owned a farm in New Hampshire that produced only stone. He had a contract with a big outfit to mine it, and every time a truck full of rock left the farm, the guy made a few dollars; and once, he said, while he was waiting in line in Woods Hole, to catch the ferry to the Vineyard, he'd seen one of those very trucks boarding ahead of him. The island was a rocky place, but not rocky enough to supply the demand of the stone workers.

I followed the wall until I came to — what else? — a new stone wall defining the property line of Nunes's neighbor. The new wall was high and beautifully constructed, a far cry from the old, rough, utilitarian one I'd been following.

It was possible but unlikely, I thought, that the prowler came in from the road. If he parked a vehicle, it would be seen; if he walked from some far parking area, he'd still have to avoid being seen by some night driver.

I walked east along the new wall, admiring its workmanship while looking for any indication that someone had come over it. I saw no such suggestion, and though I am no Abraham Mahsimba I can cut a little sign if required.

The stream bubbled out from under the wall through a nicely shaped stone arch as it entered Nunes's land. I crossed it with the help of a fallen log and went into the woods on the far side until I came to the old wall Nunes had mentioned. Here it was harder to tell just where an intruder might have entered since the wall was so old and broken that it offered no interference to any traveler, coming or going, and because much of the ground was covered with leaves and needles that could hide the footprints of any careful walker.

But what walker could be so careful at night, when he could show no light to guide his way and could only guess when he disturbed the earth with his step? We'd had recent rain, and I saw no spoor as I walked between the trees and around patches of undergrowth, stopping often to study the ground and look around me for whatever the prowler might have seen had he come this way.

When I came to the ancient way I noted no tracks. Even had there been some, I'd not have known whether they were those of the prowler or of some innocent walker of old trails.

I crossed the path and worked my way south, moving slowly, seeing no sign, until I came to the old mill pond. A pair of ducks watched me, then paddled across to the far side of the pond.

Evening was approaching, and birdsongs were beginning. As I listened I thought of Bonzo, my brain-damaged friend, who loved fishing and birdsong above all things, and of friends who had returned from Africa with stories of their wonder at the night sounds of the bush: the chatter and cheep and howls of monkeys and birds, the cow-like moo of hyenas, the bass grunts of hippos and the occasional trumpet of an elephant, the splash of crocs near the riverbank.

Circling the pond, I studied the soft soil surrounding it and finally, after recrossing the stream over the old mill gates in the dam, I found the sign I'd been seeking. The prowler had come onto Nunes's land from the woods to the south, along a path that followed the stream and led through the state forest behind the fenced land belonging to Nunes's southern neighbor. He'd then gone up through the meadow behind Nunes's outbuilding, done his work, and returned whence he'd come. Behind him, in a small patch of dirt he'd left a clear print of a medium-sized, low-heeled shoe that could have belonged to either a man or a woman. The soil was soft but the print wasn't too deep, which suggested someone of little weight. No matter, since small people could be as dangerous as large ones.

I followed his trail by the edge of the stream, along the old path that had probably originally led to the mill, and noted that the farther the intruder was from Nunes's land, the more careless he'd been with his track. A half mile or so to the south I came to the Edgartown–West Tisbury

Road, where the stream flowed through a culvert and bubbled on toward the Tisbury Great Pond.

There were houses in sight both ways along the road, and there were driveways leading off it to unseen homes. There was also room to park a car beside the stream, and there were hiding places for a moped or a bike.

It would be a good spot to wait for the intruder, and I wished I had a helper, someone to stay here with a walkie-talkie while I watched and waited with another one back at Nunes's place, but I didn't.

So I walked back along the path, listening to the tinkle and gurgle of the brook beside me, until I was again on Nunes's land. There I worked my way west along the new stone wall marking his southern neighbor's boundary and wondered if this neighbor was somehow engaged in a stone fence duel with the neighbor to the north, because this wall was even higher than the one I'd followed earlier. I imagined Frost looking at the walls with pixie grin and ironic eyes.

I found no sign that anyone had come over this new wall or over the old one paralleling the paved road, when I followed it back to the ancient way where I'd begun my circumnavigation of Nunes's land.

The only sign I'd cut was on that path along the brook. Unless I'd missed my guess, the prowler had always come in along that path and, since habit is strong and success leads to repetition of action, it was reasonable to presume he'd come that way again. As I walked to the house I thought of what I'd seen and not seen.

Nunes was seated on a mat in front of his house. He looked like pictures I'd seen of mystics seeking nirvana. He turned his head toward me as I approached and flowed to his feet, smiling.

"I'm about to have tea. Will you join me?"

"Tea sounds good."

He went into the house. I was double-checking the grounds when he came back out, carrying his single chair.

"Use this," he said. "Unless you're used to sitting on a mat, the ground can be uncomfortable."

He gave me the chair and went back inside. Moments later he returned carrying a pot and cups.

"It's green tea," he said. "I have no milk or sugar, I'm afraid."

"I don't need either, thanks."

He poured for both of us and then sank easily down onto his mat. The tea was mild and refreshing.

"Your face says you found something," he said.

No wonder I have so much trouble winning at poker.

"Yes," I said, and told him of my wandering and discovery.

"Ah," he said. "I've followed that path myself, more than once. It's a good back entrance to this place, as is the ancient way that goes east into the forest."

"The ancient way was clean of tracks. It's rained since your last walkers came through from there."

"Yes. It's been a few days, and we've had rains since. Have you decided where to wait for my visitor?"

"Yes." I pointed to the southern edge of the meadow. "That oak tree yonder will give me cover and a good view of your whole place, including the mill pond. If he comes I should see him and he shouldn't see me. If he gets close to the buildings I'll be able to get photos of him before he can do any damage, then I can do one of two things: I can make a racket and scare him off or I can take him down. Which do you prefer?"

The Monk didn't have to think that one over. "Make a racket," he said. "I've had enough of taking people down."

"Good," I said. "Me too."

"It can be chilly at night," said Nunes. "Do you want a blanket?"

"No," I said. "I'd rather be cold and awake than warm and asleep."

He nodded. "It's the choice I'd make." Then he smiled. "I plan to take advantage of you and sleep deep and warm."

"I won't mind. It's what I'd do in your place."

An hour later, as the sun disappeared, I took my spy gear and walked up to the oak tree.

4

The darkness came slowly and the birdsong gradually lessened and was replaced by the sounds of night creatures. When it was dark enough, I experimented with the glasses and camera and thought I could handle them.

I wondered who the prowler was and what his motives were. Was he just a vandal bent on terrorizing a lonely man in the woods, or was he, as Carole Cohen suspected, the agent of unscrupulous people after the Monk's land? Or was he someone else with an agenda as yet unknown to Carole or me? I wondered how much it would take to persuade him to take his business elsewhere.

I remembered an impeccable response to a threat. A large, young, and powerful lawyer, had, in the security of his own office, threatened a visitor with both lawsuits and physical mayhem. The visitor was a tiny, frail old man, without apparent resources, but in response to the lawyer's threats, he produced a small pistol and pointed it at the lawyer, saying that if any suit was filed or if he experienced any damage of any sort, he would immediately kill the lawyer. He pointed out that he was an old man without much longer to live anyway, so he wasn't afraid of the police or of a trial or of jail. The lawyer, rightly, believed him and never took action of any sort against him.

Too bad I didn't know who the prowler was and that that fearless old man wasn't with me.

I directed my glasses to the mill pond and thought of Grendel, descendant of Cain, cursed by God, who haunted the moors and wild marshes and came to Herot seeking blood. But I saw no one in the infrared night, and swept my eyes over all of the empty meadow before settling down for a long wait.

Above me the sky was filled with diamonds, but it was the dark of the moon and not even the light of many stars could brighten the landscape in front of me. In the darker darkness of the oak's shadow, I sat back against the tree, and listened to the music of the night: the hoot of an owl, the scurry of little creatures hurrying through the grass and leaves, the distant laughter of the stream.

Then a circle of light came dancing down the pathway leading to the house from the west. I lifted my glasses and saw that it was a woman with a flashlight making no effort to avoid being seen. She went to the cabin and knocked. A moment later Nunes opened the door and stepped out. She spoke and he replied. She gestured toward the open door and they went in. Some time later, they reappeared. They spoke and after a bit she touched his arm and walked up the path, following the circle of light back toward the highway. He looked after her, then glanced my way, then went back into the house.

So that explained the fragrance of lavender.

The woman definitely was not the prowler, but it was still a good night for a prowler to prowl and it was therefore important for me not to get too comfortable; somehow, however, I managed to doze off anyway, because when I jerked awake and hurriedly put my night glasses to my eyes I saw Grendel coming, moving through the night, full of hate, up from the swampland, sliding silently toward the great hall where Beowulf's men slept.

But of course it was not Grendel creeping toward Herot, it was a smaller creature, a human being, dressed in dark clothing as I was, moving confidently across the meadow behind the Monk's house. Was it a man or a woman? I couldn't tell, because the person's face was smeared with black, and the individual wore a dark, hair-hiding, stocking cap.

In one hand the prowler was carrying an infrared flashlight that accounted for his or her assured movement over the dark meadow. In the other was a small canvas case. As the prowler came closer, I set my glasses aside and took up the camera. I began snapping pictures as the person knelt near the spirit house and took a flat, round tin from the canvas bag. The figure removed a tight-fitting plastic cover, and then swiftly rose and hurried the last few yards to the corner of the house and placed the open tin on the ground. As the prowler turned and started back whence he'd come I took more pictures, then put down the camera, rose to my feet, flicked on my flashlight so he'd know I was there, and shouted, "You! Stop! You're under arrest!"

But the prowler did not stop. Instead, with the speed of a deer, he fled toward the mill pond, flicking his light in my direction as he did, but never losing a step.

Shouting loudly, I ran after him, following

the bouncing circle of light from my flash-light, but he was fast and I had legs scarred with shrapnel and he pulled away. Down across the meadow we flew, past the mill pond and into the darker darkness of the path beside the stream, where I lost sight of him completely.

Was I up to a half-mile run? Was he? My breath was already short and my adrenaline was lessening, but I ran on, slower but still fairly well, and the dark trees flowed by me on either side. I was in a coal mine, an end-less long barrow, a tunnel leading down to the center of the earth. I pounded on.

Why was I doing this? I'd done my job already. I had the pictures and I'd given the prowler a scare that should keep him from coming back very soon, if at all.

Enough of this running. I decided to stop. But my decision was seconds too late. As I pulled up, panting, a dark figure appeared at the rim of my flashlight's beam and I looked up in time to see an arm pointed at me just before I felt a powerful blow to my chest.

The blow melted me. I was turned to liquid and flowed down onto the ground unable to control any part of my body. My mind, too, turned to mush. I knew I'd been shot.

I heard a sound like distant surf and wondered what it was. Gradually the surf turned into voices speaking words I could understand. I listened to them as though from afar, as though they had to do with someone distant from me, floating in space.

"Got the son of a bitch," said one satisfied voice. "Maybe we should finish him off right here while we have the chance."

"Nobody's said anything about finishing anybody off," said another voice.

"You'll kill a cat, but not a man, eh?" said the first voice. "At least not until you get paid for it."

"We didn't get hired to kill anybody."

"Not yet, anyway."

"Wait a minute. Look at him. This isn't Nunes, it's somebody else."

"What the hell? You saw the woman at the house; why didn't you see this guy? Who is he?"

"Lemme get his wallet." I felt hands turning me but I neither wanted nor was able to do anything about it. I was disconnected from all things. "Here. Here's his ID. Name's Jackson. Lives in Edgartown. You know anything about him?"

"No. Jesus. What's he doing here?"

"He must be working for Nunes. Damn! What are we going to do with him?"

Voice One had lost its bravado. "We're not going to do anything with him. We're going to get out of here. He'll be all right."

"I don't like this," said Two. "Some people die when they get hit with one of these guns, you know. They have heart attacks."

"If he has a heart attack, we'll be long gone. Besides, he'll be O.K. Look. He's breathing. Come on. I'll buy you a beer."

The voices ceased and I lay there in pieces until, slowly, my parts began to be reattached to one another and my mind began to work more coherently. After a while I sat up. It was black as the pit from pole to pole.

I put out a hand and it found my flashlight. I pushed the switch and the light went on. I was confused but finally realized that my attackers had turned it off. I wondered fuzzily about that, then, as my mind got clearer, guessed that it was because they could see very well with their infrared flashlights and didn't want my white beam to attract attention.

I sat there for a while and flashed my light around. My wallet was spilled open by my side and I got hold of it and collected its scattered contents. Nothing seemed to be missing. I stuffed it into my pocket.

I rose slowly to my feet and stood there until I was sure I wasn't going to fall over, then walked south down the path toward the Edgartown–West Tisbury Road, following the circle of light from my flashlight. My chest hurt and I was weak as a baby. I didn't think my attackers were still around, but as the fishermen say, "If you don't go, you don't know."

When I got to the paved road there was no one in sight, nor was there any vehicle of any kind. Probably just as well. I flashed my light along the side of the road but saw nothing interesting. A car came from the west, its headlights splashing over me before it passed. I wondered what its driver thought of a lone man standing there in the middle of the night. Whatever his thoughts, I hadn't been offered a ride.

I turned and walked back north along the dark path, feeling a bit better and a bit clearer-headed as I went. I was conscious of the babbling brook beside me and the billion stars above. A large bird crossed over the trail on silent wings. One of nature's hunters looking for prey. Unlike me, though, this hunter would not become the prey of his prey.

When I passed out of the trees into the meadow and found my oak tree, I was glad to see that the camera and binoculars were still there. I wished I had that blanket Nunes had offered me, but maybe it was for the best because I wanted to stay awake on the unlikely chance that the prowlers would come back.

I found my backpack and sat down, leaning against the tree. I drank some water and chewed some dried fruit and felt stronger. It had not been smart, Kemo Sabe, to chase the prowler into darkness like that. If he and his partner had used a normal gun instead of a stun gun I could be dead now.

I thought some more, then suddenly remembered what I'd seen before my chase had begun. I jumped to my feet, flicked on my flashlight, and ran toward the house, hoping I wasn't too late.

It took me only a moment to spot the flat can that the prowler had placed on the ground. I snatched it up and looked at the contents. It seemed untouched. I swept the light around the area and saw nothing dead or alive. I felt a rush of relief, then heard a slight sound behind me, whirled, and found myself facing the Monk, who had just stepped out of his door. He held a hand up in front of his eyes to protect them from the light.

"Mr. Jackson. I startled you. I apologize."

I lowered my light. "You startled me all right. Sorry to wake you."

"I've been awake since I heard you shout earlier. What have you there?"

I lifted the can. "Cat food."

"For Mr. Mephistopheles? How kind. He's inside."

"Not kind at all. It's a gift from the prowler."

Nunes was silent for a moment, and then said, "The guy has a light foot. I didn't hear him."

"A light foot and a fast one. Do you have something to cover this can? I want to have its contents tested."

His voice never lost its gentle tone. "Do you think the food is poisoned?"

"I don't know, but I want to find out." The idea of poisoning a cat filled me with rue and anger.

"When I heard your voice earlier," said Nunes quietly. "I came to the door and saw your light down near the pond. Were you chasing the man who left this can of food?"

"Yes."

"You will forgive me, I hope, for observing that that was probably not a wise decision. Did you catch him?"

"Not exactly." Without thinking, I put my hand to my sore chest.

"You're hurt." He peered at me then said, "Come inside. We'll cover that can and have a look at you."

Inside the cabin there was candlelight, and I saw Mr. Mephistopheles lying on the double bed. He yawned in response to my gaze. Nunes covered the can with some paper and fastened it with a piece of string, then turned to me.

"I'm all right," I said.

"One of the things I got in the army was a bit of medical training," said Nunes, with a small smile. "Let me look at you."

I sat on the couch and he peered into my eyes, took my pulse, then opened my shirt and studied my chest. His hands moved swiftly and gently.

"What happened to you?" he asked.

I told him everything I could remember, and when I was through he said, "You took a chance you shouldn't have taken. I thank you for doing it, but I hope you'll stop chasing prowlers into dark places."

"We got some benefit out of it," I said. "I learned some things that might be useful."

"That's true," he said, thoughtfully. "You learned that the prowler has at least one partner and that they have an employer who's paying them for their work. You also know that for the moment at least they're not willing to use fatal force, although they said they might in the future if they get paid for it. And you know that they didn't use their advantage to rob you or inflict additional injury upon you."

"On the downside," I said, "they seem to be getting more violent, to the point of poisoning your cat, if I'm right about this can of food. I'll have a friend send the can to a lab to check that out. I don't know how big a step it is between killing cats and killing people."

"And they know who you are," said Nunes.

I nodded. "There's that, but I have the prowler on film and your sister says that may be enough to identify him. If so, that might end your troubles."

Nunes nodded. "Let's hope that she's right. Meanwhile I thank you again for what you've done but now I want you to go home and put this job behind you. You've done what my sister asked, so your task is completed."

"I think I should hang around for the rest of the night, at least."

He smiled. "There's no need for that. I've lived alone here for a long time. I'll be fine."

"You haven't had a stalker before. I'll spend the night up under the oak tree and leave in the morning."

He pressed his palms together. "If you

wish." He went to a shelf and brought back a blanket. "But at least take this with you." He picked up the can of cat food. "I'll put this where Mr. Mephistopheles can't get at it. In the morning I'll trade it to you for the blanket."

I left him and walked back to the oak tree. The camera and binoculars were where I'd left them. The faint light in the cabin window went out and the night seemed darker than before. I swept the meadow with the glasses and saw no movement. I leaned my back against the oak thinking he was a trusty tree, and wrapped the blanket around me.

I woke before the coming of the sun, full of guilt for having slept. My chest was sore. I watched the brightening eastern sky, then saw two deer down by the mill pond. They were unalarmed. The woods came alive with the cheeps and chirps of wakening birds.

A little after dawn I carried my gear to the house. Nunes was up and had soup and tea already prepared. We sat outside, on the sunny side of the house, and ate breakfast.

"A lovely morning," said Nunes.

"Yes." Another beautiful day on the beautiful island of Martha's Vineyard. I wondered if the prowlers and their boss were awake to see it.

When I left, he thanked me yet again and told me I'd done my duty and should go back to my normal life.

"I'll see your sister and return her equipment," I said, "and I'll give this can to my friend to have it analyzed."

"Let's hope that they find nothing."

A consummation devoutly to be wished, but one I didn't expect. "I'll let you know what I learn."

I drove to John Skye's farm and found him and his wife Mattie over coffee. They were early risers. The twins, Jen and Jill, were, as college students will, sleeping late.

"I thought you might be up," I said.

"You must be bored," said Mattie. "Zee and the kids will be home in just a few days, if you can hold out that long. Have some coffee."

"The bachelor life is not the life for me," I said, putting the can on John's desk as Mattie went to fetch another cup.

"We don't have a cat," said John, eyeing it.

"If you did, I wouldn't give you this stuff," I said. "As I recall, you have a pal up at Weststock who's a toxicologist. Is that right?"

"Not all of us professorial types are in the liberal arts," said John. "Yes, my colleague

George Faulk is in love with poisons. Why, is this cat food full of cyanide?"

"I don't know, but I want to. Do you think your friend will test it for me? The quicker, the better."

John eyed the can, then eyed me. "Tell me your tale."

I told him of the earlier vandalism and then described how I'd seen the prowler put the can on the ground beside the cabin, but I didn't mention names or tell him anything about what had happened on the trail beside the stream.

Mattie returned with my coffee cup just as I ended my narrative.

"Now you can say everything again," she said, pouring. "John filters stories sometimes and I want the original."

So I repeated myself and when I was through she said, "Don't these people you work for have names?"

"They do," I said, "but I can't tell you what they are. Call it client confidentiality."

"You're not a lawyer or a doctor, J.W. You can't claim confidentiality."

"How do you know I'm not a lawyer or a doctor? Maybe I'm just too modest to have mentioned it before."

"Ha!"

"Maybe I'll tell you someday. Meanwhile,

I'd like to have the contents of this can analyzed."

"Why don't you take it to the police?" asked John. "It seems to me that they're the ones to do the test. If somebody's trying to poison a cat, they should know about it."

"My client doesn't want the police involved."

"Why not?" asked Mattie.

"Ask my client."

"How can we ask your client if we don't know who your client is?"

I smiled at her.

John tapped his forefinger on the table. "Say, I think Sam Myers is driving up to the Kittery Trading Post today. I'll bet I can get him to drop this off at Weststock on the way. All I have to do is tell him it's a suspected poisoning. That'll catch his interest." He looked at his watch and got out of his chair. "I'll call him and George right now and tell them the situation."

He went into the house and Mattie looked at me. "You're infuriating sometimes," she said.

"And you're gorgeous all the time," I said. I tried fluttering my eyelashes, but all I got was a laugh.

A while later John returned, smiling. "We're in business," he said.

5

Carole Cohen worked at Gull Realty, one of the countless real estate companies that kept busy buying and selling property on the Vineyard. The two growth industries on the island were building mansions and selling property so more could be built; Carole was in the right profession.

I found her in her office, poring over papers while she talked on the phone with a client. She waved a manicured hand at me and pointed to a chair. Her desk was piled with papers, many adorned with photos of houses, and her diplomas and certifications were hung on the wall along with photos of her and happy-looking people I took to be satisfied customers, standing in front of a variety of buildings, both domestic and commercial. A matching but unoccupied desk sat beside hers, and similar diplomas and certificates on the walls proclaimed Jordan Cohen to be an equally qualified Realtor.

There were even pictures of small places, to prove, I guessed, that even the little people could depend on Carole to do well by them. Not that really little people could thrive on the increasingly pricey Vineyard, where a house for less than six big figures was getting very hard to find.

It was no wonder that people were after Roland Nunes's land, and although terrorism was still not a usual ploy to encourage a sale, perhaps it would become more popular. I thought of my own acres, purchased long ago by my father when Ocean Heights would have been considered to be on the wrong side of the tracks if Edgartown had had tracks, and land there was cheap. Lately, though, there was no cheap land on the island and more than one Realtor had come inquiring about the possibility of me selling some of mine for very nice money. So far, I'd always said no, but my taxes were getting so high that I didn't know how much longer I could hold out. Adam and Eve had been forced to give up Eden, so it could happen to anyone.

When Carole finally hung up her phone, I gave her the camera and binoculars.

"Thank you," she said. "You just missed Jordan. He's out with a customer. Shut the door, will you? Did you get some pictures already? That was fast."

"I'm not sure they'll be much use," I said, returning to my chair. "The guy had blackened his face, so he might be hard to identify."

"But you saw him. You caught him in the act. Good. Did you scare him off?"

"Yes, I scared him off. I yelled and he ran."

"Good. Maybe he won't be back. I'll have this film developed right away." She smiled. "Thanks. The job didn't take as long as I thought it would. I'll give you a check." She found her purse and pulled out a checkbook.

"I wouldn't be too sure he won't be back," I said.

She'd been reaching for a pen, but now her hand stopped. "Why do you say that?"

She was paying me for my work, so I told her everything that happened, finishing with my arrangement with John Skye.

She stared at me. "You were shot? You have to see a doctor! My God, I didn't imagine that you'd be in danger!"

"It wasn't your fault, and it was only a stun gun. I'm fine. The point is that those two guys, whoever they are, are not pussy cats. I think that if their boss decides to keep

70

pushing this thing and pays them enough, they'll be back. I think it's time for you to take this to the cops."

She paid no attention to that suggestion. "They wouldn't dare do anything else, would they? Now that they've been seen."

"Some people will take a lot of chances if the money's right."

"But one of them has been photographed!"

"He doesn't know that."

"But they must know someone might be waiting for them if they go back."

"They don't have to go back," I said. "Your brother goes to work every morning. They just have to wait for the right moment and they can catch him away from home. He rides that moped wherever he goes, and a man on a moped hasn't got much protection."

"You don't think they'd really hurt him, do you?"

"Someone apparently wants his land pretty badly, if your theory is right. If something happened to your brother . . ."

"Something fatal, you mean!" she interrupted.

"Yes. If that happened, your cousin would own the property."

She sat back, frowning first into space,

then at me. "If the prowler knew we have his photo that would make a difference. We'll have to let him know before he does any more damage."

I was annoyed with her. "I don't know how you're going to tell him that, but I do know you should be talking with the police. This is vandalism at the very least, and it has the potential of being a lot more."

"No," she said vehemently. "No police. I don't want to take a chance on having my brother arrested. I don't want to hear any more about the police!"

"I made a mistake taking this job," I said, getting up. "I never should have agreed to leave the police out of it, but I thought it would be just a simple matter. But it isn't, and now if something happens to your brother the police will be involved whether you like it or not and you and I will both be at fault for not talking with them earlier!"

She spoke in short, staccato sentences. "Please. Sit down. Don't leave. Let me think. I need help. I need someone I can trust. I trust you."

I felt my teeth clenching, but then I looked at her desperate face and the tension eased. I sat down. "You have to take this to the police," I said. "They don't have any reason to look back thirty years, so they may never find out about his past. Besides, even if they do, it'll be better than having him hurt or killed."

"I won't tell them if I don't have to, but I will tell them if I do. Will that make you happy?"

"You should tell them right away. It's the best advice I can give you."

"No," she said, frowning into the air. "We can wait at least a day. Those prowlers will have to report back to their employer, won't they? And they probably didn't do so last night, so that means they can't do it before today. And then they'll have to agree on what to do next, and that means they won't do anything before tomorrow at the earliest, so we have at least today to work before we have to tell the police." She brought her eyes down to mine. "I think that if the man you photographed knows about the photos, he'll want out of this business. I think that if he can be identified he may want to spill the beans rather than take the full responsibility for what he's done. Does that sound right to you?"

"Fall guys rat out their friends pretty often, but how are you going to let him know he's on film?"

Her eyes grew bright. "I'm not going to let him know. I'm going to let his boss know.

If his boss knows we've got his picture, he won't want him hanging around where he can be found and might talk. I think he'd rather send him away and drop this whole business. What do you think?"

"It could work like that. But how are you going to find his boss?"

"If I'm right, there's a chance the boss is my cousin or one of Roland's abutters. You can start with them."

"I thought my job was over."

"You took the pictures. That's about all you'll have to say." She looked at her watch. "You can see all three of them today. You have plenty of time. I think you should start with my cousin Sally. She's right here in town. Will you do it?"

I thought she was right about having one more day before the cops had to be called in.

"It might be good to have the photos developed first, so we know what we have," I said.

"Actually, it may not make any difference," said Carole. "What's important is that they believe we have the photos."

She was probably right, especially since the prowler might be unidentifiable. "If we have a face to show them, we'll have a stronger argument," I said, feeling stubborn.

"You can drop the film off downtown right now," she said. "They have a fast service and you can pick the photos up in an hour, before you go see Sally."

"Where will I find her?"

She gave me an ironic smile. "In a realty office, where else? Prada Real Estate, right up the street."

There were a lot of Pradas in Edgartown. Several of them worked for the town, but one, at least, had gotten into a more lucrative profession.

"Who are the other two suspects?" I asked.

"Give me a minute," she said, and opened a file cabinet. In not much more than the requested minute, she pushed two eight-by-eleven envelopes toward me. "Names, ranks, and serial numbers."

I opened one envelope. In it were typed pages and photographs. "This is a pretty good dossier."

"The long arm of real estate," said Carole. "We know everything and everybody."

She leaned forward. "Well, are we still in business?"

"For today, at least."

"Thank you."

"One more thing."

"What?"

"Where is your brother working?"

She told me and I left her office with the camera. Because I'd been lucky enough to get a parking space, and was unlikely to find one farther downtown, I walked to the photo shop.

"Well, J.W.," said Sam, the proprietor, when I handed him the camera, "are you in the Carpe Noctis business now?"

"Not so you'd notice. I don't trust myself to unload this camera, so I'm going to let you do it. And I'd like to see the prints in an hour or so, after I feed my cats. Can you manage all that?"

"I can indeed," said Sam. "Feed them well."

I drove home and found Oliver Underfoot and Velcro irked by having been abandoned for the night, but in a forgiving mood, especially when I refilled their dishes and gave them fresh water.

"It won't be long before everybody's home," I said to them. "Only a few more days."

They thought that was good news.

I watched them eat, tails in the air as they scoffed up their food, and I thought of the can of food left by the prowler. I hoped I was wrong about the poison, but stories of cat killers are not rare and I couldn't forget the remark I'd heard as I lay dazed on the ground. I could understand and sometimes forgive people killing other people, but I had no grasp of cat killers. Such people were a cruel and dismaying mystery to me.

And in this case, I now realized, the possibility that the prowlers were willing to poison Mr. Mephistopheles was one reason I was still on the job. I wanted them stopped, not because they'd shot me — that was understandable, given the circumstances — but because I suspected they were cat killers.

By such small emotions are our lives changed. I once read about a diplomat who was so offended by Hitler's halitosis that he couldn't bear to talk with him and thereby lost a chance to try to prevent the invasion of Poland. Just as Hitler's bad breath may have caused World War II, so my suspicions led me into trouble I might otherwise have avoided.

I went out to the garden and picked enough beans for supper, then drove back to Edgartown. Along the bike paths the galloping moms were pushing their tri-wheeled baby carriages and walkers were taking their morning constitutionals while dodging the occasional amateur biker. The pro-bikers in their skintight pants and racing helmets of course scorned the bike paths and insisted on riding on the highway. Bike paths were too slow and dangerous for them; they didn't want to dodge walkers and families on rented bikes, they preferred to force irritated automobile drivers to dodge *them*.

Prada Real Estate had a small parking lot behind the office. I left my truck there beside a lovely little Mini Cooper and walked down to the photo shop.

The photos were ready and I gave them a quick study. They were not Pulitzer contenders, but a couple did show the shadowy face of the prowler as he'd glanced my way for some reason. In one shot, I could see the cat food can in his hand, and in another he was placing the can on the ground beside the cabin.

I showed the best shot of the prowler's face to Sam, the proprietor. "You know this guy, by any chance?"

Sam looked and shook his head. "Looks like one of those Seals or Special Forces guys who sneak onto beaches in the movies. That black cap and the black clothes and that black face camouflage. You a combat photographer or something like that these days, J.W.? Is Martha's Vineyard being invaded by the Marines?"

"Nothing like that. Just somebody sneaking around at night."

"And you caught him in the act, eh?"

"The camera isn't mine," I said. "I just brought it down here for a friend who wants to know who the guy is."

"I'm afraid I can't help you," said Sam. He studied the photo again and added, "I doubt if anybody else can, either, what with all the stuff the guy's got on his face."

"Can you make me some more copies of these?"

"Sure."

When he came back with the copies, I said, "You're a photo pro. Do you happen to know anybody who can clean that camouflage off this guy's face? I read someplace that they can do that sort of thing with computers these days."

"They can do almost anything with computers these days," said Sam. "I'm not a photo manipulator myself, but I know a guy who is. Lives right here in town, in fact. He can erase what you don't want and add what you do and you'd never know the picture had been changed. You want me to see what he can do with these?"

I gave him the best photos. "Give him these and let's see what he can come up with. The quicker the better."

Sam grinned. "I'll tell him it has to do with Homeland Security. That might speed him up."

"Tell him whatever you want, Sam." I thanked him and carried the camera and the rest of the photos back up the street and stashed them in the truck. Then I went into the Prada Real Estate office. Looking at the little Mini Cooper, I remembered when VW Beetles were all the rage and Beetle drivers would hold rallies to celebrate their cars. I'd heard that Mini Cooper people did the same. We are odd animals.

A neatly dressed receptionist eyed me and put a smile on her face even though I did not have the look of a normal customer-to-be since I get most of my clothes from the thrift shop. On the other hand, there are a lot of scruffy millionaires around these days, so she couldn't be sure who she was talking to. I told her I wanted to speak to Sally Oliver. She said that Ms. Oliver was with a customer and asked if she could be of any assistance. I said no, I wanted to see only Sally Oliver. She smiled and said of course and asked me my name. Then she spoke into a phone, apologizing for intruding and saying there was a Mr. Jackson waiting. She listened and hung up and waved me to a chair. I wondered if it hurt her face to smile so much.

It was another room adorned with pictures

of houses, buildings, and properties available for purchase. This one, however, also included photographs of an attractive and muscular young woman running, swimming, biking, and accepting a trophy. The magazines mostly dealt with home design, architecture, lifestyles of people far richer than I was, and gourmet cooking. I was reading one of the latter, amazed at how long and complex some recipes could be, when an office door across the room opened and a large young woman, who was surely the same one in the photographs, ushered a middle-aged man out with many a smile and encouraging word. When the man was gone, she turned to me and said, "Please come in, Mr. Jackson." She put out a manicured hand. "I'm Sally Oliver. How may I help you?"

Her hand was powerful but businesslike and somehow friendly. Did people teach you how to shake hands like that in real estate school? Was there a course in hand shaking? In smiling? In looking honest and concerned and caring? If so, Sally Oliver had graduated cum laude.

"I have an interest in some land in West Tisbury," I said, after she'd shut the door behind us and we'd taken chairs across her desk from one another. "I'd like to talk with you about it." Sally Oliver's eyes lit up. I must have said the magic words.

6

"Of course," she said. "Are you buying or selling? We handle purchases and sales all over the island. Tell me about the property you're considering. Perhaps I'm familiar with it."

"I believe you are," I said, and told her where it was. "A cousin of yours lives there. His name is Roland Nunes."

Her warm smile cooled a few degrees.

"What is it that you're getting at, Mr. Jackson? Are you interested in buying the land?"

I didn't deny it. Instead, I said, "I'm here because I think that as a trustee of that land you should know what's been going on up there. Are you aware of the vandalism that's occurred?"

Her eyes became hooded. "Vandalism?"

"You don't know about it?"

She eased back in her chair and her voice became careful. "No. My cousin and I aren't in close contact. What's happened?"

I told her of the damage to the garden and the shed, and of the dead skunk in the water barrel.

"And what's your interest in this, Mr. Jackson?"

"I was asked to go up there with an infrared camera and get photographs of whoever was doing the damage. I did that." I put the photo of the prowler on her desk. "I have more of these, but this one's typical. Do you know this person?"

She seemed torn between curiosity and caution, and didn't look at the photo although one hand inched toward it before she drew it back. "Why do you think I might? What are you suggesting?"

I skipped the most obvious reason and created another one that might actually be true. "My guess is that whoever hired the guy in this picture is trying to scare your cousin away. Probably to scare him into selling. You're the trustee of the land. You may be next on his list."

She looked at the photo but still didn't touch it. "Why would I know this man?"

"He knows who your cousin is and he may know you. If he does, you may know him. Do you?"

She finally picked up the photo. "Does Roland recognize him?"

"You're the first to see the picture. I just had it developed. Roland sees it next."

She studied the camouflaged face, then shook her head. "I can't really tell what he looks like. Do you know who he is?"

"No."

"What's he doing?"

"He's putting a can of cat food on the ground beside your cousin's cabin. A cat lives with your cousin. I suspect the food in that can contains poison. I'm having it tested."

She stared. "He tried to kill the cat!? I have a cat!"

I didn't think there was a real estate class in how to look horrified, so I took advantage of her shock and told her about my chase after the prowler and its abrupt ending. "The point is," I then said, "that these guys are not kidding around. One of them considered killing me right there while they had the chance and the other one's only argument for not doing it was that they hadn't been paid to kill anyone yet. Emphasis on yet. Your cousin is in somebody's sights and you may be too. You're sure you don't recognize this guy?"

"Anybody who would poison a cat would do anything!"

Like many people, both men and women,

she was more appalled by cruelty to an animal than to a human being. My problem was not knowing if she was shocked because the prowler was both cruel and unknown to her or because he had used techniques she hadn't imagined when she hired him.

"The cat is fine," I said. "But we don't know what will happen next. Look at the photo again. Take off that camouflage in your imagination. See the face underneath it. Have you seen that person before?"

She put her teeth over her lip and stared and frowned and shook her head. "No, I don't recognize him."

"There are experts who can clear that gunk off his face," I said, not knowing if I was right, "and I've gotten my photos to one of them today. Once we ID this guy, we can learn who he's working for. After that the police will make some arrests and this business will be done."

"Do you really know someone who can strip away that makeup?"

"Sure," I lied, "but it may take a day or two to get it done, and we may not have that long before more violence occurs. You might be able to save us some time."

"How?"

"Can you think of anyone who's so interested in getting that piece of land that he'd hire a couple of thugs to frighten your cousin into selling?"

"No! I don't know anyone who'd do a thing like that!" Her voice was firm, but her eyes looked full of thoughts.

"I'm going to be talking with the people on either side of the land where your cousin lives. Can you tell me anything about them?"

She seemed almost offended. "You're off base there. Neither of them would break the law just to get the land. They're both rich enough to buy what they want legally."

"Not unless the owner can sell what they want to buy, and in this case it's my understanding that your cousin doesn't plan on moving."

She grew angry. "But I want him to. You know that, don't you? You know that I want to sell the land. Is that why you're really here? Because you think I hired those killers? Is that it?"

"They aren't killers yet. At least they haven't killed anybody that I know about."

I watched her anger flare like fire then slowly ebb and become smoldering coals of resentment. "If you think I hired them, why are you here? Why are you telling me all this? Why did you show me your precious photograph?" She flipped the photo back onto the desk.

"I don't know who hired them," I said, "but whoever it was should know I've got the photos and that I plan to ID the guy in the pictures and that when I do he'll tell the cops who hired him and that person will be smart to deny everything and drop the whole plan before he does something that'll land him in jail. Tell me about the people who live beside your cousin. All I know about them is that they like stone walls and can afford to build long ones."

She became sulky. "You think that I did it. You think that I hired those men."

I felt like a bully. "If you didn't, you're in the clear. If you did, you aren't."

"I didn't!"

"I've never said you did, but if the police get into this they'll be interested in asking you some questions because you're bound to be on their short list of suspects."

"The police?" Her brow knotted.

I retrieved the photo, and decided it was time for the carrot.

"Look," I said, "I want to keep the police out of this, too, but I need your help. Can you think of anyone who might have hired those men? If we can find the employer, both you and Roland will be better off."

"I honestly can't think of anyone. I wish I

could help."

"You're sure it's not the abutters? They both want the land, I'm told."

"No. I've met them both, and I don't think they're the sort who'd do such a thing. They'd be more likely to offer so much money to Roland that he couldn't afford not to move. Then they'd buy the land from me." She frowned at me. "By the way, just who are you working for? You seem to know a lot about Roland and me. How'd you find out about the prowler?" She grew bolder. "Are you a private detective of some sort? Do you have some identification I can see?"

"I'm not any sort of licensed investigator," I said. "I was asked by a private party to photograph the intruder and I was told what I know about the situation by the person who hired me."

"And who was that?"

"If you wish, I'll ask if I can reveal my client's identity. If the answer is yes, I'll tell you who it is. Until then, it's confidential."

"You need a license to be a private investigator."

"You don't need one to ask questions." I dug out my wallet and handed her my driver's license. "I can understand why you might be upset by this business, and I want to be square with you. This is me. I live up in Ocean Heights. For what it's worth, I used to be a cop in Boston."

I watched her scribble my name and address on a piece of paper, then frown slightly and look at the information again.

"You wouldn't be the Jackson who owns that nice piece of property up by Felix Neck, would you?"

The air in the office seemed to change. "I own a few acres there," I said. "My father bought them when the land was cheap."

Sally Oliver was suddenly back in her professional role. "I imagine your taxes must be pretty high these days. I'm sure I can get you top dollar for any land you'd be willing to sell."

"I'm hanging on to it for the time being," I said. "Can I have my license back?"

"Of course." She handed it back along with one of her cards. "Please let me know if you change your mind about selling."

Her hostility and her curiosity about my employer seemed to have melted away in the warmth of a possible sale. I put the license and card in my wallet and returned the wallet to my pocket. "I'm going to talk with the abutters this morning," I said.

"They're not the people you're looking for."

"You may be right," I said. "If you think

of anyone else I should see, I hope you'll let me know. My number's in the book. I don't have an answering machine, I'm afraid."

"I can't imagine anyone who'd hire vandals." She leaned forward. "You seem to be very intent. You must be making good money."

"It's not just the money," I said, getting up. "It's personal. I got shot with a stun gun last night. I may have deserved that, but the guys who did it talked about killing me if the money was right. They know who I am and now I want to know who they are before they decide to finish the job."

I started for the door, then turned and said, "Can you think of any enemies your cousin might have? This business may not have anything to do with real estate."

She shook her head. "He's the last person in the world to have enemies. They call him the Monk, you know, and some people think he's a saint. How could anyone hate a saint? You might think that I'm his enemy, but I'm not. I just want him to move so I can sell that piece of land."

I went out thinking but not saying that sanctity was no immunity to hate. The fate of holy martyrs was evidence enough of that.

I glanced at my watch; then, following Carole Cohen's directions, drove up-island to the site of yet another Chilmark mansion-to-be. It was a huge place overlooking Menemsha Pond with workmen steadily framing walls, pouring cement, and shingling roofs. No wonder simple islanders who wanted a garage repaired or a new dormer built found it so hard to get people to do it; all the island's carpenters were busy building castles.

I spotted Roland Nunes's moped among the workmen's pickups and Jeeps, parked my truck, and walked into the organized chaos. Nunes was working on a deck that thrust out above Menemsha Pond. It was big enough to hold my whole house and provided a splendid view of the pond and the Elizabeth Islands on the far side of Vineyard Sound.

I watched him work for a while, taking note of the smooth rhythm of his movements and seeing once again the beauty in anything being done well, whether it is a dancer's arabesque allongée, a short-order cook flipping eggs for the morning crowd, or Zee making one of her perfect casts off Wasque Point. He worked steadily, wasting no motion or energy, using his air-driven nail gun like a maestro, never missing a beat. Lovely.

I crossed the unfinished deck and came

up behind him. He sensed my presence and turned and smiled.

"J.W. What brings you here?"

"Somebody's going to have a nice view."

"Yes. The world is full of them."

I showed him the photos. He studied them and shook his head. "I don't know him. The camouflage looks pretty conventional. Half the Special Forces in the world look like that, so he could be anybody."

"You're sure you don't recognize him?"

He handed the picture back. "I'm sure. I think you should let this business go now."

"I may do that, but first I'm going to talk with a couple more people." I told him of my conversation with Sally Oliver.

"I don't think that Sally is involved," he said in his gentle voice.

"Do you have any enemies?"

"We have met the enemy and he is us." He smiled.

Another Pogo person. "Aside from that," I said.

"I had many long ago," he said. "For the last thirty years I've tried to avoid making new ones."

"What became of the old ones?"

He looked down at his hammer. "Most of them are long dead." He lifted his eyes. "We were warriors then," he said. "I'm no longer one of those. I'm just a man."

"What about the woman who was at your place last night?"

"I'm not celibate."

"Maybe she has a lover who doesn't like you taking his place."

Some sort of light flickered deep in his eyes, but he smiled. "She wears a diamond, but I've never asked her whose. She's full of life and fills me with it, too."

You can't have too much joy. "What's her name?"

But he shook his head. "Sorry. When I was young, I was taught that it's improper for a man to discuss his women friends."

It was an inconvenient scruple for me at that moment, but I wasn't up to contesting it.

As I walked away I heard the rhythmic sound of his nail gun begin again.

7

A widow named Carson owned the big house north of Roland Nunes's land. The stone wall I'd admired while circumnavigating Nunes's place also extended across the front of the Carson acres, and as I drove between the granite posts and open gates that stood at the front of the driveway I could see that in fact the wall encircled the whole estate. The widow Carson or her deceased husband was clearly a big fan of stone walls but apparently not of Robert Frost.

The driveway was made of crushed stone and led to a modern house with a breezeway that linked it to a three-car garage with a small barn at its far end. The combination was some modern architect's version of the linked buildings you often see on old New England farms, that allowed the farmer to move from his home to his principal workplaces without having to give battle to rain or snow.

It was a large, white clapboard house, but not in the same league with the mansions that were now going up all over the island, and I wondered if Mrs. Carson wanted Nunes's land so she could build her own castle and not have to tear down this house to do it. Maybe she was the sentimental type, who cherished the past while moving into the future.

I parked in front of the breezeway, put on my most honest-looking smile, and tapped on the front door of the house, using the handsome bronze scallop-shell knocker that was centered there. After a bit, the door opened and a white-haired woman looked at me, then swept her gaze down to my feet and back up again.

"Yes?"

She was wiping her hands on a towel and was wearing a stained, full-length apron. Under it were old rich-lady clothes that were informal and comfortable but had originally been pricey, so I knew she wasn't the cleaning woman.

"My name is Jackson," I said. "I'd like to speak with Mrs. Carson about a matter that may interest her. It has to do with the property that adjoins hers." I waved a finger toward Roland Nunes's land.

"I'm Babs Carson," said the woman. "I'm in the middle of something. Will this take long?"

"I won't take up much of your time."

She thought about it for only a moment, then smiled and said, "Well, a short meeting is usually a good meeting." She opened the door and stepped back. "Come in, Mr. Jackson, and sit down in there. I'll get rid of this apron and be right with you."

I did as she asked and found myself in a sitting room, facing a lovely antique coffee table. It was a medium-sized room with windows looking out at a rose garden and, on the opposite wall, a fireplace and bookcases alternately holding books and small objects d'art. Over the fireplace was a painting of a much younger Mrs. Carson. She had been a beauty then and she still was. I suspected that she'd been Babs since her boarding school days. I'd never known a poor girl called Babs.

A few moments later she came in and sat down opposite me.

"Now, Mr. Jackson, please take the podium."

"I gather that you're a potter."

"You gather correctly. My studio is in back of the house. I was working there when you arrived."

"Wheel or slab?"

"Both."

"Do you make your own glazes?"

"Sometimes. Are you an artist yourself?"

"Not at all, although I'm pretty vain about some of the fishing lures I've made."

She smiled and I immediately liked her. "You're a fisherman, then. So was my husband Chris. So am I."

"I'm a surfcaster."

"Blues or bass or both?"

"Both, but mostly blues. I don't like to catch and release and you have to do a lot of that when you're bass fishing because of the size limit for keepers."

She nodded. "I totally agree." Then she leaned forward a bit and said, "The fact is, though, that when I catch a bass and nobody's looking I usually keep it whatever its size because I like to eat what I catch!"

A woman after my own heart. We looked at one another with satisfaction.

"One more question before we get down to business," I said. "Out of curiosity, was your husband related in any way to Kit Carson, the famous scout?"

She seemed pleased. "As a matter of fact, he was a descendant of the same family. It's my understanding that his great-grandfather was so happy to be related to old Kit that he named his first son Christopher and that the name has been passed down to first sons ever since. My Chris was number three and our son, if we'd had one, would have been number four. If my husband was alive, he'd be very happy that you asked." She leaned back in her chair. "But that's not what you came here to discuss."

"No it isn't. I'm here because your neighbor, Roland Nunes, has been the victim of several attacks of vandalism recently. I'm wondering if you've experienced any here at your place."

She frowned and shook her head. "None. My husband's stone wall would make it difficult for a vandal to get in here even if he wanted to, and at night our gate is shut. You no doubt think that Chris had a fortress mentality and in a sense that's true. He was a great fancier of medieval culture — castles and armor and knights and ladies and that sort of thing — and he always liked the idea of a walled house, so the first thing he did when we got this place was to build that wall you see. What sort of vandalism are you talking about, and why are you involved?"

I answered her second question first. "His sister asked me to find out who was intruding and why. Last night I stayed near the house with an infrared camera and I got some pictures of the prowler before he ran away. Here's one of them. Do you recognize him? Try to look through the camouflage on his face." I handed her the best of my photographs.

I studied her as she studied the photo, shook her head, and returned the picture. "I don't recognize the face. Who is he?"

Her expression had revealed nothing devious to me. "I don't know yet, but I've given my photos to an expert who may be able to get rid of that camouflage and reveal the face underneath. After that I may be able to ID him. If I can do that and if he's still on the island I may be able to find him, and if I can find him I may be able to get him to tell me who hired him."

"There are a lot of *mays* in your plans, Mr. Jackson. Just what has this vandal done?"

I told her, including the part where I'd gotten myself shot and had heard the prowlers talking and my suspicions about the cat food.

"Good heavens," she said, "that's pretty extreme stuff, don't you think? You should go to the police."

"I gave my client that same advice, but she doesn't want the authorities involved because her brother leads a very private life. I believe she sees him as a sort of saint."

She gave a short, almost bitter, laugh. "My horny daughter might not agree with you. She spotted him as soon as she got here and is making a mighty effort to add him to her list of conquests. With some success, too, or so she says. Melissa has the ethics of an alley cat, but she's rarely thrown out of bed."

"Why, Mother," said a silky voice from the door. "How sweet of you to speak of me so nicely."

I turned my head and saw a woman coming into the room. I'd seen her before, at Roland Nunes's house. She was wearing white tennis shoes and socks, white shorts, and one of those pastel green and pink Lilly Pulitzer shirts. She had a large diamond on her left ring finger and a tennis racket in her hand. I guessed she was about my age, which is past the flower of youth, but she was very pretty. She put her racket on a chair and extended a tanned hand.

"Hi! I'm Melissa Carson, the alley cat. Who are you? One of Babs's lovers?"

"I'm afraid not. My name is Jackson."

She took my left hand and looked at my wedding ring. "Is this real, or do you just wear it to frustrate us girls?"

"It's real." I looked at the giant diamond

on her ring finger. "Is that?"

"I certainly hope so. My fiancé is in serious trouble if it isn't. Do you like it?"

"I like mine better."

"How sad for me."

Her mother, who had listened to this exchange with a faint smile, now said, "Mr. Jackson is here to ask about vandals, dear. We've just met, and I lack your swiftness of attack on new potential prey." She looked at me. "I actually don't have or want any lovers, but Melissa is like a cheetah stalking a deer when she meets a new someone she fancies. She's been that way since she was in school, so we no longer expect her to change. Isn't that right, my dear?"

"Yes, Mother, and it's made things much easier for all of us." Melissa ran her eyes over me rather like a butcher eyes a side of beef. "You're sure you're really married, Mr. Jackson? And even if you are, I hope you're not the faithful-and-true type. They're so mysterious."

"I'm tempted but taken," I said, feeling a smile on my face. "Would you like to see a picture of my wife and children?"

"The competition? Of course. Let's look at the sweet little wifey and the darling kiddies."

I dug out my wallet and showed her the

photo I carry.

"Dear me," said Melissa, "she really is a beauty, and so are the two little ones. The boy looks a lot like you and the girl looks like her. How nice. What's her name?"

"Zeolinda. Most people call her Zee."

"Tell me, is wifey as good as she looks? In bed, I mean, of course."

"Of course that's what you mean."

She heard my unsaid words and sighed. "Ah. How nice for you. How disappointing for me. Here." She handed me the photo and gave another theatrical sigh. "I've tried marriage, you know, but none of them worked out. Roland Nunes acts like he'd like to marry me, but I already have sort of a commitment. What if he really is a monk, like some people say? Although if he is, celibacy isn't part of his religion. He may not have gotten any promises out of me yet, but I still might give him one if he'd move from that shack. Did you hear the phone ringing just now, Mother? It was Alfred and I told him I couldn't see him tonight because I had another appointment. He guessed it was with Roland and seemed a bit put out. Poor Alfred. Roland is the only thing that's keeping me from being bored completely to death."

"You might try getting a job," said her

mother dryly.

"Oh, Mother, how gauche. I have Grandpa's trust and I'll never be able to spend it all if I try. Did you know I was rich, Mr. Jackson? Now that you do, am I any more attractive than I was a few minutes ago?"

"You were attractive when I thought you were just a poverty-stricken tennis player."

"I'm glad you think so. Did Mother mention my math degrees to you? No? I can offer you not only beauty and money, but brains to boot. Does that appeal?"

"If we'd met twenty years ago we might have had a damned good time together."

"Too late now, though, eh? Dear me." She collapsed gracefully into a chair. "Maybe I should mention my money to Roland. Maybe that would perk him up even more."

"It certainly perks Alfred up," said her mother. "I know he isn't at all happy about you flirting with Roland Nunes."

Melissa waved a languid hand. "Oh, Alfred, Alfred. Just because I have his ring and we've shared the past few months, he's positive that I'm really going to marry him. He's too jealous for his own good. I may just abandon him to that mistress of his. They deserve each other."

"Alfred is the current fiancé," explained Babs. "He's not my favorite of my daughter's fiancés or husbands, so my feelings won't be hurt if she does break off the engagement."

"Oh, don't be so hard on poor Alfred," said Melissa. "He can't help it if he's a blah. He does have that touch with money, though, and they love him for it up in Boston."

"Alfred is very successful in stocks and bonds," explained Babs. "He has a nice hideaway in Aquinnah and owns the Noepe Hotel there in Oak Bluffs." She smiled at her daughter. "Isn't that where you met him, dear? At that New Year's blast he puts on every year? But you're right. He is a blah. You have a tendency to attach yourself to blahs, my dear. I hope that Roland Nunes isn't another one. You should raise your sights."

"I raised them to Mr. Jackson here, and it did me no good at all."

"How well do you know Roland Nunes?" I asked her.

She pouted. "Not as well as he'd like."

"Have you ever heard him mention any enemies?"

Her eyes brightened. "Enemies? That sounds interesting. Does Roland have enemies? Oh, you must be talking about those vandals Mother mentioned when I came in.

Has Roland been vandalized? He's never mentioned it. Tell me all about it!"

I told her what I'd seen and done.

"My goodness," she said. "So you were shot? I think you're the first person I've ever known who's been shot. Does it still hurt?"

"No. Real bullets hurt a lot more a lot longer. Has Roland ever mentioned any enemies?"

"No. Have you been shot by real bullets? How exciting!" Her eyes were actually shining.

"There's nothing exciting about being shot," I said. "Can you think of anyone who might be behind this vandalism?"

Melissa cocked her head in a thoughtful pose and then looked at her mother. "Well, there's Mommy, of course. She'd like to have Roland's land. Isn't that right, Mother?"

8

"My daughter has more than one bad habit, as you see," said Babs Carson. "She not only covets her neighbor's manservant and maidservant, she doesn't honor her parents, either. I doubt if she has many commandments left to break. I really should throw her out of the house, for the sake of the family image."

"Oh, Mother, you don't care a whit about the family image," said Melissa. She looked at me. "Mother is an artist and you know how artists are. They just don't give a damn about propriety."

"Neither do some mathematicians," said Babs cheerfully.

"You should spend less time on my romances and more on your own, Mother," replied her daughter. "Rob Chadwick has been eyeing you ever since Joanna left him for that slimy prince of hers. Now that she's gone with half of Rob's money, he'd love to climb into your bed. And why not? You know you like him. The two of you could have a splendid golden years affair. Or you could even get married."

"Then you could marry Roland and we could combine the three properties and have a genuine estate. How splendid."

Melissa smiled. "What an excellent plan! Maybe I will marry him. I'll give the idea some real thought. Maybe I'm already weakening." She gave me a girlish smile. "We ladies can be so indecisive sometimes."

"I take it you're talking about the Robert Chadwick who owns the land on the other side of Roland Nunes's place," I said. "Has he been trying to buy Nunes's land, too?"

"I wouldn't know," said Babs.

"Of course he has," said Melissa. "And he has even more money than we have. Or at least he did before Joanna got half of it. Tell me, Mother, do you suppose Rob hired those men who shot Mr. Jackson? Come to think of it, did you?"

"How sharper than a serpent's tooth," said Babs. "No, dear, I didn't hire anyone to vandalize Mr. Nunes's property and I'm certain Rob Chadwick didn't either. In fact, you're the only person I know who might hire a thug to do that sort of dirty work. You didn't try to poison Roland's cat, did you, darling?"

"Why, Mother! How could you think such a thing? I might pluck a man's eyes out, but I'd never harm his cat! You've hurt my feelings."

"Poor baby. Well, Mr. Jackson, have we entertained you enough for one morning?"

I handed Melissa the photo of the vandal. "Before I go, I'd like to show you this picture I took last night. Do you recognize the man?"

"Oh, is this the man who shot you? How thrilling." She frowned at the picture, turned it this way and that, sighed, and handed it back. "I'm afraid not. Is that how a killer looks?"

"Killers mostly look like ordinary people," I said. I stood up and glanced at Babs Carson, feeling a smile on my face. "It's been grand. I may want to talk with you again. If you think of something that might help solve this vandalism issue, please let me know. My number's in the book."

"I will," said Babs.

"And if you change your mind about me, I hope you won't hesitate to call," said Melissa.

"I'll be sure to do that," I said.

"I'll be holding my breath," she said, running her tongue over her lips and looking at me from beneath lowered lids.

I heard her laughter answering mine as I left the house.

Robert Chadwick's home was surrounded by another of those high stone walls that were becoming all the rage. I thought of pictures I'd seen of cities on the Mediterranean and in South America where even higher walls surrounded the homes of the wealthy. It was an ancient practice for the rich and powerful to separate and defend themselves from the people in the streets. I didn't think that Chadwick or the island's other castle builders had to fortify themselves against assaults by the Vineyard's peasantry, but maybe I was wrong.

I parked in front of his large brick house and knocked on his door. Eventually the door opened and a large, ruddy-faced man peered out at me. He looked to be on the cusp between late middle and early old age, which, I'd read somewhere, was between sixty-five and eighty these days. He was wearing sandals, khaki shorts, and a T-shirt that had "Trust Your Professor" printed across its front. His thick legs and arms were hairy but his head was bald except for his ears, which sported tufts of hair growing out of them. Reading glasses hung from his neck.

"Mr. Chadwick?"

"Yes?" He gazed beyond me at my battered old Land Cruiser and then back to me.

"My name is Jackson. I've talked with your neighbor Mrs. Carson about vandalism that's taken place on the land between yours and hers, and I'd like talk to you about it, too."

"Yes. I just got a phone call from Babs. She said you might be stopping by. Come in."

I followed him into a library filled with books that looked like they'd actually been read and took a leather chair opposite his. At a desk was one of those captain's chairs that colleges give to retiring professors.

"Babs told me that vandals have been damaging Roland Nunes's place," he said, "and that you've been asked to look into it. What can I do for you, Mr. Jackson?"

I handed him my photo. "You can tell me if you recognize this fellow."

He donned his specs and studied the photo, then gave it back to me. "No, I don't recognize him. Is this the vandal?"

"He's one of them. There's at least one more, but I didn't get his picture."

"How did you happen to get the photo of this one?"

Leaving out Carole Cohen's name and relationship to Nunes, and what I'd been told about Nunes's desertion from the army, I started from the beginning and told him how I'd gotten involved, what I'd been told, and what I'd experienced the previous night, concluding with my efforts to get an analysis of the cat food.

He listened without saying a word. When I was done, he said, "It sounds like a matter for the police."

"I agree, but my principal doesn't want them involved. She says Nunes is a very private person and she doesn't want him to have to deal with the police."

Chadwick pursed his lips. "What do you suppose is your principal's real reason? Do you know?"

I made a small gesture with one hand. "My advice was to call the police, but my principal said no."

He rubbed his chin. "Curious. Dealing with the police would seem to be much preferable to dealing with the vandals." He eyed me. "But we all have secrets, I suppose."

"I have a couple," I said. "Have you had any vandalism here at your place?"

"You've seen my stone wall."

"You don't have a front gate."

"I have a motion light out there. Anyone coming in at night would set it off."

"Babs Carson has a wall and a gate. Do people need that much security up here in the wilds of West Tisbury?"

"Probably not, but crime is hardly unknown here on the island, and I happen to be a wealthy man so my house would be a temptation to an enterprising thief. Ergo, the wall and the motion light. I also have a security system here in the house." He arched a brow and smiled. "You aren't actually casing the place, are you?"

"No," I said. "Not many college professors are wealthy. How did you manage it?"

"I did it the old-fashioned American way: I inherited my fortune. A good thing, too, because I'm really not very good at handling money. Fortunately, I have bankers to do that for me. That allowed me to do what I really liked: teaching history. I'm retired now, but I had a fine time for forty years. I've noticed that you've been eyeing my books. Are you an academic yourself?"

"I'm a fisherman. Can you think of anyone who would have reason to hire people to vandalize Nunes's property?"

He nodded. "The two most obvious people are Babs and myself. We're both interested in buying the land, but Roland

Nunes won't move off it. If we could frighten him into moving, it would be to our benefit. Is that why you're here, Mr. Jackson? To ask me if I employed the men who shot you last night?"

I felt a smile on my face. "I wasn't going to be quite that straightforward, but now that you mention it, did you?"

"Of course not. But I'd say that anyway, wouldn't I?" He returned my smile. "The fact of the matter is that I wouldn't know where to look for a vandal if I wanted one. I dare say I could find one if I set my mind to it, because I'm a wealthy man and wealth opens many doors, but to date I've never done that."

"Can you think of anyone else who might have hired the two men? Anyone who might have a grudge against Nunes?"

He spread his big hands. "They call it an ivory tower, and it is. I know more about books than about the real lives most people lead. Even though Nunes has been my neighbor for years, I know almost nothing about him except that he seems to be a very gentle man who lives an incredibly simple life. He appears to be the least likely of men to have enemies."

"Is it possible that your ex-wife might know something that you don't know?"

He gave a short, ironic laugh. "Joanna knows more about a lot of things than I do, including how to become wealthy by marrying and then divorcing, but I can't imagine her knowing or caring about anything having to do with Roland Nunes. She always had her sights set higher on the social and economic food chain. I'm told she's in Cannes now, with her little prince, so I don't think you'll have an opportunity to question her. Even if she were here I think you could scratch her off of your list of suspects."

"What do you know about Melissa Carson?"

His eyes widened for a second. "Ah, Melissa. She's certainly a woman who knows what she likes. I'm actually very fond of her, if you want the truth. In a fatherly way, of course. I'm more interested in Babs as a partner, as I'm sure Melissa must have told you."

"I believe she did mention something like that."

"Mention? Ha! I'm sure she portrayed me as drooling at the thought of Babs, and that she urged Babs to join me in bed! Did you know that Melissa has a masters in math? She's a very bright woman, but her hormones are her guide. What did you think of her? I suspect she invited you to enjoy her charms. Am I right?"

"I'm past my days as a wolf, I'm afraid."

"I believe that Melissa has her eyes on our friend Roland Nunes in spite of that rock Alfred Cabot gave her. Melissa likes to have a man who's nearby, and Alfred's usually up in Boston tending to financial matters in the family bank. He should either move down here or move Melissa up there if he wants to add a gold band to that diamond on her finger." He glanced at his watch. "Good heavens, it's almost noon. Would you care to join me for lunch? I can offer you beer or wine or whatever else you might like with vichyssoise and a sandwich. I make my own vichyssoise and I'm very vain about it. What do you say?"

"Thanks. I'll help you make the sandwiches."

"Splendid."

I followed him into a bright kitchen and created a couple of ham and cheese with tomato and lettuce sandwiches on homemade white bread while he got the soup out of the fridge and set a couple of places on a patio table outside the sliding doors leading to his backyard.

We accompanied the food with cellar temperature Theakston's Old Peculiar, a rich, hearty brew I rarely drink but always enjoy. It could be argued that Old Peculiar is too heavy a drink to have with vichyssoise, but it suited both of us just fine.

From the patio I could see the far woods but not Roland Nunes's property.

"Do you know a man named Jed Mullins?" I asked, thinking that if he knew Mullins that he might know more about Nunes than he'd admitted.

"Never heard of him," said Chadwick. "Who's Jed Mullins?"

"Someone I'll be talking to. He's a friend of Roland Nunes."

"Another suspect on your list?"

"I'm just groping around trying to get a lead on who's behind this business. Mullins may know something useful."

He nodded. "It's sort of like what scholars do: They grope around in libraries and piles of dusty papers looking for something that might turn out to be important. I like doing that sort of thing myself."

"What's your specialty?"

"Ancient civilizations. I probably should have studied archaeology, but I had too many history books to read. When I travel, I go to see the remains of old cultures. I think I learn about them through my feet, by walking through the ruins and standing where the people who built them stood."

"Where have you been?"

"Oh, to Britain to see Stonehenge and Avebury and as many other sites as I could manage. There are standing stones from Land's End to the Orkneys, you know. And I've been to Carnac in France, and to Malta and Greece and Turkey and Israel, and Egypt of course. And, let's see, to Great Zimbabwe and Machu Picchu and Chichén Itzá and Mount Alban and Angkor, and a lot of places here in the U.S.: the Anasazi ruins in the southwest, the mounds along the Ohio and Mississippi, the great snake mound, Mystery Hill up in New Hampshire. Places like that. You like to travel?"

"I've been a few places, but I don't get off the island too often."

"They say that Roland Nunes was in Vietnam, but that he hasn't left that place of his since he got back. I guess Vietnam got the wanderthirst out of his system."

"I guess it did." I finished my beer and got up. "If I think of anything you might know, I may come back and ask you about it. If you recall anything, I hope you'll give me a ring. I'm in the book."

"Drop by any time. If I'm not off somewhere looking at an old pile of broken stone, I'll be here."

"If you're gone so much, why are you interested in buying Roland Nunes's property?"

He walked me to his door. "Joanna was my second wife. I was a widower. I have two children by my first marriage. I don't necessarily want them living with me here, but I'd like to have them and my grandchildren nearby. If I had Nunes's land I'd build a couple of houses there and see if I could entice them to move to the island, or at least summer here." He put out his hand. "Nice to meet you, Mr. Jackson. Glad you could stay for lunch."

As I drove toward Vineyard Haven I wondered if I was getting sentimental in my old age, and if my liking the last three people I'd interviewed that morning was clouding my judgment. It's usually not wise to become fond of suspects in a case.

On the other hand, as Jung might agree, our emotions and intuitions are sometimes sounder than our pure reasoning.

I wondered if Nunes's old buddy, Jed Mullins, would be at home.

9

Jed Mullins was not at home, and thus my string of finding people where I wanted them to be was snapped at four. However, his wife told me where he was working so I drove there. Mullins was unloading lumber from the back of a sixteen-wheel flatbed. He handled his big forklift as if it were a dancing partner and the two of them were alone on a spotlighted dance floor while a good orchestra played Strauss. When he backed away from the stacked lumber I got his attention and he turned off his engine.

He looked to be about Nunes's age and sported a huge, gray, waxed mustache that curled upward and compensated nicely for the lack of hair on the rest of his head. He was large in all directions and his arms and face were browned by the sun.

I told him my name and said, "Carole Cohen has hired me to see who's been vandalizing Roland Nunes's place up in West Tisbury. She says that you're Roland's friend. I'm hoping that you may be able to give me some idea about who might be behind the guys who have been doing the vandalizing."

Mullins studied me with expressionless eyes, then said, "You say Carole hired you, eh?"

I had anticipated his carefulness, so I dug a scrap of paper out of my pocket and handed it to him. "You've got a cell phone there on your belt. Here's her number. Give her a call and check it out."

He took the paper. "I'll do that."

"I'll give you some privacy," I said, and walked to the shade cast by the piled lumber. I leaned against the yellow boards, inhaled their sweet smell, and watched as he spoke into his phone. Everyone in the world had a cell phone these days. Even Zee and I shared one. Originally we'd gotten it to carry in the Land Cruiser when we were on the beaches, in case we got stuck out there somewhere and needed help; later we used it elsewhere because it was occasionally convenient; now one or the other of us seemed to use it regularly; as is often the case with gadgets, what had once been a luxury had now become a necessity.

When Mullins returned his phone to his belt, I walked back to him.

"When it comes to Roland, I'm careful about who I talk to," he said.

"Carole told me about her brother going over the hill," I said. "She said you were the only other person who knows about it. I'm hoping that if you know that much, you might know more. Maybe something that will give me a line on who's been giving him grief."

He frowned. "I haven't seen Roland for a while. What kind of grief?"

I told him of my adventures, my intent to get the photos analyzed, and of my talks with Robert Chadwick and with Babs and Melissa Carson.

When I was through he gave a snort and said, "Jesus, Roland doesn't deserve that sort of crap, but I don't think I can steer you toward anybody who might be behind it. You say the guys who stun-gunned you didn't seem to have any problem with killing somebody if the money was right?"

"I was sort of dizzy at the time, but that's the way I got it." I gave him my photo of the intruder. "You recognize this guy?"

He frowned at the picture and shook his head. "Damned camouflage hides a lot." He handed the photo back to me. "That's pretty heavy stuff, killing somebody for money."

"People have enemies sometimes. Can you think of any Roland Nunes might have? You know him from way back."

He squinted at me. "Thirty years ago I might have been able to guess at a few. You know anything about Roland back then?"

"I know the gossip and what Carole Cohen told me: that he was some kind of major-league warrior who put in several tours in Vietnam before he decided he'd had enough and left without saying good-bye."

He eyed me. "What do you think about that? About him going over the hill?"

I shrugged. "The whole command pulled out not much later. I don't fault people who've had their fill of war."

"Were you over there?"

"Not for long. I got mortared on my first patrol."

"Where were you?"

"I'm not even sure. Somewhere around Tay Ninh."

He smiled slightly. "Get to see the Khmer ruins up there?"

"I didn't know they were there until I read about them later."

"I spent a little time along the border. We bombed a lot of the temples and did some major damage, but that's where the Cong were hiding out, so they got a lot dropped on them. Roland and I mostly worked up north of there, out of Dakto and Ben Het."

"You sound like you worked with him."

"We did the same kind of work, but he was better at it. In fact, he was the best I ever saw. He liked his job better than being back on R & R at China Beach. He was testy back then and rubbed a lot of people wrong, but out in the field he was in his element. I think it took his mind off the Dear John letter from his girlfriend. I used to wonder if he became a sniper because he really wanted to kill the girl. Beer makes you think odd thoughts."

"I've heard that he was a very gung ho, dedicated guy. They say his medals could sink a ship."

Mullins rubbed his mustache and gave one end a twirl. "We'd been friends here on the island when we were kids and we did a lot of hell-raising together. The police suggested that it might be a good idea for us to join the army before they had to throw us in jail. Then, like I say, his girl dumped him for another guy, and that nearly killed him, so we enlisted together." He shook his head. "Seems like a long time ago, but I guess things haven't changed too much. Kids are still raising hell."

"Some of them," I said. "I joined up when

I was seventeen. I was bored and I thought being a warrior would be interesting."

"Yeah. High adventure. Anyway, Roland and I ended up over there as snipers." Mullins looked me in the eye. "Roland killed seventy-five people that I know of. Had a special rifle. He'd lie up there and pick people off as they came near our fire support base. One time he killed twenty people in one day. They came along and he shot the officer in front, then he shot the guy who tried to lead a retreat back up the trail. The patrol took cover and one by one he shot everybody who tried to make a break or showed himself any other way."

"I've heard a few sniper stories. I don't know if I could have done it."

"The two of us worked together sometimes. He was the best shot I ever saw. When they pulled us back for R & R he mostly lived in brothels. He was surly and had a bad mouth and just wanted to get back on duty so he could keep killing people. He was popular with the brass because he was so good at his work, but the grunts stayed away from him. I stuck with him, though."

"What happened to change him?"

He shook his head. "I don't know. Maybe he just got tired. I know I did. In my case when I got tired I got careless and got myself shot." His hand strayed to his massive chest. "Roland carried me out of there and saved my ass doing it. It took him two days and the Cong were looking for us all the way back. We'd hide and hear them going by, then move on and hide again. He got the Silver Star for that.

"Later he came to see me in the hospital and told me things were fine, but his eyes were different. Something had changed in him. When he left he said good-bye instead of see ya, which was what he usually said when we went different directions.

"Next time I saw him was years later right here on the island. He wasn't the same person at all. There wasn't any wildness in him. I kidded him about it. Told him he reminded me of a priest. He said he wasn't any kind of priest and told me about going over the hill. A separate peace he called it. He'd given up booze and only drank tea. He only ate vegetables. Said he was going to build himself a house up there on land his aunt had bought, get himself a job of some kind, and try to live a quiet life.

"Around here people treated him like a hero when he first got back, but he slipped away from them as quick as he could and built that little house of his. I go by sometimes and we talk. He may think I'm the only person who understands him because of what we did in 'Nam, but I don't think I really do. What I do is listen and make small talk."

"That's probably quite a lot."

He shrugged. "After forty years, it may have added up. Did you know there's a woman who's been waving herself at him, and that he seems interested in her?"

"Melissa Carson? I met her earlier today. She's a case. She says he's more interested in her than she is in him."

Mullins frowned. "Can't say that sounds too good. She's a looker, though. I've seen her."

"She is that, all right." I switched gears. "Over the years you've never heard Roland mention anyone who might have it in for him? Never heard of any enemies of any kind?"

He shook his big, bald head. "Like I told you, forty years ago I could have named a few here on the island and over in 'Nam, too. But since he got back? No. Nobody. Although those neighbors and his cousin Sally Oliver would all be happy to see him sell out and move on."

"Does anyone else know about his desertion?"

"Nobody that I know of. The only people

who know are me and Carole Cohen and now you. Why?"

"I thought there might be an angry vet out there who'd think he was fair game."

He considered that, then said, "I think a mad vet would probably just rat him out."

"One may have decided that Roland might not give a damn if he was ratted out, and to try a little terrorism first."

He shrugged. "I go to the VFW every now and then. I've never heard anybody bad-mouth him. He never goes there, and half the gang doesn't even remember him."

"And as far as you know he hasn't left any angry women in his wake."

"You mean that hell-hath-no-fury stuff? No, as far as I know, there haven't been any women until this Melissa Carson."

"How about the places he works? Any trouble with anyone there?"

"Not that I've heard of. Maybe you should ask people who've worked with him. He's been framing with Milt Jorgensen for a couple of years. Ask Milt."

"I will." I told him I'd be back in touch if I thought of something he might know and asked him to call me if he remembered anything that had slipped his mind.

"I'll do that," he said, putting out a beefy hand. "Roland saved my life and I owe him.

Besides, he's a friend."

I got back into the truck, wondering if I had learned anything new. If, perhaps, someone from long ago in the Monk's past was now reemerging to take revenge for a slight or crime forgotten by everyone else. I thought of the folklore that said Italians preferred their vengeance cold, and of the cask of amontillado.

At home I prepared a cream of fridge soup for supper, which is a meal that is always good but never quite the same, depending as it does on what you have in the way of leftovers in your refrigerator. I put the soup in the freezer to chill and had a Sam Adams while the cats and I socialized, agreeing that the place was empty without Zee and the children. When the soup was cold, I ate two bowls of it, each sprinkled with a few Herbes de Provence. Delish! Then I drove to West Tisbury, parked, and walked down the ancient way to the Monk's house.

He was seated on a mat on the western side of his house, taking in the rays of the setting sun. Mr. Mephistopheles was lying beside him, looking very comfortable and wise the way cats do.

I sat on my heels and told him most of what I'd done that day, who I'd seen, and what they'd said. When I was done, he smiled that gentle, amused smile of his and said, "I can think of no one I've offended at work. But ask Milt, if you wish; maybe he knows something I don't know."

"You haven't exactly made a friend of Melissa Carson."

The smile became broader and gentler. "So you found out about Melissa. She's charming, but I don't think she's interested in my kind of life. I really have nothing to offer a wife." He waved a hand at his house. "What woman would choose this house when she could choose another?"

"A nun?"

He smiled. "Melissa is hardly a nun!"

"True. She's had a couple of husbands already and she's sporting a diamond from a guy named Alfred Cabot, but she isn't sure she wants to marry him, either. She seems to like you, though."

He shook his head, and I heard tension in his voice. "I want that to be true. Your ring says you're married. When I think of Melissa, I think of marriage. But she keeps me at an emotional distance and I think she'll shortly give me up and go after better game."

I thought he might be wrong about that, but only said, "I haven't decided whether or not to park myself out yonder again tonight.

I doubt if those guys will be back so soon, after what happened last night. I think they'll want to talk to their boss and decide whether they even want to keep on hassling you. If one of the people I talked to today is the boss, they know I have those photos because I told everyone that I did. In any case, what happened last night should cause them pause for a day or two at least. Maybe for good, especially if the experts can clear away the camouflage from that one guy's face."

"That makes sense to me," said Nunes. "I think we can both get a night's sleep, and I'll keep Mr. Mephistopheles inside. We can talk again tomorrow if you wish, but I believe it's all over."

"I hope so."

I walked back to the Land Cruiser and drove home. Later that night, when I put out a hand and Zee wasn't beside me, I recalled the old agnostic saying that sleeping alone in a double bed is evidence that there is no God.

The next morning as I was weeding in the garden I heard the telephone ringing and for once actually got to it before it stopped. It was Carole Cohen.

"Did you hear?" she asked, her voice sharp and worried. "They found a body this

131

morning beside the highway, at the end of the ancient way we took when we went to my brother's house. It was Melissa Carson. They say she was murdered."

10

"I think you'd better get a lawyer for your brother," I said. "The police will be talking to him and he may need one. Did you know that he and Melissa Carson were lovers?"

"What are you talking about? My brother's been celibate for thirty years. He's like a priest, for heaven's sake."

"Maybe he's a priest, but he hasn't been celibate recently. Her mother will tell the police about the affair and Roland will automatically become a suspect, especially if they found her body on his land."

"I don't really know exactly where they found her, but that's what I heard. Oh, dear! You're right. I'll call a lawyer right now."

"Good."

"Can you go up there and find out what happened? Tell the police that you're working for me. Find Roland and tell him to say nothing until the lawyer's with him."

"All right, but I won't have any influence.

The police will have no reason to tell me anything."

"Then just tell Roland to say nothing! He's so honest that he may get himself into trouble without realizing it! Please go now! I'll be there myself as soon as I can."

"This might be a good time to tell the police about the vandalism. That would give them something to think about besides Roland."

"No, don't do that yet. No one should say anything until we talk with a lawyer. Please just go up there and make sure that Roland stays quiet while you find out what actually happened. I'll see you up there. Hurry!"

The phone buzzed in my ear.

I hung up, found Ann Bouchard's number in the book and called her. Ann was a reporter for the *Gazette.* In the days before I met Zee, Ann and I had spent some time together. Now both of us were married to other people, but we were still friends. I thought if I tipped her about this killing she might pass me off as an assistant when she went up to cover the story. But Ann was already gone, having been tipped earlier. So much for the latest of my best-laid plans. I got into the Land Cruiser and drove west.

Carole Cohen had a right to be worried, even if her brother was innocent as a dove.

It was possible that the police wouldn't look back forty years into Roland Nunes's past, but if they didn't it was likely that some newspaper reporter would. Ann Bouchard, for instance, would see a story in the fact that a war hero turned reclusive monk was now a principal figure in the murder of a sexually charged woman who had been his lover. If Ann dug very deep both she and the United States Army would discover the truth about Nunes and the military would be sure to prosecute him for desertion.

Unless, that is, the real killer was discovered quickly enough to cause both the police and the reporters to lose interest in Nunes so that his past remained unexamined.

Both sides of the paved road were lined almost bumper to bumper with cruisers and civilian cars when I got to the site, but I found a spot where I could park and walked toward the center of activity, where local and state police were holding back curious civilians and trying not to contaminate the crime scene encircled by yellow tape. There was no body, which meant that the ambulance had come and gone, but detectives were still looking for anything that might help clarify things for them. They were being careful trying not to join the ranks of investigators who infamously destroy more evidence than they find.

Ann Bouchard and another reporter were talking with Sergeant Dom Agganis of the state police while Dom's underling, Officer Olive Otero, kept an eye on what was going on inside the tape. Olive and I had wasted a lot of time and energy over the years disliking each other with irrational intensity, but recently that had changed and we had become friendly due to a small, unlikely discovery: We were both fans of old Tarzan movies starring Johnny Weissmuller as the ape man. Warmed by that revelation, our ancient animosity had melted away and stayed away. Now, seeing me, she waved a hand before turning back to watch the detectives at work.

Dom was an old acquaintance, a tall, thick man with fingers the size of sausages and an aura of command that allowed him to do his tough job without actually having to use force very often. In one locally famous incident, for instance, a drunken bow hunter had loosed an arrow in the direction of his ex-wife's house and fled into the woods with several very nervous members of the Edgartown police in pursuit. All of them wanted him disarmed and taken into custody but after surrounding him none wanted to risk getting shot with a hunting arrow, a possibility that frightened them much more than being shot with a bullet.

The standoff, with the hunter shouting drunken threats and the police reluctant both to shoot or be shot at, lasted until Dom, in civvies, unshaven, and irked because the call he'd gotten had forced him to stop fishing just as the blues were beginning to hit, appeared, grabbed a speaker, stood and looked right at the perp, and said, "Dave, this is Dom Agganis. Put down that goddamned bow and come here right now!"

And Dave, cowed, did just that.

I walked over and listened to what Dom was saying to Ann. It wasn't much, since Dom, like many police officers, liked to play his cards close to his vest until he knew more about what was going on.

Now, seeing me, he said, "J. W. Jackson. I guess I should have known you'd show up. What is it about you and trouble? Every time we have a situation, there you are."

"Not every time," I said.

He patted his shirt pocket. "I haven't got your name here on my list of people to talk to. Should I add it?"

"I doubt it," I said. I nodded to Ann. "Hi, Ann. How are things with the fourth estate?"

"Enlightening the ignorant, keeping an eagle eye on the authorities, and entertaining the masses, as always," said Ann. "What *are* you doing here, J.W.? Are you so bored living alone for a week that you're offering your sleuthing services to the police these days? By the way, how did you find out about this killing?"

"Yeah," said Dom. "How did you find out? Ms. Bouchard here has snitches working for her, but you don't. Or maybe you do."

"I got a phone call," I said. "Is it a killing? Is it murder?"

"The ME will let us know," said Dom. "Who phoned you?"

"A woman I know."

"Who? And how'd she find out? And why did she call you?"

"Carole Cohen. I don't know how she found out. She called me to ask me to come up here and see what was going on. What is going on? Is it true that Melissa Carson is the vic?"

Dom looked at me with his flat cop eyes. "Why is Carole Cohen so interested?"

"You can ask her."

"Don't dance with me, J.W. Why is she so interested?"

"Roland Nunes is her brother." I gestured with a thumb. "He lives down that path about a quarter of a mile. She thinks he's a saint and she doesn't want you to bother him."

"What's that got to do with you?"

"I'm supposed to keep him out of your clutches until she gets here with her lawyer." I held up a hand as Dom's brows drew together. "I told her that I didn't think I'd swing much weight with you, but she insisted and you know what a sucker I am for women's tears."

"Ha!" said Ann.

"You're right about swinging no weight," said Dom. "Hey, Olive!" Olive trotted over. "Olive, I want you to go down that path there and find a guy named Roland Nunes. Bring him back here so I can talk with him."

"I'll go with you," I said.

"No, you won't," said Dom. "Get going, Olive."

As she left I said in a loud voice, "Just make sure you Miranda him!"

Dom tipped his head a bit to one side. "Why the advice, J.W.? Does Nunes know something I'd like to know?"

I shrugged. "I doubt that he knows anything, but his sister doesn't want him talking without her lawyer being there. I guess she's heard stories about you guys and your rubber hoses."

Ann was scribbling in her notepad, taking all this down just in case it might mean something or at least add color to her story.

"You never did tell me if the vic is Melissa Carson," I said.

"That's right, I didn't," said Dom.

"Well, I guess I can ask Babs."

"No, you can't," said Ann. "Babs had chest pains when they told her about Melissa, and they've taken her to the hospital."

"So it *was* Melissa," I said to her, ignoring Dom. "Was it murder?

Ann nodded. "I'm no doctor, but before they took her away, I saw bruises on her jaw and her head was at a funny angle. Looked like a broken neck to me." She looked up at Dom. "Any comment on that, Sergeant?"

"Nope. So far it's just an unattended death, causes unknown. We'll be questioning the neighbors to see if anyone saw or heard anything that might be useful to us."

"But the victim is definitely Melissa Carson."

"Tentatively identified," said Dom. "I wouldn't put that in my paper just yet, Ms. Bouchard."

"Call me Ann," said Ann. She looked at me. "How well do you know Babs Carson, J.W.?"

"Are you working for the police now?" I asked.

"It's just that you seem to know Melissa and Babs. I didn't know you moved in those elevated circles."

My meetings with the Carsons and Rob Chadwick weren't going to be unknown for long after the police talked with them, so I said, "I've spoken to them."

"When was that?" asked Dom.

It's been argued that it's better to always tell the truth so you don't have to try to remember later what you said the first time. I wasn't sure about the always part, but this seemed to be one of those honest times, so I said, "Yesterday."

"About what?" asked Dom.

I thought the whole business of the vandals was going to come out very soon in spite of Carole Cohen's hopes that it wouldn't. Babs Carson and Rob Chadwick both knew about it because of me, if for no other reason.

"Somebody's been vandalizing Roland Nunes's property," I said. "Carole Cohen hired me to try to catch them in the act. I did, the night before last. Yesterday I talked with the neighbors trying to find out if they knew anything about it. They said no."

"You should have called the West Tisbury

police in the first place," said Dom.

"That's what I told Carole, but she wanted to handle it herself."

Dom snorted. "Amateurs. What did you do with the night crawlers after you caught them?"

"Well, I didn't exactly catch them."

"What did you exactly do? You'd better start from the beginning."

I looked up and down the road, but Carole and her lawyer were not in sight. Alas.

Feeling only faintly guilty about it, I started from the beginning, leaving out all references to Nunes's past, Jed Mullins, and Melissa Carson's sexuality, but relating the rest of what I'd seen and heard, including Carole Cohen's theory about the motive for the vandalism and the photos I was having cleaned up. When I was done, Dom was looking thoughtful and Ann was scribbling fast.

"So you got yourself stun-gunned. You should have reported that."

I shrugged.

"And you heard these guys talk about killing somebody but only if the money was right?"

"I might not have been hearing straight, but yeah."

"And now you're having those films worked on?"

"Yes."

"Lemme see that one you've got." I gave it to him. He glanced at it and put it in his own pocket. "I'll just keep this. When you get those other copies back from the guy who's trying to clean them up, I'll want them, too."

"Sure." But I'd have copies made for myself first.

"So the Cohen woman is coming up here with her lawyer and she wants you to keep her brother's mouth shut until they get here," said Dom. "What's she afraid he'll tell us?"

I shrugged. "She thinks he's such an innocent lamb that he might say something that can be used against him later by you wolves."

Dom glanced down the ancient way. Just coming into sight were Olive Otero and Roland Nunes.

"You've talked with Nunes," said Dom. "What's your impression of him?"

"You mean does he seem like the killer type? No, he doesn't."

"Did he strike you as being a saint?"

"I don't know many saints. Some people call him the Monk."

"Oriental or Occidental?"

"I didn't see any saffron robe."

"Just a normal sort of man?"

"What's normal these days? Anybody see a car parked here last night? The killer had to get here somehow."

"Nobody we've talked to saw one. Besides, maybe Nunes did it."

We watched while Olive and Roland Nunes came to us. Nunes's eyes were taking in the tape and the police.

Before anyone could speak, I said, "Roland, your sister has asked me to tell you not to say anything until she and her lawyer get here."

"You two leave right now," said Dom, waving a large forefinger at Ann and me. "Mr. Nunes, I'm Sergeant Agannis. I'd like to talk to you. Olive, did you Mirandize him? Good. Let's step over here, Mr. Nunes."

Ann and I moved one direction and Agannis, Olive, and Nunes moved the opposite way and stopped beyond our hearing.

"I knew Melissa Carson," said Ann. "She led a pretty active life. Did she put the moves on you yesterday? It would have been just like her."

"I didn't take her too seriously. Zee is woman enough for me. I liked Melissa, though. She was smart and had a lot of moxie."

"Did Nunes know her? He's a good-looking guy and he lived right next door."

"You'll have to ask him."

She studied my face, then smiled.

"Oh," she said.

We hadn't been an item for a long, long time, but she could still read me pretty well.

11

A car stopped on the pavement and a guy with a necktie stepped out. Carole Cohen was the driver, and another man was in the front passenger seat. I guessed that the man who got out was her lawyer. I was right. As Carole drove on, looking for a parking place, the man walked directly to Dom, Olive, and Roland Nunes and did his best to bring their conversation to a halt.

A few minutes later, Carole and the other man came trotting back along the roadside. Carole looked a bit hot and bothered. I didn't think she'd get any cooler when she learned that I'd told Dom about the vandals, and I was right. When I fessed up, she was furious.

"I told you to say nothing! I thought I could trust you!"

"I'm a disappointment to a lot of people," I said, "but in this case the secret hasn't been a secret since yesterday when I spilled the beans to the neighbors just in case one of them was behind the vandalism. Remember our talk? We wanted them to know we had those photos so they'd be scared off."

"But now the police know!"

"And they'll get the information again as soon as they interview Rob Chadwick and Babs Carson. Better they don't think we're hiding anything."

She got hold of herself, but she was still annoyed. "Maybe you're right."

The man with her finally managed to get in a word. "I'm Jordan Cohen," he said, putting out his hand. He had a firm grip. I gave him my name and said, "Of course, we're still withholding some things. Or at least I am. I haven't mentioned Jed Mullins or said anything about Melissa jumping Roland's bones, because Mullins might be squeezed enough to reveal his separate peace, and any lover is a suspect in a murder case."

The last of her anger became concern. "Can we keep that from them?"

"I doubt it," I said. "Babs Carson knows about Melissa and Roland, and sooner or later somebody's going to remember that Mullins and Roland are close. It's only a matter of time."

"I know my brother didn't do this!"

Considering the seventy-five Vietnamese

that Nunes had killed long ago, I wasn't sure that another killing was an impossible act for him. I didn't think the police would have much trouble deciding that it wasn't.

"I don't think he's in any danger of being arrested right away," I said. "The police will have to ask a lot more questions and there's lab work to be done before anyone can be charged, if it turns out that this is a murder and not death by some other cause."

"You mean it might not be murder?" asked Jordan Cohen.

"The police are acting like they're pretty sure, but I didn't see it happen."

I looked and saw the little cluster of people consisting of Dom, Olive, Roland Nunes, and the lawyer beginning to break up, with Dom and Olive watching as Nunes and the lawyer came toward us. Carole Cohen embraced her brother.

"You didn't tell them anything, did you?"

He brushed back her hair with one hand and smiled. "Nothing that seemed to help them."

"You shouldn't have told them anything," said the lawyer. "From now on, don't say anything unless I'm with you."

Nunes looked down at his sister with serious eyes. "They asked me if Melissa Carson visited me last night, and I said yes, but that she hadn't stayed long. They asked me how long she'd been there and when she'd left. I told them I don't have a watch or clock, but that it was after dark. They asked me if we were or ever had been lovers and I told them yes. They asked me if we'd argued and I said no. They asked me if I'd gotten angry and I said no. They asked me if she'd gotten angry and I said I didn't think so. They asked me where she went when she left and I said she'd walked this direction along the ancient way and that I presumed she was going home. They asked some of these questions several times and then Mr. Sharkey here arrived and told me not to talk anymore." He put his hands on her shoulders. "The truth can hurt but I don't think it did this time."

I thought but didn't say that it could hurt more than he guessed.

Sharkey didn't think anything should be said to the police unless he was there and said it was okay.

"Did she have a flashlight with her?" I asked.

Sharkey glared but Nunes said, "Yes. She came with the last of the daylight, but she used it when she left."

"Did you see anyone else?"

"No."

"That's enough," said Sharkey to Nunes. "I want you to say nothing more, not even to your sister. If you have something to say, say it to me and I'll decide who else should hear it."

Nunes gave him an enigmatic look, then turned back to me. "Mr. Sharkey wants me to go with him to his office so we can talk in private. Will you do me a favor?"

"If I can."

"You know where I've been working. Go there and tell Milt Jorgensen that I won't be coming to the site today. Tell him why, if he asks."

"No, don't tell him why," said Sharkey sharply. "Just tell him that something has come up. Come along now, please, Mr. Nunes. Carole, Jordan, let's go to your car."

"Tell him I'll be there tomorrow," said Nunes before he turned and walked away with his escort.

I went over to Dom and Olive. "Do you know any lawyer jokes?" I asked.

"Sharkey isn't a joke," said Dom. "It's gonna cost the Cohens a few bucks to hire that guy. I noticed you gabbing over there. You learn anything we don't know?"

"I learned Melissa had a flashlight when she left Nunes. Maybe that means she didn't plan to spend the night."

"Wild guesses are your specialty."

"Yeah. Nunes says he didn't see anybody else around, but I'd like to know where the vandals were when this happened."

"Why would they want to kill Melissa Carson?"

"I have no idea. I've been wondering if one of her ex-lovers might be the perp. She had a lot of them, apparently."

"You know any of the names? Save us the trouble of tracking them down for ourselves?"

I shook my head. "Not a one. You're on your own."

With thoughts running around through my brain like chickens with their heads cut off, I walked to my truck and drove to the building site in Chilmark where I'd found Nunes working. The view of the pond was still beautiful and I once again decided that if I didn't live where I lived I'd live in Chilmark if I had a choice. With its hills and ponds it's the prettiest township on the island; its only disadvantage is that it's fifteen miles from the nearest liquor store.

Milt Jorgensen was leaning over blueprints spread out on the hood of his pickup. When I introduced myself, he seemed reluctant to take the time to talk with me, but he was polite about it. I told him that Nunes wouldn't be coming to work today.

"Too bad. He's a good worker. Not sick, is he?"

"No. Something came up unexpectedly. He should be back tomorrow." I paused, then said, "His sister has hired me to help her deal with some vandalism that's occurred at Roland's place. Maybe you can help me."

"Vandalism? Roland's never mentioned it."

I told him what I'd been told and what I'd seen and done.

His eyes widened "Jesus," he said. "You were shot? Have you gone to the police? Are you all right?"

"I'm fine and the police know about it," I said. "I'm talking with everybody I can think of, trying to find out who might have hired those guys. You've been working with Roland for a while. Does he have any enemies that you know of? Anyone with a grudge? Anyone who doesn't get along with him?"

He shook his head. "He's never been in an argument or even raised his voice to anybody while he's been working for me. He's the quietest guy I've ever seen. Not unfriendly or anything like that, just quiet. The crew likes working with him. He'll do anything you ask him to, and do it well. He hasn't got an enemy in the world."

"He seems to have at least one."

"I can't imagine who it could be."

I tried cynicism. "He sounds too good to be true."

Jorgensen frowned at me. "I know what you mean, but he's the real thing. Nothing put on or fake. I've been working with people all my life and I know a fake when I meet one. He's the real McCoy."

"That's my impression, too," I said. It was true, but I'd been fooled before. Besides, I didn't believe in saints.

I thanked him and drove back down-island.

At home our lawn needed mowing, so I did that first and then phoned John Skye and asked him if he'd heard anything about the cat food from George Faulk, up at Weststock. John said no. Then I phoned Sam, down at the photo shop in Edgartown, and asked if his friend had had any luck cleaning the camouflage off the prowler's face. Sam said yes and I said I'd be right down.

I finally found a parking place at the far end of South Summer Street and walked back downtown dodging people decked out in tourist clothes and wearing cameras hung around their necks. They looked happy and full of energy and were busily looking this way and that as they admired the village's bright gardens and wandered in and out of shops.

The photo shop was busy with people having photos developed from their digital cameras, so I had to wait my turn before Sam was finally free to show me the results of his friend's work. I was surprised that the face that now looked out of the photos was so clear. It was as though it had never been camouflaged at all. It was a young face, clean-shaven, with careful eyes and slightly pursed lips. Its owner appeared to be listening and looking intently as he did his work. I had never seen him before.

"You ever see this guy?" I asked Sam.

He shook his head. I had him make me a second set of pictures plus a dozen copies of the best shot of the man's face. I put the twelve copies in my shirt pocket, left the other pictures in the truck, and walked up Main Street to Prada Realty, where I was lucky enough to find Sally Oliver in her office. She was not anxious to talk with me but on the other hand she wanted to handle the sale of my land if such a sale ever occurred, so she put on her best professional face when I handed her one of the refurbished photos. She looked and shook her head.

"I've never seen him," she said. "Who is he?"

"The vandal. I don't know his name yet."

I left her and walked to Gull Realty just in case Carole or Jordan Cohen had finished their meeting with her brother and their lawyer. They hadn't, so I peeked in her phonebook and found a Paul Sharkey listed under Lawyers in the yellow pages.

Sharkey's office was in Vineyard Haven, above one of those stores that changes hands every summer or two so a new renter can try to sell enough goods to pay for the outrageous rent the building's owner requires and still make a profit. Not an easy thing to do. I parked in the Stop & Shop parking lot and a bit later walked into Sharkey's waiting room.

His receptionist was a middle-aged woman with well-pinned gray hair and a face that was at once friendly and rather guarded. There was a small nameplate on her desk identifying her as Yvonne Yeats.

I told her my name and she told me that Mr. Sharkey was unavailable at the moment but that she would be glad to make an appointment for me.

I nodded toward the closed door at the

end of the room and said I thought her boss and his clients would want to see me. "Tell them I have a photo that might interest them," I said, tapping my shirt pocket.

She eyed me with mistrust, which suggested that I didn't look much like most of Sharkey's clients. Maybe I should make a return visit to the thrift shop to get some new clothes.

"I was with them earlier this morning," I said. "Just tell them I'm here. If they don't want to see me, I'll leave, no questions asked."

"Very well."

She got up and went to the door where she tapped lightly then went into the room. A moment later she stepped out, smiled doubtfully, and waved me in.

Jordan and Carole Cohen and Roland Nunes were seated at a large table, and Paul Sharkey was coming toward me, hand extended. I shook it.

"You have a photograph, I understand."

I gave a copy to him and one to each of his clients.

"This is the vandal," I said. "Sans camouflage, thanks to another miracle of modern science. Does he look familiar to any of you?"

They studied the face and shook their

heads. I wasn't surprised.

"Well, keep the face in mind just in case you run into the guy by accident," I said. "I'll get out of your hair." I went back into the receptionist's office, smiled at Yvonne Yeats, and descended the stairs to Main Street. The Bunch of Grapes bookstore had Bill Tapply's latest novel in the window. I was tempted but too cheap to buy it. I'd get a copy from the library.

I drove to Oak Bluffs and went into the state police office on Temahigan Avenue as Olive Otero came out of a back room. We greeted one another with a friendliness that still seemed strange after our years of bickering. I gave her a set of the photos and two extra copies of my favorite photo of the vandal, and said, "These are computer-enhanced pictures of the photo Dom got from me this morning. You ever see this guy?"

She studied the photo. "Can't say I have, but can't say I haven't. There's something about him looks familiar, but he's got one of those faces that you see everywhere. You know what I mean?"

I did. There are certain facial shapes that appear over and over. Some movie actors have them. There's a James Dean face, a Marlon Brando face, a Marilyn Monroe face. You see them on regular people fairly often. The vandal's face was a variation of a young Paul Newman's. I wondered if Paul knew his face was archetypal.

"I'll check our files and the computer and see if we can ID this guy," said Olive. "For some reason I think of Boston when I look at him. I'm not sure why. You used to work in Boston. Do you recognize him?"

"Olive, I left the Boston PD twenty years ago. The lowlifes I knew then are all at least as old as I am now. This guy was in diapers when I wore blue."

"Just asking," said Olive. "Well, maybe Dom will recognize him. I'll let you know if I learn anything." She paused, then said, "You be careful, J.W. We've got vandalism and a probable murder on our hands. Someone is playing a very rough game and you're at least on the cusp of it."

"I'll keep my eyes open and my ears up," I said.

I left the station and drove to the hospital, which was only a block away. In the ER, where Zee usually works, I learned that Babs Carson was being kept overnight so they could monitor her condition. They preferred that she didn't have visitors.

As I was leaving I met Robert Chadwick hurrying in. He gave me a quick nod and trotted right by. I paused in the doorway long enough to hear him ask about Babs Carson. His voice was full of concern. I turned back and went to him.

12

Chadwick, too, had been refused admission to Babs Carson's room. As he turned, frowning, from the desk, I said, "I came to visit her, but I guess we'll both have to wait until tomorrow."

"They should let me see her," he said in a hollow voice. "She needs to have a friend by her side. She must be devastated. Poor Melissa. My God!"

"I don't want to intrude on you," I said, "but I'd like to show you a photograph. It may be related to Melissa's death. Let's step outside."

"All right," he said in his faraway voice. "I guess . . ." I never learned what he guessed because his voice faded as he followed me out the door.

"This is a cleaned-up version of the photo I showed you yesterday," I said, handing him a copy. "He's one of the vandals we discussed. Do you know him?"

He stared dully at the picture and shook his head. "No. What's he got to do with Melissa's death?"

"Maybe nothing, but he committed violence at Roland Nunes's house earlier and Melissa visited there last evening. There may be a link. Maybe she saw him lurking there or maybe he killed her as a final warning to Nunes."

"That doesn't make any sense. Why didn't he just go ahead and kill Nunes and be done with it? Why kill Melissa if Nunes was his target?"

"I don't even know if this guy was involved with Melissa's death, but I'd like to know who he is. Will you show this photo to Babs tomorrow, if they let you in to see her? Tell her it's the vandal I discussed with her yesterday and ask if she's seen him."

"All right." He put the photo in his pocket so mechanically that I wasn't sure he'd remember he even had it. "Poor Babs," he said. "Why won't they let me see her?"

"Go back in and ask to speak with her doctor," I said. "Tell them you're her neighbor and friend and that she has no family on the island. The doctor may give permission for you to visit."

"Yes," he said. "Yes. I'll do that right now."

He turned and hurried back into the hospital.

I suspected that he was in love and hoped that he'd be allowed to see her. Both of them needed to comfort and be comforted during this bad time.

Melissa Carson's face and form floated through my memory and I remembered the lightness of her footfall and the way I'd liked her cheerful outrageousness and intelligence. It vexed me to think of her now dead and lying primly on a cold table.

I drove to the Edgartown–West Tisbury Road and followed it west until I came to the spot where it crossed the stream that ran through Nunes's place and where the path parallel to the stream ended. I parked there and spent some time going to every nearby house and asking if anyone had seen the man in the photograph. No one had. I asked if anyone had noticed a parked car or any activity at the end of the path during the night. No one had, but most had seen cars parked there during the day when walkers liked to use the path. I got a lot of curious looks and questions that I answered by saying no I wasn't involved in the police investigation of Melissa Carson's death but that I'd been hired to investigate some vandalism in the neighborhood and that the police might be asking them the same questions I was asking.

By the time I'd visited the last house, I was tired and little wiser than I'd been before. All I was certain of was that the vandals hadn't driven to the path in a car; otherwise someone surely would have noticed it. They'd, therefore, come by foot or bike or had been dropped off and picked up again by an associate who'd not lingered in the area.

I walked up the path, hearing the brook laugh and gurgle off to my right, and looked for something, anything, that might be useful to me. But I found nothing. There were enough footprints on the ground to show that a lot of people had used the path in the past few days, probably to link up to the ancient way that led on into the state forest. I didn't see the single, clear, unique shoe-print that would prove that the villain and only the villain had been there the night of Melissa's death. Rats.

I walked out into Nunes's meadow. His cabin and shed looked small and forsaken. No one was in sight. I crossed meadow and stream and followed the ancient way into the forest. Beneath my feet the leaves and pine needles made a soft walkway. Around me a gentle wind sighed through the trees.

Now and then I heard a birdcall and wished, not for the first time, that I knew what I was listening to, for in spite of my years on the island I'd never really become a birder.

I thought of Bonzo, my friend — who had been a promising lad before bad acid had reduced his brain to that of a child — and who now worked at the Fireside Bar cleaning the floor and tables and bringing beer and booze up from the basement. Bonzo's great loves were fishing and birdsong. He had tapes of songs that he'd recorded himself, using mikes he'd set up on beaches, and in bushes, meadows and forests. He knew the call and music of every bird on the island. If he was here, he could tell me what I was hearing. Good old Bonzo. I should go by the Fireside and have a Sam Adams and say hello.

Bonzo and beer. I stopped in my tracks, remembering the vandal's last words: "Come on," he'd said to his companion. "I'll buy you a beer."

There are a lot of bars and liquor stores on Martha's Vineyard but they're all in the island's two wet towns, Edgartown and Oak Bluffs. If you're going to buy your friend a beer, you can only do it in those two towns.

I turned and walked back to my truck, glancing at my watch and noting with surprise that it was only noon. I'd been so busy since getting Carole Cohen's phone call that it seemed more time had surely passed. A lot of the bars would be open for luncheon patrons, so I had a chance to both eat and ask questions.

I drove to Edgartown and managed to find a seat at the bar in the Newes from America, a good pub on Kelly Street. I ordered a Sam Adams and a hot pastrami sandwich and asked the bartender if a couple of guys wearing dark clothes had come in for beer just before closing time the night before last. He said he didn't know because he hadn't been on that night, but he thought one of the waitresses now bustling between tables had been. When he got her attention, she came to the bar and I put my question to her. She thought back and shook her head.

"The only men in here just before closing were tourists wearing summer clothes. No men in black. You looking for Johnny Cash or the Blues Brothers, J.W.? They're not around anymore, in case you hadn't heard."

"I heard," I said. "I'm looking for two other guys, but all I know about them is that fairly late, the night before last, they were wearing dark clothes and were planning to have a beer. I'd like to talk with them. If you have any pals who were slinging booze or food in other places last night, will you ask them if they saw a couple guys like that?"

"What's in it for me?"

"A toothy grin and a hearty thank-you."

"That's more than I get from a lot of people. Okay, I'll ask around and let you know. Oops, I gotta go. Say hi to Zee."

She went away and when I'd finished my beer and sandwich, so did I.

For the next two hours I went from bar to bar and liquor store to liquor store in Edgartown and got nothing for my troubles other than an increasing certainty that I'd have to come back that evening and make the rounds again, this time talking to the people on the after-dinner shift.

It was midafternoon when I parked in Oak Bluffs and began working my way up Circuit Avenue asking my same question and getting no useful answers.

Bonzo was pushing a broom in the Fireside. The place was fairly empty, so I managed a few minutes with him while I sat at the bar and had another Sam Adams.

"Jeez, no, J.W.," he said after furrowing his brow and casting his thin thoughts back to the night before last. "I don't remember seeing no guys like that, and I was here past closing time because, you know, I got to keep things clean as a whistle so I stay here and work after we close up." He nodded seriously. "It's summer, you know, and we're busy, busy every night. Why you want to see these guys, J.W.?"

"I just want to talk with them. If two guys like that come in, will you let me know?"

"Sure, J.W." His dim eyes brightened. "Say, you want me to have them call you?"

"No, no. I want to surprise them. You just let me know they're here."

His smile was bright. "Sure, J.W. I can do that. I like surprises. They're fun! You going to have a party?"

"I'm not sure about that."

"If you have one, can I come?"

"Sure, Bonzo. If we have one, you can come."

He clapped his hands in happiness.

Good old Bonzo.

I worked my way up Circuit, then followed Kennebec back down to the harbor. No one on duty in the bars and liquor stores had seen the two men.

It's said that a true scholar must have a love of drudgery. Similarly, a lot of successful police work has nothing to do with brilliance, but is the result of patient plodding and prodding. Thus, I wasn't surprised when, at the end of my day, I hadn't learned anything useful.

At home, the cats and I relaxed together on the balcony, where I sipped a vodka on the rocks and looked out over our garden, over Sengekontacket Pond, and over the barrier beach where cars were departing after their owners had enjoyed another sunny, Vineyard day in sand and small surf. Beyond the beach, in Nantucket Sound, white sails moved across the wind and the white wakes of power boats drew lines over the blue water as their skippers headed for harbor.

As far as those happy people were concerned, it was the close of another beautiful day. Although domed by the same warm sun and blue sky, Babs Carson's day held no beauty at all. I hoped that Rob Chadwick had gotten to see her.

I was very conscious of how far removed I was from my years of bachelorhood before I'd met Zee, and found it almost impossible to believe I'd been happy before my marriage. I put out an arm, but of course Zee was not sitting beside me. Oliver Underfoot and Velcro, lying nearby in the evening sunlight, glanced up at me with veiled cat eyes and said nothing.

I thought about Roland Nunes living alone for thirty years, seemingly content to do so, and I wondered if he had made his life an atonement for the killing he had done in war. I knew that I couldn't live such a life, that I'd need companionship other than my own, that I was not made to be a monk. I thought of Melissa and the fragrance of lavender and was sad for both her and Nunes.

Downstairs the phone rang and kept on ringing. When I got to it, John Skye was at the other end of the line.

"I just heard from George Faulk," he said. "There was strychnine in that cat food. I think you should contact the police right away. You've gotten involved with some evil people."

I felt a jolt in my psyche, for I'd been hoping that my suspicions were wrong. I said, "Ask him to fax his analysis to you right away, and to secure that cat food as possible evidence in a criminal investigation. I'll come over now and get the fax and take it to Dom Agganis."

I hung up, full of that anger and fear most people feel toward the killers and mutilators of animals. Cruelty to humans is occasionally understandable and even forgivable, but cruelty to animals somehow seems beyond redemption. The argument of a distant book flashed through my mind: that children who tortured cats, like fire starters and some bed-wetters, often grew up to be criminals, and I wondered if the vandals had torn the wings off flies for youthful sport.

I finished my drink and drove to John Skye's farm. He met me with a frown and handed me the fax he'd just received.

"I don't like this business," he said. "I think you should get out of it before something else happens."

"You may be right. I'll take this up to Dom, and he can decide what to do with it."

"Good. The police are the people to be handling this whole affair. You go home and clean house. Zee'll be back in a couple of days."

"My house is always clean," I said, feigning shocked surprise. "Well, almost always." I thanked him for his help and drove to the state police station.

There I found both Dom and Olive looking at photographs of known perps. I gave them George Faulk's fax and told them that Faulk had secured the cat food as possible evidence.

Dom read the fax without expression. When you've been a cop as long as Dom has, it takes a lot to shock you. Olive read the fax and her lips twisted. She muttered a nasty word.

"There's another thing," I said, and told them about remembering the one vandal's offer to buy the other a beer, and about my afternoon travels to bars and liquor stores.

"We can get help from the Edgartown and Oak Bluffs police to chase that lead," said Dom. "It's a long shot, but something may come of it. Do me a favor and don't go back to talk with bartenders and waiters tonight. Leave that to us."

I pointed at the pile of mug shots. "I guess you haven't ID'd my prowler yet?"

"Not yet, but the day isn't over. You have any other tidbits for us to chew on?"

"No. You have them all. Do you think the vandal and the murder are related?"

"Time will tell. Go home and clean house. Your wife will be home soon and you can surprise her."

Where was all this messy house stuff coming from? Just because I was batching for a week didn't mean I was a slob. Should my feelings be hurt?

I went home and had supper. As I was rinsing and stacking the last of the dishes in the drainer the telephone rang.

The voice on the other end sounded faintly familiar.

"Is this Mr. Jefferson W. Jackson?"

"Yes."

"You're snooping too much for your own good. Stop it. If you don't, the next time I shoot you I'll use real bullets. I know where you live."

"I'd like to talk with you," I said, but the phone clicked and buzzed in my ear.

13

I felt cold and less than human when I hung up the phone. The prowler — maybe the killer — knew much about me but I knew little about him. One thing I did know was that someone I'd talked to had told him, deliberately or accidentally, that I was looking for him and his companion in crime, and that he wanted to deflect the heat. Another was that he was willing to try threats before actually killing either me or Roland Nunes.

Melissa Carson was another matter; if she'd been murdered, it was apparently by someone who hadn't hesitated at all. That made me wonder if there was any link between her death and the acts of the vandals, or whether, perhaps, they were professionals and Melissa's killer was an amateur.

Professionals usually don't kill people without good reason (money being one such good reason), because they know that killings bring cops and that cops are a real danger to them. When they do kill they try to do it carefully so that they'll not be suspects or will have good alibis. Amateur killers, on the other hand, either don't believe they can get caught or don't think about that possibility at all and make stupid mistakes from the word go.

Melissa's body had been found at the end of the ancient way leading to Nunes's house. If she'd been killed there, it was surely the act of an amateur because no professional would have run the risk of being seen killing her beside the road. On the other hand, maybe she'd been killed somewhere else and her body had been dumped there for reasons known only to the killer. In either case, the location of the body seemed possibly significant because, if nothing else, it drew attention to Nunes, who was already the focus of interest for the prowlers and others who might want him gone.

I needed to know what the Medical Examiner had to say about Melissa's death, but I wasn't about to get that information tonight, so I got my old police .38 out of the gun case, put it in my belt, and, ignoring Dom Agganis's advice, went out to talk to night-shift people in the pubs and liquor stores.

I was in about my fourth Edgartown bar when Chelsey Fisher came up to me, balancing a tray of dirty glasses on her shoulder.

"Hey," she said, "Marty Goldman tells me you're looking for a couple of men in black. Didn't they make a movie with that name?"

"I don't know about the movie," I said, "but, yeah, I am looking for a couple of guys in dark clothes who may have been having a beer just before closing, three nights back. Did you see them?"

She put the tray on the bar and the bartender took it and carried it toward the wash station. "I was on that night and I do remember a couple of guys who fit that description," said Chelsey. "They came in late and sat right over there in that booth. Drank Rolling Rock. Left a good tip. Haven't seen them since."

I pulled the photo from my pocket. "Is this one of them?"

She turned the picture in the dim bar light until she could see it fairly well and nodded. "Yep. That looks like Angie, the younger one. The other guy was a bit older. Some gray around his ears."

"Any sense of their size? Weight? Height? Any distinguishing marks?"

"They were sitting down, J. W. They looked about average." She grinned. "The one in your picture asked me if I'd like to come up to Charlestown. Said he'd introduce me to his mother and we could get married right away. I said I couldn't imagine trading Edgartown for Charlestown in the summer, but if his mother wanted to come down, I'd be glad to talk with her."

"You can't blame a guy for trying. I imagine you get a lot of offers. Did you get the other guy's name?"

"Fred. Angie's the young one. Fred wore a wedding ring. Yeah, when you sling drinks you get all kinds of offers and the wedding rings don't always mean much, but Fred was only interested in having a beer. Kept looking at his watch."

"They mention where they were staying?"

"Nope. If it wasn't for those black clothes I probably wouldn't have remembered them at all. Nobody much wears black clothes in the summertime. When I looked up a while later, they were gone."

"And you haven't seen them since?"

"No. I thought Angie might come back, but not so far. Haven't seen his mother, either!" She laughed.

"Where does Marty Goldman work?"

"She's at the Lighthouse. She wants to

176

get off day shift so she can make better tips. I gotta go." Chelsey headed back into the crowd.

I was tired, but I went on to the Lighthouse to see if Fred and Angie has stopped there, too.

No one remembered them, but I got a description of Marty Goldman and remembered asking her about the men in black. I wondered who else she'd told about my questions.

I made two more local stops, in one of which I found Sergeant Tony d'Agostine of the Edgartown PD in civvies, working a special shift and asking the same questions I was.

"What are you doing here?" asked Tony. "I heard about your adventures up in West Tiz, but Dom Agganis told me you were going to stay home from now on and take care of the cats. I should have known better."

"I have my reasons," I said, and told him about the phone call I'd gotten.

"Jesus," he said. "That's a good reason for you to pull in your head and stay in your shell. You recognize the voice?"

"Maybe it was the guy who stun-gunned me," I said, "but I'm not sure. He didn't say much. Before you slap my wrist and send me packing, I'll give you a little information that might mean something." I told him what Chelsey had told me.

He scribbled in his notebook. "Fred and Angie, eh? And maybe Angie lives in Charlestown. It's not much, but it's something. I'll pass it along to Dom. You know anybody who knows the crooks in Charlestown?"

As a matter of fact, I did. "I met Sonny Whelen a couple of times, but we're not what you might call close."

He pursed his lips and raised his brows. "Sonny Whelen isn't a guy you really want to be close to."

True. Sonny was the biggest wheel in the Charlestown mob. Our roads had crossed briefly years before, but we'd not been in contact since.

It was late, so I went home to bed, where Oliver Underfoot and Velcro joined me in snuggling down. They were good company but no substitute for Zee.

In the morning, after giving him time to recover from the night before, I phoned Quinn at his *Boston Globe* desk. Quinn and I went back a long way, to when he had been a young reporter and I had been a young Boston PD cop. He was groggy but not beyond speech.

"You should get married," I said. "Your wife will tuck you under the covers at a reasonable hour and you can give up this dusk to dawn womanizing that's aged you beyond your years."

"As soon as I can talk Zee into leaving you, I'll do that in a New York second," said Quinn. "Why are calling me in the middle of the night?"

"Are you and Sonny Whelen still on speaking terms?"

"No thanks to you."

"He and I have balanced our books and I don't want to unbalance them, but I need a couple of IDs. Maybe he has them."

"Fat chance he'll give them to you even if he has them. Sonny keeps things to himself."

"Use your interviewing skills as a member of the fourth estate." I told him about my encounter with the two crooks, described them as best I could, and gave him the information I'd gotten from Chelsey. Then, as spice, I told him about the death of Melissa Carson. "I don't know if there's any link between the crooks and the killing, but maybe the stun gun will narrow things down. How many perps use stun guns these days?"

I could almost see Quinn's ears perk up.

He was always interested in a crime story. "How soon do you need this information?"

"Yesterday would be nice. Maybe you can tell Sonny you're doing a story on some of his opposition. That might encourage him to say a few words."

"You'll owe me. Are the bluefish still around?"

"There are still a few."

"I want a fishing trip and I want first dibs on this story."

"I think the local papers already have the jump on you."

"I mean first major metropolitan newspaper dibs. I want you as my inside source and I'll want to know everything you know. Deal?"

"Sure," I lied. "And maybe Zee will even smile at you when you come down. Of course that would be hard on your heart."

"The joy that kills. I'll let you know what I find out, if I find out anything."

He rang off and I wondered how long Roland Nunes's past would remain a secret once Quinn got involved in the story. Quinn was a deep digger and very good at his work.

I phoned Dom Agganis and left a message on his machine, repeating the information I'd given to Tony d'Agostine and asking if the police were checking hotels and inns to see if they could find out where Fred and Angie were staying. I was pretty sure such inquiries would be made, but doubted if much had been done yet, since the names and descriptions, such as they were, were new information. Besides, the police had plenty of routine work to keep them busy and it would take time to shake free personnel to check with the clerks at hotels and inns, to say nothing of the island's ever-increasing number of B and Bs.

I didn't think that Fred and Angie were the B-and-B type, but you never knew, so I prepared myself psychologically for a long day and stuck my .38 in my belt under my loosest shirt, where it wouldn't be too noticeable. Then I told Oliver Underfoot and Velcro to be wary of strangers, and left.

My first stop was at the hospital, where I learned that Babs Carson had been released and had been driven home by Rob Chadwick. I pondered driving up to talk with her but decided to give her more time to grieve before I saw her. Instead, because I had to start somewhere and I was already in Oak Bluffs, I spent the morning going to its inns and hotels in search of Fred and Angie.

It was a learning experience. I had summered on the Vineyard since I'd been a child and had lived here full time since I'd left the Boston PD for a quieter life, but though I knew where all of the island's bars were, I now discovered that I was totally ignorant of the variety and number of establishments offering rooms for rent in Oak Bluffs alone. When I commented on this to a clerk a couple of hours after I'd begun my search for the men in black, she was not surprised.

"It's because you live here and don't go to hotels. It's the same with restaurants. When people ask my husband and me where to get an inexpensive place to stay or eat, we can't tell them because we live in our house and don't eat out much. I recommend this place, of course, but not because it's inexpensive, because it isn't, even by Vineyard standards."

"Not much is inexpensive by Vineyard standards."

She smiled a crooked smile. "Freight," she said. "That's why everything costs more. It has to come over on the boat."

"Absolutely." Ask the owner of a liquor store why his bottle of booze costs several dollars more than the same bottle sold in Falmouth and he'll tell you, "Freight." The same is true for gasoline and everything else: "Freight." Another name for monopoly capitalism. You'd think a Communist revolution might flourish on Martha's Vineyard, but it doesn't. The Communists here have too much money to revolt. They're limousine liberals, like most of the island's Pinks and Reds. The Vineyard's working class, like most working classes, is too busy to rebel.

I didn't know whether Fred and Angie could afford that particular hotel, but according to the friendly clerk, they weren't there, so I went on my way.

Just before the twelve o'clock crowd came in, I went to the Fireside for a Reuben and a Sam Adams and got a booth in the back where I could keep an eye on the door in case the crooks happened to come in and I happened to recognize them. They didn't; or if they did, I didn't identify them. Instead, the room filled with working stiffs and a mostly young male vacationing crowd who were full of loud, cheerful talk of fishing, women, the Red Sox, and other familiar topics. Soon, the scent of marijuana floated across my nose, and at the dart board someone pinned a photo of George W. Bush on the target.

When Bonzo wasn't busy wiping tables, he was washing glasses behind the bar; wearing that studious expression he often wore when doing a job at the edge of his abilities. He took his Fireside job seriously, and had only had time to wave hello when I'd come in.

When I finished my lunch, I went to the bar and managed to catch his eye again. I showed him the photo from my pocket.

Bonzo's hands were sudsy, but he leaned forward over the bar and peered at the picture. Then he beamed and nodded.

"Sure, J.W. I seen that guy in here a couple times. He likes them black shirts like he's got on there in your picture. I served him beer once and he left a good tip." He leaned closer. "Not everybody does that, you know." He straightened and smiled again, happy to have been of use.

"Does he come in any particular time, Bonzo?"

He frowned, thinking hard, then shook his head. "No time special, J.W. Just now and then. You know what I mean?"

"I know what you mean. Say, if he comes in again, will you give me a call?"

"I sure will! You can trust me, J.W.!"

I left and went on to the Noepe Hotel, so called, I presumed, in honor of the original Wampanoag name for the Vineyard. It was not far from Ocean Park, and was one of those multicolored Victorian structures that make Oak Bluffs such a lovely, gingerbread town. A little bell rang in my brain as I walked into the lobby.

14

The lobby was nicely decorated with eighteenth- and nineteenth-century paintings of the sea, Victorian lamps, leather chairs, and oriental carpets. The woodwork was hand-carved and polished. On either side of the front door were stained-glass windows in the Pre-Raphaelite mode, and on one side of the front desk a curved staircase led up to a second-floor balcony. As I entered, a cleaning woman carrying the tools of her trade reached the top of the stairs and went silently out of sight down a hallway.

From behind the desk, a clerk came through a doorway that was curtained with strings of Victorian beads. She smiled at me in spite of my clothes.

"May I help you?"

I smiled back. "I hope so. I just learned that a couple of friends of mine are on the island and I'm trying to track them down.

You wouldn't happen to have a couple of Boston guys staying here, would you? A young guy with dark hair and one a little older, beginning to gray? Fred and Angie? Been here maybe a week?"

The smile stayed on her face. "I'm sorry, sir, but it's our policy not to reveal the names of our guests. I hope you understand."

I nodded and looked around. "Sure. Privacy should come with a place like this. So this is Al's Vineyard property, eh? He said it was nice and he was right. Small and personal with everything first class."

The clerk's expression was slightly changed when I looked back at her.

"You're a friend of Mr. Cabot, sir?

I grinned. "I like to think so, but you know what the old poem says: 'The Lowells speak only to Cabots and the Cabots speak only to God.' "

Her smile returned. "I take it that you're denying that you're God?"

"You take it correctly. Well, when I see Al I'll be sure to tell him that you're defending the gates. Say, can I leave a message for Fred, just in case he happens to come by? Do you have a sheet of paper I can use?"

She dimpled. "Of course, sir. Just in case he comes by." We shared a jesting, conspiratorial smile as I took the paper.

I wrote: "Fred, sorry to have missed you. I'll catch up with you later." I signed it "J.W.," folded it, wrote "Fred" on the outside and handed it to her.

"No last name?" she asked.

"If he comes by, just Fred will do." I winked.

"I'll make sure he gets it." She grinned. "If he comes by."

I thanked her and headed for the door, then turned and said, "Say, Al isn't around, is he?"

She beamed some more. "I'm afraid I can't comment on who's staying here."

I smiled in turn. "Of course."

I went out, then stepped quickly along the porch and peeked in through a window. The clerk had opened my note and was reaching toward a telephone on the counter. I walked on around to the back of the building, where I found the parking lot, the rear exit, and the narrow fire stairs leading down from the second and third floors. From the back, the hotel looked less smashing than from the front, but it still cut a good figure.

There were four cars in the lot: a VW Rabbit, a forest-green Hummer in a private parking spot, a dark-windowed white Mercedes sedan, and a nondescript middle-aged

Chevy pickup. I guessed that the pickup belonged to the cleaning lady and the VW belonged to the clerk. Of course I knew I might be wrong since there are more millionaire plumbers than doctors on the Vineyard these days and, for all I knew, cleaning ladies and desk clerks might be driving Cadillacs.

I walked back to my truck and drove around a few of the many narrow, one-way streets that wind between Oak Bluffs' lace-trimmed cottages until I found a parking spot where I could keep an eye on both the hotel's front door and the parking lot exit.

Nothing happened for a while, then the Mercedes came out of the lot and drove away. I followed it.

The car moved slowly, which is the proper way to navigate in Oak Bluffs. In this case, hesitations at side roads and excessively long pauses at stop signs also suggested that the driver was unfamiliar with the town's streets. I stayed well back until the Mercedes found its way to the Oak Bluffs–Edgartown Road and turned right toward the state beach. Then, to make sure I wouldn't lose it in the heavy flow of traffic between the beach and Sengekontacket Pond, I moved closer.

Under the high blue summer sky the

beach was full of bright umbrellas. The beach side of the highway was lined with parked cars, while on the pond side the bike path was busy with walkers and bikers. The highway itself was a slow-moving parking lot, crowded with cars, motorcycles, scooters, and mopeds moving in both directions and slowed still more by people creeping along looking for parking places or trying to back their cars into those spaces when they found them. When we got to the big bridge, I found it crowded with the traditional laughing and screaming teenagers jumping off the railing into the water, and noted that the channel was, as usual, lined with fishermen who probably didn't care whether or not they caught anything.

The driver of the Mercedes moved cautiously along and I followed suit, careful to brake for street-crossing beachgoers and ever alert for children who might dart into the road. It was a cheerful picture, all in all. Very Vineyardish. I wondered if the person I was following appreciated the noisy innocence of the scene.

Traffic picked up speed a bit after we crossed Crab Creek. The Mercedes drove into Edgartown, crept through the Stop & Shop/Al's Package Store traffic jam, then turned right onto the West Tisbury road.

I paused before turning onto the road to give the driver a good start, then followed. To my surprise, he wasn't too far ahead of me and seemed to be loafing along.

Hmmmm?

He turned left onto Meshacket Road and I wondered briefly if he was going to do some shopping at Morning Glory Farm, but he kept on going. I turned after him and followed the winding road. He turned into the Island Grove housing development. I drove past the entrance, turned around and drove back to the farm's parking lot.

Island Grove has only one entrance, so unless the driver was really going to an address there, which I didn't believe because I was pretty sure he'd spotted me and was double-checking to make sure he was right, he'd have to come back out the way he came in. Not seeing me on his tail any longer, he'd have to decide whether he'd been right about me and then he'd have to decide whether to return past the farm or go on along Meshacket to Clevelandtown Road and eventually on to where he actually wanted to go.

My guess was that being unfamiliar with the island he'd come back past the farm where, if he'd noticed me at all, he might have been fooled into thinking I'd been after fresh veggies all the time. If he went the other way, of course, I'd lose him.

About ten minutes later the Mercedes came past the farm and turned left toward West Tisbury. The car's darkened windows prevented me from seeing the driver, but didn't prevent him from seeing me if he was looking, which I imagined he was since I certainly would have been in his place.

I pulled out after him but this time didn't find him dawdling along in front of me. Instead, he'd apparently decided to take advantage of the fact that he had a Mercedes and I had an ancient, rusty Land Cruiser and had put the pedal to the metal. I saw his car disappearing over a far hill and by the time I got to the top of the same hill he was out of sight.

There are a lot of side roads and driveways leading off that highway, including those leading to Oak Bluffs and into the county airport itself, and he could have taken any or none of them. My tailing skills were obviously not up to snuff and now I was paying the price. I mentally flipped a coin and drove on to West Tisbury on the off chance that he might be returning to the scene of the crime for some reason.

But I didn't find him near Roland Nunes's place or anywhere else in the neighborhood.

Unfortunately for me, even if I'd been right in following him that far, he might have taken any of the several roads leaving West Tisbury, including the three leading through Chilmark and the two you could follow back toward Vineyard Haven. I drove up Music Street, where I admired David Mc-Cullough's white picket fence, then followed Panhandle Road around to Scotchman's Lane where I took a right and then a left, and was headed back to Edgartown. Alas, the driver's destination, wherever it was, was going to remain a secret from me for the time being, at least.

Still, all had not been in vain. I had the Mercedes' license plate number.

In Edgartown I stopped at the police station where, as a bow to Homeland Security, you now had to punch a button to gain admittance through the front door. I punched and was admitted by Kit Goulart, who had not grown smaller since last I'd seen her. She was my height and outweighed me by several stone. I asked her if the chief was in and she allowed as how he was.

I went to his office and tapped on the open door. He was sucking an empty pipe and looked up from a pile of papers.

"Don't tell me," I said. "I already know that computers have created more paperwork than you had before they were invented and that you think you'll move to Nova Scotia for the summer. Have you ever actually been to Nova Scotia?"

He sat back. "We went up there one fall, in fact. Great place. Bright-colored houses and all the lobster you can eat. Bagpipes and fiddles. We loved it. Like the island was forty years ago. What are you doing here again? I just saw you yesterday. I thought you spent the summers either up there in the woods or out on East Beach."

"I need a favor," I said.

"I should have known. Something legal, I hope."

"I want to know who owns a white Mercedes sedan." I gave him the license number.

"This wouldn't have to do with the business up in West Tisbury, would it? Naturally, you're probably mixed up in that somehow."

I admitted as much and told him about Zee and the kids being gone and being bored and everything except the part about Roland Nunes's desertion.

Of course he picked up on that and eyed me over his pipe. "How come Carole Cohen didn't want you to go to the police in the first place?"

"You'll have to ask Carole Cohen."

"You don't know?"

"Would you believe client confidentiality? Anyway, the police are involved."

He snorted. "And so are you. You just can't keep your nose in your own business. You know, about half of my work would end if two or three families would move off this island. Yours is one of them. Not because of Zee or the kids, just because of you. Wait here." He got up and went out of the room.

It wasn't the first time I'd heard the two-or-three-families statement, because it was almost as true for Edgartown as it was for most small towns: A few people from a few dysfunctional families caused half the grief in their communities, with trouble passed down from one generation to the next. The drunken father produces a drunken daughter; a son beats up his girlfriend and steals from his mother, and both women lie to the cops about who did it; the kid who drives his car too fast and kills his buddy when they hit a tree is the same kid who deals coke in the high school halls and has a baby or two in the junior class. When the police get called out to tend to trouble in any of its many forms, they're rarely surprised by who they find at the scene.

The chief came back into the office and tossed a piece of paper to me. I caught it in the air.

"There," he said. "Does that help?"

The car had been rented in Boston by Frederick McMahan of Charlestown.

Fred.

"Do you know anything about this Fred McMahan?" I asked.

"No."

"Do you think you could find out?"

"I could if I had some time to waste, which I don't. Maybe your reporter pal on the *Globe* can help you out. Anyway, you should be dealing with the West Tisbury cops, not me. That's where you got in trouble and the Carson woman was killed."

"I think this is one of the guys who put that stun-gun shot into me. If that was him making the phone threat I told you about, he may use a real one the next time."

The phone threat had come to someone in his town, which made it his business. He chewed his pipe stem and I knew he wished he was still puffing tobacco, because years after giving up the weed I, too, sometimes still had an urge to stoke up my corncob.

"I'll see what I can learn," he said finally.

"While you're at it, see if he's tied to the guy called Angie. And maybe you could spread the word about that Mercedes. We have ten police forces on this little island and one of their minions might see it somewhere and have a chat with the driver."

"Anything else you want to tell me to do that I was going to do anyway?" asked the chief. "If not, good-bye." As I left, he added, "Be careful."

I drove back to Oak Bluffs and checked the parking lot behind the Noepe Hotel. The Hummer was gone but the VW and the pickup were there along with a couple of cars I hadn't seen before. The clerk and the cleaning lady were still at work and they had some new customers to deal with. I was sorry I hadn't written down the Hummer's license plate number and compensated by writing down those of the two new cars in the lot. Maybe Fred had imported a couple of friends to help him.

I was conscious of time flowing past. Zee would be home in a few days and I wanted this business over and done with before she and the children came on the scene. Not for the first time I felt that having a house and family was, like love itself, not only the greatest of blessings but the greatest of dangers.

I glanced at my watch, got back in the truck, and drove to West Tisbury.

15

When I knocked on Babs Carson's door, Robert Chadwick answered, filling the doorway with his body. I thought, from the look on his face, that he was exhausted and unsure whether or not to let me come in.

"How is she?" I asked.

"Devastated, of course."

"I'd like to talk with her."

"Well . . ." He wasn't sure it was his place to defend her gates.

I empathized with him. "You're wearing yourself out emotionally," I said. "She's a strong woman and she'll be all right eventually, but right now you need to keep your own energy up so you can help her past this hard place she's in."

He took a deep breath. "Grief wears you out," he said. "So does trying to help but not really being able to do it. I'm afraid I'm not very good at being soothing."

"I think you're probably what she needs

right now," I said. "Does she have any woman friends? Maybe you should have one of them come over, too."

"I've asked her if she wants that. She just shook her head."

"I'll come back later if I can't see her now," I said. "But the colder a trail gets, the harder it is to follow. I want to know about the men in Melissa's life."

His big body still blocked the doorway. "The police have already been here. Babs answered all their questions."

"They won't be telling me what they learned," I said. "I'm too involved in this prowler business to walk away and do nothing, and I liked Melissa enough to want to catch her killer. Babs is my best bet to learn about her daughter's past."

He thought for a moment, then stepped back and let me in. He led me to a studio attached to the rear of the building, where Babs Carson was sitting in a tall chair in front of a painting of bright flowers, dabbing at the canvas now and then with a thin brush. She wore a long, paint-stained apron.

The easel was set up in what was obviously a potter's studio, and I wondered if it was significant that Babs was painting instead of potting. Was she avoiding her life's work, just as she was avoiding thoughts of her daughter's death?

She looked at me with indifference, and I had the impression that nothing really interested her, not even the painting in front of her.

"You remember Mr. Jackson," said Chadwick.

"Of course. You were here just the other day."

"Yes. I met your daughter, too. I was very sorry to learn of her death."

She nodded, and touched her brush to her canvas. "Yes. Thank you."

"I liked her."

"I loved her."

"I don't mean to be intrusive, but I want to ask you about the men in her life."

"I told the police everything I know, which isn't a lot, really. Melissa enjoyed shocking people, but she really wasn't one to entertain with intimate stories of her affairs."

"You implied that she'd been married more than once, and that she led an active social life," I said. "It's not unusual for an abandoned lover or spouse to want to harm his ex-wife or mistress. Did any of Melissa's men ever say or do anything to suggest that he was going to get even for being abandoned?"

Her voice was weary. "The police asked

the same questions and I told them no. My daughter was married three times, but the last divorce was almost four years ago. She kept on good terms with all of her exes, curiously enough. In fact, she got along with them better after their divorces than before. I've heard that's not unusual. People can be good friends as long as they're not married to one another."

My first wife had divorced me because she couldn't stand the tension of being a policeman's wife, ever fearful that her husband might be shot. Now, years later, some of the love we'd felt for one another during our marriage still lingered even though we'd both remarried and begun new lives.

"Was she on good terms with her ex-lovers, as well?" I asked.

"I know less about them. She brought some men to the house to meet me, and I found some of them clever and entertaining, but not most. She liked personable men and so do I, so I hit it off with those quite well." She paused. "Of course there were a lot I didn't care for, such as Alfred Cabot, for example, but she usually shed them fairly quickly. I wondered sometimes if she wasn't using me as a measuring rod. You know, as a test of her judgment. If Mother didn't approve, daughter would find a new man. Melissa never admitted to such a thing, of course, but that's how it sometimes seemed to me." She studied her painting, then wiped her brush, dipped it in a bit of yellow on her palette, and touched it to her canvas.

I said, "But even if you approved, she didn't keep the latest man on her string."

"No, it was more as though my approval didn't guarantee a long relationship, but my disapproval guaranteed a short one."

"But when I was here, she was wearing an engagement ring, and it was my impression that you didn't care for the man who'd given it to her."

"Alfred Cabot? Your impression was correct. Alfred is a money man. He was born with it, he studied how to make more of it, he makes it, and he plans to continue making it, although he'll never be able to spend what he already has. I consider him a complete blah."

"Why do you suppose Melissa agreed to marry him?"

"I simply can't imagine." Babs looked directly at me. "Anyway, as you know, being engaged to Alfred didn't inhibit Melissa from pursuing other men such as yourself and Mr. Nunes. I personally believe that the engagement wasn't going to last, and that was fine by me."

"Maybe it was his money."

She shook her head. "No. She had all the money she needed. A trust fund. She didn't have to work, although I believe she'd have been happier if she had." She looked at her canvas. "People need to work at something, I think."

"Some people never have enough money."

"That would be Alfred Cabot, not Melissa."

"Do you know if Cabot is on the island right now?"

Her tired eyes seemed to brighten. "No. Why?"

"Do you know what kind of car he drives?"

"I don't know what you call them. One of those big, square things that take up most of the road."

"A Hummer?"

"That's it. I understand they're very fashionable, although I can't see why. Maybe it's another one of those conspicuous consumption items that you buy so people will know that you're rich. Alfred likes being rich and he likes to have people know that he is. Money and the things it will buy are his standards of success."

"Maybe he thought of Melissa as a trophy."

"I can understand him wanting her; I can't understand her wanting him. My best guess is that it was just her private joke."

"What do you mean?"

She studied her painting. "He's a man who uses people to make money and thinks that money will buy him what he wants, which it usually does. I thought that she might have decided to play with him the way he plays with other people, to use him the way he uses them. To let him think he was buying her, too, and then to drop him for someone without any money. It would have amused her."

"For someone like Roland Nunes?"

She shrugged. "Or you, although she gave up that idea faster than I thought she would. She usually didn't pay much attention to men's wedding rings."

"Were there angry wives?"

"I wouldn't know. If so, Melissa never mentioned them. I suspect that when she handed their husbands back, the wives were no longer interested in her." She smiled a strange smile. "You attracted her but she seemed to know very quickly that you weren't available. It was unusual for her to admit defeat so rapidly."

I could see Melissa in my mind and felt again the affection I'd had for her in spite of, or possibly because of, her cheerful hedonism. "I found her very attractive," I said, "but I'm very married. Can you think of anyone at all who might have wished your daughter harm?"

She shook her head and her eyes grew empty as her brief energy left her. "I cannot."

She sat there like a gray ghost, staring sightlessly at the painting in front of her.

Robert Chadwick moved into my vision. "I think that's enough for now, Mr. Jackson."

I thanked her for her time, but got no response before I followed Chadwick out of the room. At the front door, I stopped and said, "You know something about Melissa. Do you agree with her mother's assessment of her husbands and lovers and the lovers' wives? Were they all so benign? So lacking in anger when she moved on to her next conquest?"

"I don't know," he said with a frown. "But there is one thing I do know that I've already told the police and that may interest you as well. The night she died, after I watched the news, I took a nightcap out to the patio. While I was sitting there, enjoying the air, I heard voices on the other side of my wall. Male and female voices, arguing. I couldn't make out the words, but there was no doubt about the tone. The argument went on for a good five minutes, then seemed to stop. I thought it was over, but a few minutes later it started again. The voices weren't really loud, but they were bitter; it was as though both of them were trying to keep from attracting attention. I thought about going over to the wall and telling them to go somewhere else before they woke up the rest of the neighbors, but then the argument stopped again." He paused. "The next morning they found Melissa's body right about where I'd heard the voices. I think I may have heard the murderer speaking just before he killed her."

"What did the police have to say when you told them what you'd heard?"

"They wanted to know about the exact time and what was said and they wanted me to describe the voices, but I couldn't do any of that. They asked me to try to remember and to tell them anything that I can recall, but I can recall nothing. Angry voices, bitter laughter. That's all I remember."

"Something may come back to you. If it does, even if it seems insignificant, tell the police. I'd like to know, too."

"All right, but I'm getting old and my ears

and my memory aren't as good as they used to be." He glanced back toward the studio. "I'd better be getting back. I don't want Babs to be alone."

I went to my car, hoping that Chadwick's friendship would be a comfort to Babs in the long loneliness that follows the death of a child. I couldn't imagine ever recovering from the death of one of mine.

I drove the short distance to the place where Melissa's body had been found, parked outside the yellow police tape that still surrounded the spot, and walked down the ancient way to Roland Nunes's house. He and his moped were gone, probably to work, since the world continues to turn after a murder just as it did before.

The site was peaceful and serene, showing no sign of new intrusions. I went into the unlocked house and began a search, looking for anything that might give me a clue about possible enemies or aspects of his or her character that had eluded me so far.

I found nothing helpful to me. No revelatory letters, no enigmatic possessions, no remembrances of things past. Only a few books, a small ivory Buddha, a string of wooden prayer beads, clothing, and utensils for cooking and eating. The double cot still smelled faintly of lavender. Aside from that,

Nunes's home was as simple and unadorned as the man himself. He was what he appeared to be: almost a monk. Except, of course, for his involvement with Melissa.

Who would want to terrorize a monk?

Who would a monk want to terrorize?

I ran murder possibilities through my mind. Was it Nunes's voice that Chadwick had heard that night, arguing with a woman? Was Melissa the woman? It was a good guess that she was, since Nunes had reported that she'd left him after the late summer darkness had finally fallen.

Maybe Nunes had changed his mind about being seduced and had gone after her only to discover that she'd also changed her mind about him. Maybe they'd argued and he'd killed her in a fit of rage. Such things had happened before.

Or maybe she'd met the killer when she'd reached the road. It seemed unlikely that such a meeting would have been purely coincidental: Lone woman meets killer by chance and is murdered on the spot. Things like that also happen, of course, but rarely.

Maybe she hadn't been killed where her body had been found, but somewhere else, after which the body was placed where they'd found it. The police would know after they got the Medical Examiner's report.

Maybe they'd tell me. Maybe not.

Would she have gotten into a stranger's car and driven off with him? She was a woman who liked an adventure and wasn't afraid of much, so maybe that's what had happened. Then she'd been killed and the killer had dumped her where he'd found her and gotten well away in a hurry.

I walked back to my truck, passing near Robert Chadwick's wall, and looked around the scene of the crime just in case the police had missed a clue: a piece of paper containing the killer's confession, for instance. I found nothing.

Of course I didn't actually know that Melissa had been murdered, so maybe I was wasting my time trying to solve a crime that hadn't happened. But I didn't think that was the case.

I looked back down the ancient way, imagining that it was night and Melissa's light was coming toward me, the murderer. Who am I? Why am I here, waiting? Do I know who's coming toward me? Do I care? Am I going to kill whoever it is, because it's that time of the moon?

Or do I know it's Melissa, and I'm here specifically to meet her and no one else?

The light came nearer through the darkness and then, suddenly, I was standing in daylight again and I was alone, looking down the empty ancient way near yellow police tape that moved gently in the soft summer wind.

16

I sat in my truck and looked at Robert
Chadwick's wall. Above it, the second story
of his house could be seen. I wondered if
Chadwick had really heard the argument
he'd described.

Babs, Melissa, and Chadwick himself had
hinted that Chadwick was interested in
Babs, and certainly his actions since Melissa's death supported that idea. But what
if his overt interest in Babs hid a covert one
for Melissa? The aging professor and the
sultry student were characters in many a
tale, after all; usually one leading to a bad
end. Maybe Chadwick had been the man in
the darkness, aflame with jealousy. Maybe
he had killed his would-be mistress in a fit
of rage. Chadwick was a big, powerful man,
and she would have been no match for him.
Then he'd left her there, knowing that
Nunes would be the logical suspect, and
had returned to his house, afterward play-

ing the role of loving neighbor to the grieving mother.

All good teachers have something of the thespian in them, but was Chadwick that good an actor? Good enough to fool everyone into believing he was incapable of murder? Certainly I was fairly confident that he was what he seemed. It was a conviction I'd have to keep watch over, lest it became a blinder; so when I pushed it to the back of my mind I made a note about where to find it again if I needed to.

Since I was already in West Tisbury, I drove to the town library where, because I usually do business with the Edgartown library, I entered without getting recognized by the ladies at the front desk. I found a *Who's Who* and looked up Alfred Cabot, then went to the computer and looked him up there, as well.

Alfred had made his name by being very rich, by being a leading figure in large financial enterprises, and by belonging to clubs and organizations, philanthropic and otherwise, whose membership consisted of people much like himself, whose photos often appeared in the society pages. He had homes on Beacon Hill, in Aquinnah, and on Hilton Head, and he owned a ten-thousand-acre ranch outside Santa Fe, where he played on his private golf club, rode Arabian horses, and landed his jet at his own airport. My sister Margarite lived near Santa Fe but I doubted if she and Alfred were in the same social circle.

He had been married twice and divorced twice. No children. His photo showed a tall, attractive, middle-aged man who didn't look like the blah person Babs and Melissa had agreed that he was. I wondered if, like Chadwick, he'd been taken for a lot of money by his previous wives and if he'd proposed to Melissa because she already had money and wouldn't need his if they ever split up. Maybe I'd ask him if I ever met him.

When I returned to the Land Cruiser, I left the book on the table instead of returning it to its shelf myself, so the librarian could put it back and be confident that it was where it belonged instead of worrying about whether I'd put it on some shelf where it would be lost forever. Librarians don't need any more problems; they have enough already.

I drove down to Edgartown and finally found a parking place at the far end of School Street. Parking spots are not always easy to find in the summertime and the dreaded parking police cheerfully distribute tickets to any car parked for more than an hour, so I hustled right to the County of Dukes County Courthouse. It took most of my hour to track down the deed for Alfred Cabot's land in Aquinnah, but I was back in my truck and on my way, a map in hand, while the young summer cop who was writing tickets was still walking past the historical society. Sometimes God is on your side.

Aquinnah is the westernmost village on the island, and is the site of many beautiful houses. It's a lovely place, best known for its multicolored clay cliffs, its fine beaches, and its excellent fishing. It's also the home of the local tribe of Wampanoag Indians, which seems to be in constant confrontation with the town selectmen, and it is infamous for the no-parking signs that line the roads next to the beaches where once people freely parked so they could swim or sun or pursue the wily blues and bass. Nowadays you have to pay big money to park in the town lot before hoofing it to the shore. Worse yet, you have to pay fifty cents to use its public toilets, a policy I find offensive to both man and God.

Because of Wampanoag/selectmen arguments and the town's seemingly endless inability to get its finances or other business practices in order, Aquinnah's politics are second only to those of Oak Bluffs as a subject of laughter for the citizens of the island's other towns. Of course Aquinnah's people are, like Queen Victoria and the citizens of Oak Bluffs, not amused by this humor.

My friends Joe and Toni Begay live with their children in a small house at the north end of the cliffs, and Toni owns one of the shops at the top of the cliffs where the tour buses stop and unload hundreds of sightseers and souvenir hunters every day. When I want to fish in Aquinnah, I often park in the Begays' yard to save my children's inheritance from the parking-lot attendants. Today, however, I wasn't planning to visit the Begays. I was after richer game.

Alfred Cabot owned just under a hundred acres of land overlooking both Menemsha Pond and Vineyard Sound. I could see what I thought was the top of his house from the road, but his driveway was closed by one of those electronic gates that open only to a properly coded switch in your car or by the attendant in the small gatehouse under the trees. The gate and gatehouse were sure indications that Cabot was relatively new to the Vineyard. Old island money is never displayed so overtly; the driveways to the homes of the longtime aristocrats are usually plain, sandy lanes winding bumpily out of sight. No gates or gatehouses for them.

I parked in front of the gate and waited, but was not surprised when the attendant declined to open it, instead coming out of the gatehouse, eyeing my rusty truck suspiciously, and asking my business.

"My name's Jackson," I said, "I'm here to look at the tree."

He frowned. "What tree?"

"The one with blight. I got a call."

"Wait here." He stepped away and pulled out a cell phone. As he spoke, his frown got deeper. When he rang off, he came back and said, "Nobody called about a tree, mister."

It was my turn to frown. "Is this the Cabot place, or not?"

"It's the Cabot place, but they never called anybody about a tree. You've made a mistake, buddy."

"You got any jokers up there at the house? Somebody called me and told me there was an elm up there with blight and they wanted me to take a look at it and maybe take it down."

"Sorry, pal. Somebody pulled a fast one on you. The joker is probably some friend of yours. You've made a trip for nothing."

So much for the direct approach. Fortunately for me, Cabot's land wasn't far from Uncle Bill Vanderbeck's wife's place, so I drove there.

Uncle Bill always denied the belief of some of his fellow Wampanoags that he was a shaman who could, if he chose, be invisible and walk through walls; his explanation for why he was often unseen until he seemed to choose to be noticed was that he was so insignificant that people just overlooked him. There was no question, however, that he was a gardener par excellence whose every thumb and finger was figuratively green.

It was this love of flowers and vegetables that had led him to friendship and then marriage with the widow Angela Marcus, whose Mafioso husband, Luciano, had left her a major-league estate next to the land recently purchased by Alfred Cabot. Both Uncle Bill's and Angela's great joy was in their gardens and each other; neither was entranced by Angela's vast holdings although, being frugal, they were careful to maintain both land and buildings using Luciano's careful-eyed staff to do the work and keep things quiet in case any of his old enemies showed up.

I was a known person to the estate's attendants, so when I encountered the young man who just happened to be standing beside the driveway as I drove up toward the house, I received a nod of recognition and a friendly wave before, in my rearview mirror, I saw him lift a cell phone to his ear.

The house was a white slash built into the side of the hill, half underground, very modern, and filled with the best that Luciano's money could buy. I found Uncle Bill and Angela in the vegetable garden, kneeling side by side before a row of peas and filling a basket with their finds.

"How nice to see you," said Angela, smiling from under her straw hat. "Is the rest of the family with you?" She peered around me.

"Would you like some peas?" asked Uncle Bill. "We have more than enough for us and the crew."

I had plenty of peas in my own garden, but a few more wouldn't hurt. I could make a meal of fresh peas alone.

I explained where my family was and said I'd love some peas. "What I really want to do," I said, "is snoop on your neighbor. Do you mind if I walk up to the top of the hill and have a look at his place?" I told them about being rebuffed by the guard at the gate.

"There's a new fence up there," said Uncle Bill, whose tone indicated that it was the most natural thing in the world for me to want to spy on Alfred Cabot. "A hundred years ago there was a path running along the ridge, but he's closed it off."

"I don't need to go onto his land," I said. "I just want to see if there's a car in his yard."

"He drives a green Hummer," said Uncle Bill. "I thought I saw it on the road a couple days back."

"I'm interested in a white Mercedes."

"Do you want to borrow some binoculars?" asked Angela. She had been married to Luciano for a long time and was used to odd comings and goings.

"No," I said. "I have my own."

"Well, we'll be done here before you get back from your walk. Come into the kitchen and your peas will be waiting for you. Do you want someone to go up with you?"

"No, I'll find my way."

I walked up toward the hilltop through the trees. I could see Menemsha Pond on my right, and when I paused and looked back, I could see Squibnocket Pond and beyond Squibnocket beach to the misty horizon where the ocean met the sky. Far out, a trawler was spreading its wings like a tiny insect as it moved across the blue-gray water.

When I reached the ridge I looked out over Vineyard Sound to the Elizabeth Islands, and on across Buzzards Bay to the mainland where a smoky haze hung over New Bedford. In the slanting, late afternoon light, the sound was still busy with boats.

I turned left and started along the ridge, following an ancient track kept open by deer. Soon, I came to the fence Uncle Bill had mentioned. It was still bright with newness, a tall mesh of woven wire topped by two strands of barbed wire, more appropriate for a factory complex or power plant than for a house. A narrow path paralleled the fence on the other side. The trail I was following passed under the fence and faded into the trees on down the ridge. I didn't think a deer could clear the fence. Maybe Alfred Cabot had a phobia about Santa Claus and wanted to keep him and Rudolph and the rest of the team off his land. Didn't he remember that they could fly?

I walked along the fence until it crossed a rock ledge above a steep slope that fell away to the west. Across a meadow at the foot of the slope were Cabot's house and outbuildings. All were new and slightly oversized, as was the mode for the island's current mansionizers. I guessed that Cabot had a grand view in three directions.

A forest-green Hummer was parked on a circular drive in front of the house. One of the ubiquitous Mini Coopers was there, too. Maybe I was the only person left who didn't own one or the other. I didn't see a white Mercedes, but that didn't mean much because there was a four-car garage attached to the near side of the house and a barn to boot, in either of which might have been several parked cars.

I surveyed the scene with the trusty old WWI German field glasses I'd inherited from my father, who'd gotten them in an Army-Navy store before I was born. They were heavy and bulky, but the lenses were wonderful. I sat down and watched things for a while, not knowing exactly what I expected to see. What I finally did see was a flash of sunlight dancing off something. I looked harder and saw a scope looking back at me. In short order, a door in the barn opened and an ATV drove out. In a scabbard attached behind the driver was a black stick. The driver glanced up the hill in my direction and sped out of sight into the trees to my right.

I thought the black stick looked a lot like a shotgun. I listened to the sound of the

ATV coming up the ridge and decided that it was time to move. A hundred yards east of the rock ledge I lay motionless behind a fallen oak tree and watched through my binoculars while the ATV came along the path paralleling the fence and stopped near where I'd been. The black stick was definitely a shotgun, and I couldn't think of any hunting season going on. The driver looked carefully around but his eyes passed over me without stopping. He studied the ledge and looked down at the house, then took a short drink from a canteen and sat in the shade. He didn't seem to be going away, so I did.

17

"Here are your peas," said Angela, handing me a paper bag.

"Thanks," I said. "I'll have them for supper."

"Did you see what you wanted to see?" asked Uncle Bill.

"No Mercedes, but I did see a couple of other vehicles." I told them about the ATV rider coming up the ridge to investigate.

Angela and Uncle Bill looked at each other. "Maybe I should send Mario up there to take a look at things," said Angela. "That's probably what Luciano would do."

"Have any of us walked that fence since Cabot put it up?" asked Uncle Bill. "We probably should. Mario can do that."

I hadn't mentioned the shotgun, but now I did and suggested that they tell Mario about it before he went fence walking.

"Maybe I'll send Sean along with Mario," said Angela, frowning slightly.

I knew I was the cause of the frown, and felt regret. "I've brought you a problem," I said.

"Oh no," said Uncle Bill. "No problem. Neighbors used to get together to walk the stone walls between them and make repairs. Sean and Mario will just be checking out the new fence. Maybe they'll have a chance to chat with the man on the ATV. If he asks about you, we'll tell him you were a guest out for a walk, looking for birds."

He smiled a shaman smile and I wondered if he was thinking about walking through the fence and on down to the Cabot place to see things close up. There were real benefits to being invisible, sometimes. Not for Claude Rains, of course, but it doesn't snow on the Vineyard in the summertime.

"I'll be on my way before I cause more trouble," I said.

"You're never any trouble, J.W.," said Angela, giving me a kiss. "When Zee gets home, you've all got to come up for a cookout."

Uncle Bill walked me to my truck. "You be careful," he said. "You said you gave your real name to the guard at the gate. It might have been smarter to have used another one." He cocked his head to one side. "Unless, of course, you wanted Cabot to know you were there."

"I'll be careful," I said.

I drove back home through the falling light, thinking about what I knew and didn't know and hoping that Carole or Jordan Cohen would still be at Gull Realty. Jordan was, and I asked him if I could borrow his night glasses and camera. He gave them to me but was worried about Carole's brother now that Melissa had been killed.

"You don't think they'll be back at Roland's place tonight, do you?"

"Probably not," I said. "But you never know."

"I don't want you chasing them again. You could be the next to die."

I smiled at him. "Don't worry. Being stungunned once was enough to last me a lifetime."

Beachgoers were streaming home as I drove out of town, and the afternoon traffic jam had formed between Al's Package Store and the Stop & Shop, caused, of course, by people making left turns. When I'm king I'm banning left turns. However, since everyone else was coming into the village and I was going out of it, I made pretty good time. I picked up the mail from our box on the highway and studied the tire tracks on our driveway. They looked like

225

mine, so I drove down to the house.

Oliver Underfoot and Velcro came meowing from their sunny spot on the front porch, making me more sure that no one was waiting for me inside. Still, cats don't make good watchdogs, so instead of going in the front door, I walked around to the back one and peeked through its window into the kitchen and on through its far door into the living room. I saw no visitors. Glad that I kept my hinges oiled, I went inside and, avoiding the squeaky board in the kitchen floor, moved through the house room by room until I was sure no one was there.

Oliver Underfoot and Velcro took turns meowing along behind me and racing ahead chasing each other, until they saw that I was through playing whatever odd human game I was playing and told me it was time for their evening snack. I gave it to them and then, for my own supper, stir-fried my fresh peas and grilled a piece of striped bass. When the peas were done, I put them on my plate beside the bass and poured Italian dressing over them. The fragrance set my taste buds dancing. Solomon in all his glory never ate so well.

I was carrying the dishes to the sink when the phone rang. It was Olive Otero, working late. "I thought you might want to know that we just got the ME's report. Melissa Carson's neck was broken by person or persons unknown."

I wasn't surprised but I was disappointed. An accidental death would have simplified things. I thanked Olive and rang off.

The evening light lingered long, so I had plenty of time to wash the dishes and rig a switch for my outdoor lights so I could turn them off and on from the kids' tree house. I then had an after-dinner cognac as I waited for guests to arrive.

I wondered if, in fact, they would arrive. I'd left my name in enough places and there was no secret about where I lived, so it was at least possible that Fred and Angie and whoever their boss might be would decide to do more to encourage me to disengage from their activities, since their phone call hadn't done the trick. And if they did, it seemed likely that they'd do it at night, as was their practice when vandalizing Roland Nunes's place. A man's home might be his castle, but it's also an easy target for enemies. Maybe that's why those ever-traveling movie cowboys I'd watched as a kid never had houses. The most they could lose was their horses when they tangled with the bad guys, and nobody would have dared shoot

Trigger or Silver.

Darkness came down and the sky filled with stars. Night sounds replaced those of the day. I checked my borrowed camera and night glasses, got my Remington 16-gauge, and mused awhile over shot size before taking a handful of bird-shot shells from the gun cabinet, and climbed into the kids' tree house in our big beech tree. It was an excellent tree house, modeled in part after the great one that Tarzan, Jane, and Boy lived in when Johnny Weissmuller was Tarzan. It had a rope you could use to swing down to the ground and a rope bridge leading to a nearby oak tree. It was not a very comfortable place for adults to sleep since there really wasn't room for them to lie down, but my family and I were very fond of it anyway. From the main room you had an excellent view of our yard.

I sat in the darkness and waited.

Nothing happened for a long time, and I began to get stiff and to wonder if I'd been wrong.

Then, as I surveyed things with my glasses, I saw movement up the dark driveway. A kneeling figure in black was staring at the house through night vision goggles mounted on a face-mask carriage. I'd once seen them priced in a military equipment magazine for about five thousand dollars, so apparently my stalker wasn't lacking in money. Certainly he was equipped with newer stuff than I was.

The figure looked for some time, then turned and seemed to speak to someone I couldn't see. When the talking was over, the figure rose and moved forward until it reached the yard. I snapped a couple of pictures of the intruder before he hustled across the open yard and hunkered down behind my Land Cruiser.

Then, for a while, nothing happened until in the woods in back of the shed behind the house a dry branch broke as a careless foot came down. Even with state-of-the-art night vision goggles you need to watch where you're stepping. The careless walker stayed quiet for a time, no doubt waiting to learn if he'd been heard. When he was sure he had not, he came on, making small sounds that suggested he was more of a city stalker than a country one.

I took his picture when he peered around the corner of the shed and studied the back of the house. Then I saw him lift a small radio to his mouth and speak into it. I shifted my glasses to the front of the house and, sure enough, stalker number one was peering over the hood of the truck at the front door and talking back. My guess was that one of them was going inside the house and the other was covering the opposite door in case I tried to run away. I looked back to the second man and changed my mind because he was now easing toward the house carrying a small fuel can.

The son of a bitch was going to set fire to my house!

I let him get about halfway between the shed and the house then shot him in the legs. He screamed and dropped his walkie-talkie as I jacked another shell into the firing chamber and flipped on the outside lights. I swung the gun and put a shot right where intruder number one had been peeking over the Land Cruiser, but he was already running fast up the driveway. I led him and shot at him; he fell down but was immediately up again and running hard. He was out of sight in an instant.

I turned back to Intruder Two and saw him, too, running, limping, back into the woods. I put the sights on his rump and squeezed the trigger, but my gun, which had been choked to hold only three shells, was empty. I plugged three more shells into the magazine, jacked a new one into the firing chamber, swung down on the rope, and ran after the second man as far as the shed, where I stopped and fired blindly into the dark woods just to keep him on his way. In the distance I heard the diminishing sounds of breaking branches. I guessed that he probably didn't know where he was running but was just putting as much distance as possible between me and him. If he didn't start running in circles, he'd soon reach the Felix Neck wildlife sanctuary, where he'd find a road that would make his running easier.

Birdshot wouldn't kill him or his friend, but it had bloodied them more than a little. When I thought of the fuel can I had a fleeting wish that I'd used buckshot.

I walked back toward the house and found the fuel can and a walkie-talkie. I turned off the radio and sniffed the can. Gasoline. Damn.

I went back up into the tree house and retrieved the night glasses and camera, then walked cautiously through the trees beside the driveway all the way to the highway, anxious to know if Intruder One was gone or was planning an ambush or counterattack. I saw no sign of him and walked back down the driveway to the house.

My truck had new dimples on its hood, but it was so rusty and beat-up anyway that a few new dents didn't make any difference.

I put the fuel can in the shed, then got a flashlight and found a bit of blood on the driveway and a bit more in the backyard. I kicked dirt over the spots, then went inside, called 911, and reported hearing at least four shots somewhere in the woods behind my house. I said I thought maybe somebody was jacking deer, but whatever was going on I didn't want people shooting so close to my house. The woman at the other end of the line said she'd have the officers on the night shift check it out.

I doubted if they'd find my stalkers but maybe they would. They'd certainly remember my call if the ER reported anyone checking in with superficial shotgun wounds.

I left the outside lights on and cleaned the Remington before putting it back in the gun cabinet, as I waited for the cruiser to show up. Sergeant Tony d'Agostine was working the four-to-two shift, and when he drove into the yard I offered him coffee, which he accepted when I told him it was decaf.

"I'm going off duty before long, and I want to go to sleep," he said. "What's this about gun shots?"

"I was reading," I said, "and I heard four shots from back there in the woods. Sounded like shotguns to me. I thought somebody was jacking deer, but when I looked for a spotting light I didn't see one."

"Most deer jackers work closer to a road so they don't have to carry the carcass too far," said Tony. "You sure it wasn't fireworks or some such thing? The Glorious Fourth isn't too far away."

I shrugged. "Maybe, but it sounded like shotguns to me."

"You ever have deer jackers back there before?"

"Not that I know of."

"You say it sounded like shotguns. More than one?"

"The shots sounded different to me. Two from one gun, two from another. Maybe I'm wrong. I wasn't paying attention when I heard the first one."

"What were you reading that took so much concentration?"

"The Second Nun's Tale."

"Chaucer? It about killed me to read Chaucer. I'd never do it for fun. Middle English. Jeez."

"I read it very slowly," I said. "If I do that, I can make it out. I'm not like John Skye; he can read it a hundred miles an hour."

"Yeah. Well, better you and John than me." He finished his coffee and handed me the cup. "Thanks. I'll take a drive up toward

Felix Neck and see what I can see."

"Protect and serve," I said, "But you're probably right. It was probably kids shooting off cherry bombs or some such thing."

"You did the right thing," he said. "That's why we have 911." He looked at me long and hard before getting into his cruiser. He was no fool, and probably hadn't believed much of what I'd said.

He drove away and I went into the house and went to bed. Oliver Underfoot and Velcro, who had no doubt enjoyed the evening's activity even less than I had, thought it was about time, and climbed up beside me. After I read for a while I turned off the inside light but I left the outside ones on.

I wondered if the intruders were Fred and Angie or two other toughs imported for the job. If they were new guys, somebody was going to considerable lengths to get me out of the picture.

I suddenly remembered the walkie-talkie and it gave me an idea. I got up and found it where I'd put it on the living room bookcase. I turned it on, pushed the send button and whispered, "Hello! Hello! Are you there?"

A whispered voice replied. "Yes, I'm here. Where the hell are you? I've been calling you. What the hell happened back there?"

"I don't know where I am," I whispered, "but I'm hurt. Somebody got me with a shotgun. Feels like small shot, but it hurts like hell. Where are you?"

"I'm in the car driving toward Edgartown. I got hit, too. He was waiting for us, damn him. Jesus Christ! A cop just turned into that Felix Neck place. Don't let him see you. You got your compass?"

"Yeah."

"Work your way west toward the highway. Watch for me. I'll drive back and forth until you hail me."

"Okay. Damn, I hurt. Over and out."

I was no longer sleepy. I got dressed, put the .38 in my belt, and went out to the Land Cruiser. I drove to the end of my driveway where I parked, turned off my headlights, and watched the midnight traffic go by. After a while a white Mercedes went slowly past, headed for Edgartown. Several minutes later it passed going the other way. Tony d'Agostine drove past, headed back to town. The Mercedes came by again, then returned again. I imagined that the driver was wondering where his partner was. I pulled out onto the highway and followed him.

18

Neither of us was hurrying. I wondered where Intruder Two really was and whether he knew enough to come toward the highway in hopes of spotting the Mercedes and getting out of harm's way. I hoped so, because I wanted the two of them together. When I got close to the entrance to Felix Neck, I backed into a driveway across the road and used my night glasses to sweep the far roadside and watch the Mercedes creep back and forth along the highway looking for Mr. Two.

By and by I saw someone limp out of the woods across the road and look furtively this way and that. Mr. Two, certainly. He ducked back when the occasional car went whizzing by, but when the Mercedes crept into view once again he lurched out as it passed and shouted. The car skidded to a halt and backed up, and Mr. Two joined Mr. One.

I could imagine their car seats turning red as the blood oozed out of their wounds, and how their conversation might go:

"Where the hell were you? I told you when we talked to meet me at the highway."

"Talked? We never talked!"

"Are you crazy? We talked after the plan went wrong. I told you to meet me here. Where the hell have you been?"

"You're the crazy one. How could we have talked? I dropped my radio when I got shot!"

"Then who . . . ?" I could see the light dawn in Mr. One's mind, as he realized who must have been speaking to him.

The Mercedes went toward Vineyard Haven. I gave it a head start and drove after it. It turned right onto County Road and I wondered if it would go to the ER at the hospital to have the birdshot dug out of the driver and his passenger, or to the Noepe Hotel where the two men could lick their wounds and decide what to do next.

I hoped they'd go to the ER because it was only a block from the state police barracks and I could have Dom Agganis and Olive Otero or whoever was on the late shift there to talk to them almost before they got the first shot removed. Instead, they turned right onto Wing Road and headed for the hotel. Their pain probably helped take their minds off possible tails, because they gave no indication that they knew I was behind them.

As we entered the village they failed to take the short route to the hotel, thus revealing their unfamiliarity with the warren of one-way streets that characterize Oak Bluffs. I, being more knowledgeable than they, took a more direct route and got to the hotel first. I parked on a nearby street where I could see the parking lot, turned off my lights and engine, and waited for them to arrive.

They pulled into the lot a few minutes later, parked, and limped toward the fire stairs on the back of the building, no doubt eager to avoid shocking the night clerk by bleeding all over the lobby. Most of their facial camouflage had been scrubbed off, I noticed. I went after them, crossing the brightly lit lot on silent feet and shucking my pistol from my belt as I went. We arrived at the stairs more or less in a clump. They knew I was there when I said, "Hi, guys. Mind if I join you?"

They spun around and the older man's hand jumped toward his waist then stopped as its owner saw my .38 looking at him.

"Who the hell are you?"

"I'm a man with a gun, Fred. Turn around and put your hands on the wall. Kick your feet back. I think you know the routine."

"I don't know what you're talking about!" He squinted at me. "I know you; you're Jackson."

I cocked the revolver. "You Charlestown thugs can't possibly be as stupid as you're acting. Turn around. If you don't, I'll probably get a medal for shooting you."

They turned around, put their hands on the wall, and spread their bleeding legs. I put the pistol against the older man's head and frisked him the way they taught me to do it long before at the Boston Police Academy.

Principal among my findings were his wallet, his walkie-talkie, a stun gun, a 9mm Glock pistol, and a pocketknife. I patted down his arms and then put the pistol against his spine and patted down his legs, getting a muffled groan from him when I did that. I then frisked the younger man and found a pistol, his wallet, and a Zippo cigarette lighter. He might be a no good son of a bitch, but he had good taste in lighters. He also moaned when I patted down his bloody legs.

I tossed everything but their wallets into the shadow beneath the stairs, then stepped away from them into the bright light of the lot and flipped through the wallets. Sure enough, their driver's licenses identified the pair as Fred McMahan and Angelo Vinci. I also found a couple of those cards that serve as room keys these days.

"I'm dying here," whined Angie. "I need a doctor."

"You need a brain," I said. "Up to your room, both of you. I'll be right behind, close enough to shoot you but too far away for you to try any funny stuff. Go."

"You won't get away with this," said Fred, but he started up the stairs with Angie, almost crying with each step, at his heels.

The fire door wasn't locked, but I hadn't expected it to be, since Fred and Angie hadn't hesitated when they'd headed for the rear stairs. I figured they'd probably taped the lock open so they could get in without being noticed and would thus have an alibi if they needed one; the night clerk, unless he was more diligent than most, would never have gone upstairs to check the door and, if the cops came around, could verify that Fred and Angie had been in their room all night.

We went through the fire door and I waved Fred and Angie down the hall while I opened the door to their room.

"Come in, gentlemen," I said, waving my pistol in an inviting way. When they did, I sat them on their beds and took a chair across from them. Their faces revealed the pain they were feeling. Angie had tears in his eyes, but Fred was made of sterner stuff.

"What we have here," I said, "is a problem. You two wiseguys are in trouble. You vandalized Roland Nunes's place, you tried to poison his cat, you shot me with a stun gun, you tried to burn down my house, and you killed Melissa Carson."

"You can't prove any of that," said Fred, through gritted teeth.

"I don't have to prove it," I said. "I just have to believe it. That's all the police have to do, too. I have photos of both of you doing your dirty work at Nunes's place and mine. I think there'll be enough evidence to put you away."

"We never killed nobody!" cried Angie. "Jesus, I need a doctor!"

"Shut up," said Fred. "You keep your mouth shut." He glared at me. "You're the one in trouble, Jackson. You kill us, you'll be up for murder. You don't kill us, even if we do some time we know where you live and you'll never know when we'll be back to get you."

I smiled and shook my head. "You've

already got bird-shot in your silly ass. You try coming back to the island, you'll get a heavier dose. Stick to Charlestown where you know your way around."

Fred looked worried but thoughtful. "If you were going to finish us, you'd have used buckshot in the first place, or you'd have done it just now down there in the parking lot. What do you want?"

"I want to know who hired you to hassle Roland Nunes and why you killed Melissa Carson."

"We didn't kill nobody!" repeated Angie. "Christ, I'm bleeding. I'm gonna die if I don't get to a doctor!"

"You're not gonna die," snapped Fred. "You're hurting, but you're not going to die. Now shut up!"

"You shut up for a while," I said to Fred. "Angie, speak to me and maybe you can go see a doctor. Who hired you to vandalize Nunes's property?"

"I don't know, I don't know! I don't know his name! Tell him, Fred! Jesus, I'm bleeding all over the place!"

"Why did you kill the woman?"

"Oh, my God! I told you we didn't kill nobody!"

"You tried to kill the cat. Man who'll kill a cat will kill a woman."

"Oh, Christ, the cat! The damned cat! I don't know what was in that can. I just put it there for him to eat. Fred gave it to me. I thought it might make the cat sick. I didn't try to kill him! I swear! I gotta get to a doctor." He pushed himself partly up from the bed then saw my cocked pistol turn toward him and sat down again. "Please, mister!"

"You're some badman," I said. I looked back at Fred. "Who hired you?"

He spoke in a tight voice. "I don't know. It was a phone call. I got it up in Charlestown. He wanted Nunes driven out. He didn't care how we did it. The money came through the mail."

"Sure it did."

"I swear."

I thought he was lying, but couldn't be sure. People sometimes withhold information for no good reason at all. I should know.

"How do you get in touch with your boss?" I asked, in my nastiest voice.

"He gets in touch with me."

"How?"

"He phones me here."

"Where'd you get the poison for the cat?"

"I found it on the hood of my car. The guy on the phone told me it'd be there."

"Why did you kill the woman?"

"We didn't kill anybody! I don't know

anything about the woman. I don't even know who the hell she was."

"You sure as hell vandalized Nunes's place and shot me. You denying that, too?"

"No. We did that. That's why I know you're Jackson and where you live. I saw you and your ID that night."

I couldn't resist. "My name is Legion," I said.

He'd been long out of Bible class. "What the hell does that mean?"

"No matter." I put on a frown. "The question I'm asking myself is what to do with you two boobs. I'd probably be smart to just shoot you both here and now, but killings can go wrong so I don't like to do any if I don't have to. On the other hand, you two jerks are a real nuisance. I don't care for that. Maybe I'll just give you to the cops."

Fred didn't like that idea, and talked tough. "You hand us in, you're the one in trouble. You tried to murder us. We got the lead in us to prove it. They may get us for vandalism, but they'll get you for attempted murder!"

Fred had a point. In Massachusetts, the law says you're always supposed to run away from trouble if you can. I didn't think the DA would consider my shots from the tree house to be flight. "You're full of crap," I said. "They'll get you for attempted arson, too. You'll do more time than I will."

Fred's jaw worked. "How about we get out and don't come back?"

"Your boss won't like it."

"Fuck him. He didn't pay us enough to get arrested or killed!"

"I need a doctor!" wept Angie.

"Shut up," said Fred. He leaned forward. "Listen. We can't go to the hospital here because they'll call the cops, but I know places at home where we can get fixed up no questions asked. You let us go and I swear we won't be back."

I pretended to think about it, then nodded toward Angie. "You think you can keep your buddy from crying himself to death on the way?"

Fred became hopeful for the first time. "There's booze over there in the mini-bar. I'll pour that down him until he stops whining."

"You ever try to get off this island in the summertime?" I asked. "You'd better be in the standby line about 5 a.m. tomorrow and be ready to pay out a lot of money to the check-in guys. Maybe you'll be lucky and get off by noon."

"We got money and we'll be there. I swear."

I pretended to think some more, then smiled a thin smile. "I never want to see you again," I said. "And if I catch some pal of yours down here trying to finish what you started, I'll come up to Charlestown and see you at home. You won't see me, but I'll see you. You got that?"

"I got it."

"One of the guys you'll be paying off is a friend who works on the ferry dock in Vineyard Haven," I said. "He'll let me know when you leave, so make sure you do." I got up and tossed their wallets and one of the key cards onto the floor. The other I slid into my pocket. "I'll keep this one in case I change my mind and decide to come back," I said. "Sit right where you are for the next five minutes. I'll be watching."

I went out into the hall, then out the fire door and down the stairs. Looking back at their window I didn't see anyone peering out. I collected the equipment I'd tossed under the stairs and walked to my truck. As I drove away, I glanced at the window again but saw nothing. Then I was out of sight.

I wished that I really did have an agent working on the ferry dock, but it's an imperfect world and you can't have everything.

As I drove home, I wondered if Legion and I were the same thing.

I thought that Fred and Angie probably really were hurting enough to stay out of my hair, and I even believed them when they denied killing Melissa Carson. But if not them, then who? And why?

With Fred and Angie gone, would their boss find someone to take their place? If so, it would probably take a little time, so I had what the current pundits called a window of opportunity when no one would be trying to kill me. I used the first hours of my window to go home and get some sleep in my giant, empty double bed.

19

Just in case Fred and Angie decided to change their minds and to wreak vengeance upon me before seeking medical aid, I tried to sleep lightly and got up when the eastern sky was beginning to brighten, to go out and reconnoiter the premises. I saw nothing suspicious. At five thirty I drove to Vineyard Haven and swung by the parking lots on Water Street. There, sure enough, was the white Mercedes, waiting to join the stand-by line. I didn't wave as I drove by.

At home, I was finishing stacking the breakfast dishes when the phone rang. It was Quinn, calling from Boston.

"What are you doing up this early?" I asked. "Did somebody throw you out of her apartment because of performance failure?"

"The fourth estate never sleeps," said Quinn. "I finally had a chat with Sonny Whelen. I told him I was snooping around for a story about how hoodlums these days compared with the boys in yesteryears, and mentioned Fred and Angie. He said all he knew about crime was what he got from the papers or TV, or the gossip he heard when he was having lunch, but that he'd been told of two guys named Fred McMahan and Angelo Vinci, who are trying to revolutionize robbery by using stun guns instead of real ones, when possible, to minimize the risk of being accused of murder if they ever got caught. Sonny said he thought that was quaint."

"Sonny actually said 'quaint'?"

"Yeah. He also said that he'd heard that they were specializing as muscle for out-of-town jobs. Their idea, he'd heard, was that as long as they worked someplace else they could always come back to Charlestown where nobody, including the cops, would be mad at them. He thought they got the idea from some movie."

"Did he think it was a good one?"

"You know Sonny. He always says he doesn't know anything about crime."

"Did he happen to say how the boys got customers?"

"Said somebody'd told him that they just spread the word in bars, then waited."

"They get a lot of work?"

"Sonny said he didn't know anything

about that, but that he'd heard they advertised in Cambridge and Boston and places like that instead of in Charlestown where somebody might think they were nosing in on territory that was already taken."

"Did honest-citizen Sonny say how he happened to know about Charlestown being already taken?"

"He said he watches a lot of crime shows on television. Besides, in Charlestown everybody knows about crime."

I wasn't sure that all Charlestownians knew about crime, but it was true that the city had the reputation of housing more than its share of gangsters and of having a particular tradition of up-and-coming young criminals proving their mettle by robbing armored cars as a rite of passage. Sonny Whelen was long past being personally involved in such heists, but there was little doubt in the minds of the local cops that he derived benefit from them and most of the other underworld activities in town.

"Does Sonny have any paternal interest in Fred and Angie?"

"Not that I detected."

"Did he mention any bars where Fred and Angie might have left word of their availability for work?"

"No, but after I left him I nosed around

myself and their names came up in some of the snitzier watering holes in Boston. I guess Fred and Angie figure that the rich want to strong-arm other people just as much as the poor do, so why not go where the money is."

"You hear of any jobs they got?"

"No, but I imagine if I hung around some of those bars long enough I'd hear somebody brag about how he got shed of his wife or his lawyer or somebody else who'd been giving him grief. It's hard for people to keep their mouths shut about their triumphs."

True. Many a crime has been solved because the perp talked about it to a snitch.

"Well, keep your ears up," I said. "If you hear anything more, let me know."

"You owe me a fishing trip," he said.

"Come down any time."

"And the inside scoop on this murder. Melissa Carson was rich and her fiancé was a Cabot. It's big news up here."

"You know as much as I do about that."

"Did Fred and Angie do it?"

"Not that I know of. They say no."

"Oh, did you talk with them?"

"Very briefly. They were headed off-island."

"Done with their work there, eh?"

"More like they had more important business on the mainland."

"What kind of business?"

"Medical problem of some sort."

"What sort?"

"My impression was that it had to do with minor surgery."

"Who's their doctor?"

"They didn't say."

"Why didn't they have it done there on the island?"

"I guess they preferred their own physician."

After I rang off, I went over what I knew and didn't know with Oliver Underwood and Velcro, who yawned as they listened and had no wise advice for me.

The house had that empty feeling that emphasizes the small sounds, creaks, and taps that you never hear when the place has its people in it. I wondered what Zee and the kids were up to, and checked the calendar for the umpteenth time to see when they were coming home. I could hardly wait. There was no doubt about it; my bachelor days were far behind me and I was now a very married man.

I started thinking about the supper I'd prepare for my family's return. Peas, of course, because that's what the garden was abundantly producing at the moment. Too bad I didn't have tomatoes, zucchini, lettuce, and other stuff for a garden salad or grilled veggies. I could buy all that, of course. What else? I had flounder in the freezer. I'd thaw that and cook it in a casserole with a roux flavored with a slosh of marsala or sherry and a little Parmesan and maybe some dill, then serve it over rice. Straight vanilla ice cream for dessert for Joshua and Diana, ice cream with strawberries and orange liqueur for the big people, followed by coffee and cognac. Yes.

I took the flounder out of the freezer and put it in the fridge for a slow thaw, then cleaned house and opened windows to the east wind that was blowing the humidity away.

When that was done, it was late enough to make visits, so I put the weapons I'd confiscated from Fred and Angie into a paper bag, got into the truck, put my own .38 under the seat, and drove to Babs Carson's house in West Tisbury. Robert Chadwick opened the door and frowned at me. I wondered if he'd gone home the previous night.

"I need to talk with Babs," I said.

"Can't you wait another day, at least? She's still pretty much in shock."

"I just have a few questions. Maybe you

can answer them."

He glanced behind him, then stepped out and pulled the door shut. "I'll try."

"Melissa was killed either by somebody who accidentally encountered her or by somebody who knew where she was that night. My money's on someone who knew. Do you know if she told anybody about her plan to visit Roland Nunes? Her mother and I knew, and so did Alfred Cabot. Did anyone else know?"

He looked uneasy. "I don't know. Can't these questions wait?"

"I'd like to know who killed Melissa, and why."

"So would I. The police have asked all of your questions. Leave Babs alone."

The door behind him opened and Babs Carson looked out. "Who is it, Rob? Oh, Mr. Jackson. Come in."

Her face had aged. I followed her into the sitting room where we'd first talked. She walked like a very old woman.

"Now, what can I do for you, Mr. Jackson?"

"Have you heard the Medical Examiner's report?"

"Yes. My daughter's neck was broken." She looked away and then brought her tired eyes back to me. "She didn't deserve to die that way."

"No. Tell me, did she make or receive any phone calls after I left the other day?"

Babs frowned. "I don't think so. I wish I could help you. Do you have any idea who might have killed her?"

"I don't know. I don't think the killer met her by accident. Can you give me the names of Melissa's husbands, and of her boyfriends and their wives and girlfriends?"

"I don't know all the boyfriends' names. I gave the ones I know to the police. Only one or two live here on the island."

"Can you give me the names of the local people?"

"I don't think any of them would have done a thing like this."

"I'm sure you're right, but I'd like to have the names."

"All right." She walked to a desk, scribbled on a piece of paper, and handed the paper to me. The names were unfamiliar to me. Two men and a woman.

"Did she have any enemies that you know of?" I asked.

"No. She was passionate and impetuous, but she wasn't the sort of person to have an enemy who . . ." She broke off and I could see her face work to reshape itself into an emotionless mask.

"I think you should go now," said Chadwick. "You can talk some more later, if need be."

"I'm sorry to have intruded," I said. "Thank you for your help."

I went out and left the two of them to stitch up the torn fabric of their lives. I drove to the state police station in Oak Bluffs, where I found Dom Agganis on the phone. I stepped out of the office and waited until he was through talking, then followed his voice back into the room.

"I won't be here long," he said.

"I don't need much of your time," I said. "I thought you should know that a couple of Charlestown guys named Fred McMahan and Angelo Vinci left the island this morning and probably won't be coming back. They left this stuff behind." I gave him the paper bag.

He looked inside at the guns and stun gun and grunted. "They must have been in a hurry."

"They're driving a white Mercedes sedan." I gave him the license number. "The front seats are probably bloody. I think they had some kind of a hunting accident."

"Where are they going? Home to Charlestown?"

"I couldn't say. Somewhere to a friendly

physician who'll pick out some birdshot from their lower parts."

Dom smiled. "You ever hear the joke about the haberdasher who got robbed and ran after the thief yelling to the cops, 'Shoot him in the pants! The coat and vest are mine!'"

"No, I don't think I ever did."

"Well, now you have. Are you the shot-gunner?"

"Absolutely not."

"I heard from the Edgartown police that somebody was shooting around your place last night."

"I reported the shots. They sounded like gun shots but maybe they were just fire crackers."

"I suppose your shotguns are nice and clean."

"I keep all of my guns nice and clean."

He leaned back in his chair. "I don't sup-pose these were the guys who vandalized Nunes's place."

"I understand that they are, although I don't know if you can prove it. You can check those photos I took and maybe you can ID at least one of them."

"Did they kill the Carson woman?"

"I understand that they deny it."

"Do you believe them?"

"I do, but I haven't taken them off the usual list of suspects. I hear they got their orders by phone and their money delivered to their hotel room, so they don't know who hired them to vandalize Nunes's place. Of course, they may be lying about that. Maybe you can trace the phone calls or the poison in the cat food. If you do, I'd like to know what you learn."

"I'll bet you would. Anything else?"

"Just these names." I took the list out of my pocket and gave it to him. "These men are island guys Melissa dated, and the woman is one of their girlfriends. Maybe one of them held a grudge."

"You should be a cop," said Dom, looking at the list. "You're a natural snoop. But in this case, as usual, we're ahead of you. Olive is out talking with one of these guys right now and I'm going to be talking to the other one as soon as I can get rid of you."

That left the woman to me. "Let me know what you learn," I said.

"Don't hold your breath," said Dom, getting up and grabbing his hat. "I'll walk you out."

20

The woman's name was Cynthia Dias, and she lived in Oak Bluffs in a small, winterized house in the warren of narrow dirt streets on East Chop. Daniel Boone, when asked if he'd ever been lost, reputedly said, "No, but I've been confused for a few days, sometimes." Like Dan'l, I've been confused more than once on East Chop, but so far have always been able to find my way home.

Cynthia Dias was hanging clothes on a line when I pulled up, and I immediately felt approval for her because I, too, have one of those solar driers and I think more people should use them. I like the way the sunshine makes dry sheets and clothes smell, and the way wind-blown washings look, so I'm irked whenever I learn of one of the increasingly popular zoning laws that ban clotheslines because they supposedly lower property values and violate the aesthetic principles of the neighbors. Such rulings were not operational on East Chop. At least not yet.

Cynthia Dias wore no wedding ring. She was a woman in her thirties, tiny, slender, dark-haired, wearing glasses on the end of her pretty nose. Behind those glasses intelligent blue eyes looked at me as I walked into the backyard. A slim hand took a clothespin from her mouth and snapped it over the corner of a pillowcase.

"Cynthia Dias?"

She took other clothespins from a pocket in her apron and hung up a matching pillowcase, then smiled at me. "Yes."

"My name's Jackson. I'm working on a criminal case that you may have heard of: the death of a woman named Melissa Carson. Her neck was broken. I'd like to ask you some questions."

At the mention of Melissa's name, Cynthia Dias's smile went away. "I read about it in the paper. I can't imagine how I can be of any help to you." She turned away and went back to hanging up clothes and bedclothes.

"Did you know Miss Carson?"

"I met her once or twice."

"She dated a man named Carl Morgan. Before that, you and Carl Morgan spent a lot of time together."

"So?"

"How did you feel when Carl left you for her?"

She looked at me with annoyed eyes. "How do you think I felt? I felt betrayed! Have you ever been abandoned by someone you loved, Mr. Jackson?"

"My first wife divorced me."

She pulled a sheet from her basket and tossed it over the line. "Did you love her?"

"Yes."

"Did you beg her to stay?"

"No."

"Did another man steal her away?"

"She married again soon after she left me."

"And how did you feel about that?"

"I got over it."

"I mean, how did you feel about the man?"

"I couldn't fault him for his choice of women."

"Well, that's not how I felt about Melissa Carson. I thought she was a witch. She stole Carl away and then tossed him back as soon as she was through with him."

"Did you catch him when she threw him?"

She hung a T-shirt. "We didn't see each other again. Fool me once, shame on you; fool me twice, shame on me."

"So much for Carl. What about Melissa?"

"What about her?"

"Somebody killed her. Was it you?"

She stopped and gave me a look of disbelief. "What? Is that why you're here? To find out if I killed Melissa Carson? Good God! She was a slut, but she wasn't worth killing!" She spread her slender arms. "Besides, look at me? Melissa Carson was no giant, but she was bigger and taller than I am. You say her neck was broken? Can you see me breaking her neck? Hell, she'd have broken mine if I'd tried!"

"What about Carl? How did he feel when she dumped him?"

"He felt like the idiot he is. He was just the toy of the day, and now he knows it."

"Was he angry?"

"At her? No. He's a lamb, not a wolf. He was too red-faced to be angry at anybody but himself."

"Maybe you should take him back, then."

She shrugged, then gave me a crooked smile. "Maybe when winter comes and my house gets cold."

I liked her for that. Life is too short for long grudges. "Let me give you a hand with the rest of that wash," I said.

"No, I can handle it myself."

"I like hanging clothes. I do it at home."

She tipped her head to one side. "All right. There's not much left to do."

We hung her wash and admired our work.

"One last question," I said, as I paused outside of her back door. "Who'd Melissa drop Carl for?"

"A guy named Cabot. Owns a hotel in the village, they say. I wouldn't know because I never stay in hotels on Martha's Vineyard. They say he has money. Maybe that's what she saw in him."

"She had her own money," I said.

Cynthia Dias shrugged. "Who knows what women want?"

"Freud wondered the same thing. I've heard three answers."

She was standing on her back porch and I was on the ground. Her eyes were even with mine. "All right, I'll bite. What are they?"

"Men can't resist beauty and women can't resist money."

"I've heard that one."

"The next one is that women want what they want when they want it."

"Who doesn't? What's the third answer?"

"Shoes."

She laughed. "I'll go along with that. Maybe Cabot owns a shoe store."

"He owns a lot of things," I said.

"Did he own Melissa Carson?"

"I don't think Melissa Carson was any-body's possession."

"Love's, maybe."

I hadn't heard that idea expressed that way for some time. "Did you like that novel?"

"My father and mother were lawyers. I found the book on a shelf in their library. I thought it was fine. Would you like to come in for coffee?"

I thanked her but said I really had to go. I felt the pull of her eyes on my back as I walked around the corner of the house, but I kept going to the truck, thinking that Carl might get a second chance.

I found my way off East Chop, drove through the traffic and street-crossing pedestrians to Ocean Park, where I turned right, then went this way and that through narrow streets until I finally fetched the Noepe Hotel. I drove around to the back and parked in their lot. The white Mercedes wasn't there, but the forest-green Hummer was in its private parking place and the Chevy pickup that I'd seen the first time I'd gone there was at the far end of the lot. I went in through the back door and on to the front desk. The same clerk was there.

"Remember me? I was here a couple of days ago."

"I remember you."

"I was looking for Fred McMahan. I left him a note. Did he get it?"

She smiled. "I couldn't say."

"Is he still here?"

She smiled some more. "As you'll recall, we don't discuss our guests."

"In that case, I'll just go up and see him."

"Is he expecting you?"

Her question told me that Fred hadn't bothered to check out when he and Angie left. I showed her the card I'd kept. "I have his key."

She touched her phone. "I should call and ask."

"I doubt if he'll answer, but go ahead."

She punched buttons and listened to the phone ring before hanging up. "He doesn't seem to be in."

"Sometimes Fred sleeps late. He doesn't like phones waking him up so he puts plugs in his ears." I grinned my version of a Burt Lancaster grin. "I'll get him up. Can't have him burning daylight like this."

I went up the stairs and down the hall to Fred's room. There was a DO NOT DISTURB card hanging from the doorknob. Smart Fred had given himself a few extra hours to make his getaway.

I went into the room and spent some time

searching the place in case pain had made Fred and Angie careless enough to leave behind some clue identifying their employer, but all I found were bloodstains. I went out into the hall and looked for the chambermaid. I found her on the third floor. She was Brazilian, as were many of the people doing basic work on the island, and her English was almost as bad as my Portuguese. Still, we finally understood one another well enough for me to learn that the master suite on the second floor belonged to Senhor Cabot, and for her to learn that I had made a troublesome discovery in Senhor McMahan's room.

While she went to Fred's room, I went down to the lobby, put an anxious look on my face, and told the desk clerk that I'd found Fred's room empty and what looked like bloodstains on the bed and a chair, and that I'd sent the chambermaid to investigate. The clerk paled.

"I think you should call 911," I said. "Maybe something's happened."

"Oh, dear," said the clerk, who clearly wasn't used to signs of violence in the Noepe. "I'd better ask Mr. Cabot what to do!"

"Of course," I said. "He'll know."

She picked up her phone, punched numbers, and looked at me with wide, unfocused eyes. Then she held the phone with both hands and spoke rapidly. "Mr. Cabot, I'm sorry to bother you, but . . . but Mr. Mc-Mahan isn't in his room and there's a report of what looks like bloodstains on the furniture. The man who found them is here now and the maid is in the room. Oh no, here she comes down the stairs! Yes, yes. I'll stay right here. Should I call the police? All right, I'll wait until you see the room. I'm terribly sorry . . ." She stared at the buzzing phone, then hung up as the chambermaid, who had been gesturing and talking and looking back up the stairway ever since she'd come into view, continued her exciting if incomprehensible tale of what she'd seen.

The desk clerk pulled herself together and quieted the maid and the three of us waited to see what would happen next. What happened next was the ring of the clerk's phone. She picked it up and said, "Yes, sir?" Then, after a moment, said it again, rang off, and dialed 911. Her report to the emergency number was short and to the point. She was admirably recomposed, I thought.

While we waited for the police, a tall, broad-shouldered man came down the stairs. He was wearing slacks and a blue, short-sleeved dress shirt, and looked like one of those male models you see in slick magazines: leonine, perfectly quaffed, eagle-eyed, and totally in control of things. Not at all my idea of a blah man, as described by Babs, but maybe I didn't know blah when I saw it. Maybe blah was one of those concepts understood only by women, like hunkiness, which Zee sometimes saw in men who looked completely normal to me.

"I'm Alfred Cabot," he said, coming directly to me. "Are you the man who told the maid about the room?"

His eyes were level with mine and they were hard to read. I nodded.

"What's your name?"

"Jeff Jackson. My friends call me J.W."

"How did you get into the room?" His tone was the sort that belonged to someone who was used to getting answers to his questions.

I put the key card in his hand.

"Where'd you get this?"

"From Fred McMahan. I guess he didn't need it anymore."

Cabot studied me. "What do you mean?"

"The last time I saw him he was planning to leave the island. He was gone when I went up to see him just now."

"Why did he give you this key?"

"Business."

He frowned, and anger flickered across his face; then he said, "I don't know the man, but apparently you do. What do you think happened up there in his room?"

"I'm not an expert on forensics," I said, "but it looks like somebody did some bleeding."

"Why did McMahan give you this key?"

"You asked me that before."

"I'm asking again and this time I want a better answer."

"We'd been involved in a business transaction," I said. "We agreed that I should have access to his room."

His voice was low but demanding. "What sort of business transaction?"

"It had to do with real estate."

He stared at me. "Here on the island?"

I ignored the question. "I went up to see if Fred had changed his mind about leaving, but apparently he's pulled up stakes. Say, do you think that really is blood up there? You don't suppose something happened to Fred, do you? Gosh, things have come to a sorry state when a businessman can get hurt just for doing business."

"Business can be rough," said Cabot, looking at me with hot eyes. "You should be careful who you deal with."

In the distance I heard sirens growing louder.

21

The Oak Bluffs police didn't make much effort to keep their initial interviews private so after I'd given my statement I hung around to see what other people would say and what else would happen. Not much did, but I managed to hear the hotel clerk tell the police that she really didn't know anything about Fred McMahan and Angelo Vinci, and to hear Alfred Cabot tell them he'd never even seen them. Fred and Angie were just customers who had taken the room for a few days and had apparently slipped away sometime during the night without informing the desk. McMahan had paid a week's rent in cash in advance. No, they had heard no sounds of violence in the room and had no idea what the blood meant. It was very mysterious and troubling.

The chambermaid, who was next in line to tell her tale, was now calmer than when she'd come down the stairs but was far from sanguine. As she listened to her superiors give their reports, she fingered her skirt nervously, and when Cabot spoke, I thought a furtive look crossed her face before her eyes dropped and her features became enigmatic.

I wondered if she understood more English than I'd presumed, and if she had her green card. I didn't care whether she had the card, but I didn't expect her to say anything that might offend her boss or make the police interested in her. She no doubt needed her job, and the members of the island's large community of Brazilians are often wary of police since back home the cops are not necessarily friends of the poor.

To combat this notion, several island police departments now had Portuguese-speaking officers to bridge the language gap and persuade the Brazilians that the island cops really do work to protect and serve, but the police on the scene did not include such a multi-lingual officer, so when the chambermaid — Delia, by name, I learned as I listened — waved her arms and explained in fractured English how I'd asked her to go to the room and she'd found — *sangue! Mãe de Deus!* — what a calamity! Where were the two *senhors?* No, she hadn't seen them since early the day before.

This morning there was a sign on the door saying not to disturb them. What a disaster! No, she knew little about them. They said hello if they met in the hall. Yes, they seemed friendly. No, she had never heard or seen any indication of violence in the room until now. *Sangue!* Seeing it, she had run right out of the room. Her eyes had flicked toward Alfred Cabot and she'd added that nothing like this had ever happened in the hotel before. It was a fine hotel that catered to only the finest of guests.

Alfred did not acknowledge the look.

A detective arrived and went upstairs. I lingered for a while longer, thinking about what I'd seen and heard, then walked out the back door into the parking lot. I went to the Chevy pickup and took note of its license number, then glanced around the lot and up at the back windows of the hotel and, seeing no one watching, opened the passenger side door and checked the glove compartment.

Has anyone actually put gloves in the glove compartment of a car? Possibly, but no one I know ever has. As I do, most people put other stuff in there, including their car registration. Delia Sanchez was one of the many. Her auto registration showed that she lived off the Vineyard Haven–

Edgartown Road in Ocean Heights, actuall
not far from my house.

When my father bought the land where
now live, Ocean Heights was where you
lived if you couldn't afford to live in a nice
area of town. Now some of my neighbor
live in big, new houses and joke about liv
ing in the exclusive Ocean Heights section
of Edgartown.

Still, there are a lot of small houses in the
neighborhood and some of them are full o
people. We didn't know just how full unti
one of the houses sold and forty-three
Brazilians had to move out and find some
place else to live. The forty-three, we
learned, had lived in shifts, one third sleep
ing, one third working, and one third taking
care of the place. They took turns sleeping
in the same beds, driving the same cars, and
leading quiet, courteous lives. When they
left, the people next door were sad to lose
such nice neighbors.

Delia lived in a neighborhood of those
small houses and probably worked at least
one other job in addition to chambermaid
ing at the Noepe Hotel, since her country
men and -women often did that: working
several jobs Americans wouldn't take, living
in packed houses in conditions that Ameri
cans wouldn't tolerate, and saving money

that Americans couldn't save, until they could afford to go back and live in style in Brazil, or buy houses and businesses of their own right here.

I exited Delia's pickup, looked around and still didn't see any curious eyes, and went to my truck to wait for Delia. I sat there for quite a while, reading my copy of John Skye's translation of *Gawain and the Green Knight.* Good stuff. Gawain, like many of us, managed to get himself into an impossible situation and ended up bending the code in an effort to get out of his predicament. The ax blow he got on his neck, however, wasn't fatal and he lived to tell his tale and even be hailed for his gallantry, which was more than most of us get when our lies are revealed.

I wondered if Delia had ever read *Gawain.* Probably not.

Delia came out of the hotel's back door just as Gawain's host's beautiful wife entered Gawain's bedroom for the first time. She got into the pickup and drove out of the lot. I followed her home, and when she parked beside three other aging vehicles in the yard, I pulled in behind her and got out. She gave me a worried look.

Good.

"Delia," I said. "I'd like to talk with you."

"I'm very tired," she said, glancing toward the house. "I've told the police what happened. You were there. You heard."

"I was there, and I heard what you said. But you didn't tell everything you know. I want you to tell me what you didn't tell them."

She stiffened her spine. "I told them everything."

"No. You lied." She paled and I put an understanding smile on my face. "Or perhaps you just forgot."

"I don't know what you mean, *senhor.*"

Behind her the front door of the house opened and three men came out and looked at us.

"If I want," I said, "I can take you to police headquarters and talk with you there. I'd rather not do that. May I see your green card or your H2B, please?"

The men behind her exchanged looks, and one of them went back inside. Not all foreign workers have green cards.

Delia clutched her hands together. "I have my card, but I've misplaced it."

I looked at her, then at the two men listening with concerned faces. They, I guessed, knew where their green cards were, if they had them. I said, "Delia, I don't need to see your green card now, but I do have to know what you didn't tell the police. If you tell me, I'll forget about your card."

One of the men on the porch said something to her in what I took to be Portuguese. She spoke back and got a reply, then she looked back at me.

"I need my job."

"I want you to have it."

"My husband doesn't know if you can be trusted. He says immigration people often lie."

"Is that man your husband?" I looked at him until he dropped his eyes.

"Yes."

"Do you have children?"

"Three."

"Then you must work for your family. I have children, too, and I must work for them and my wife. Listen to me. When Alfred Cabot spoke to the police, your face changed. Why? You must tell me the truth."

She looked miserable. "I'll lose my job!"

"No. He'll never know what passes between us here. I give you my word of honor."

The man on the porch spoke again, and she replied, then said to me, "He says that many immigration agents have no honor."

I looked at him again and this time his angry eyes did not drop. I nodded slightly, and looked back at the woman. I kept my voice gentle. "He wants to protect you, but in this case you'll have to trust me, because if you won't talk to me you'll have to find that green card right now."

"*Deus!*" She crossed herself, then took a deep breath. "Senhor Cabot said he had never seen Senhors McMahan and Vinci, but that is not so. I once saw him enter their room and heard their voices. I had been cleaning another room and had just stepped out into the hall." Her eyes were fearful. "*Senhor,* if you tell this to anyone I will lose my work!"

"Are you sure it was Cabot?"

"*Sim.* I'm sure. I saw him standing there, knocking, and then the door opened and he went into the room and I heard men's voices. He never saw me."

"Could you hear what they said?"

"No. I thought nothing of it and went on to my next job. It was only when I heard him tell the police that he had not met them . . ." Her voice faded.

I took her hand in mine and shook it gently. "Thank you, Delia. Don't worry. I'll tell no one what you've said here and if anyone asks me I'll tell them that you have your green card and showed it to me." I flicked my eyes to the man in front of the door. "And tell your husband that he has a brave and beautiful wife."

I got back into my truck and drove home. It was time for lunch and I'd had a long morning. As I drove I wondered if perhaps I should get a job working for the immigration department. Apparently I had the proper look to intimidate illegal aliens. But, no, I wasn't really intended for that sort of work. I didn't care whether Delia was here legally, and I disliked myself for having frightened her into her confession. It wasn't the first time I'd bullied someone in the name of a cause I thought was just, but this instance made me feel worse than most. I hoped I'd convinced her and her husband that she was in no danger from me.

Could most people look back at moments of cruelty and pettiness in their past actions, and still feel red-faced or worse, or was I an exception to the rule? I recalled Dostoyevsky writing that even if we tried to write totally honest memoirs and had been guaranteed that no one would ever, ever see them, we'd still lie. I thought that I probably would.

At home I made lunch, brought the cats up on the latest development in the case, and asked them whether Fred McMahan and Angie had lied to me about not knowing who had hired them, or whether Delia had lied about seeing Cabot go into McMahan's room. They said they'd give the questions some thought. I asked them whether Cabot's meeting with Fred, if indeed they had met, had anything to do with the vandalism. I told them that if I had to choose a liar, I'd choose Fred, but I've been wrong before. They agreed that I had.

Maybe Dom Agganis knew somebody in Boston who could put the screws to Angie, who seemed the weaker member of the McMahan-Vinci combo. If Angie could be persuaded to talk, we might learn that he and Fred did know their employer, and if that employer ended up being Alfred Cabot, as I now suspected, my life would be a lot simpler because my job would be over.

But was Cabot Fred's boss? Maybe not, but the odds seemed good that there was something nefarious going on between them, else why would Cabot lie about never having even seen Fred? Presuming, of course, that Delia was telling the truth, which I thought she was since she believed she might get deported if she didn't spill the real beans.

The truth was elusive because the world is full of liars.

I had a Sam Adams with my fish sandwich and salad, then drove to state police headquarters. Olive Otero was there.

"Did you hear about the business at the Noepe Hotel?" I asked.

"Yes, we did. There are some lab guys over there right now, taking blood samples and finding whatever else they can. You were there, of course. What is it about you, J.W., that always gets you involved when there's trouble?"

"I'm not always involved. I'm sometimes involved. I don't know if you got this bit of information in your report, but rumor has it that Alfred Cabot met with Fred McMahan in his room sometime in the past few days."

"Rumors aren't worth much in court, but I'll humor you. Why should we pay attention to this one?"

"Because Cabot told the OB cops that he'd never seen McMahan."

Olive became more attentive, and dug a report out of a desk drawer. "Right you are," she said, after a few pages of fingering and a pause to read. "I don't suppose you'd care to tell me the source of your rumor?"

"A high administration source who requested anonymity," I said. "I have too much integrity to name the source."

She leaned back in her chair. "Would your integrity withstand a bit of time in jail for withholding evidence?"

"Absolutely. The security of our great nation rests on the fourth estate's right to maintain the confidentiality of its sources."

She smiled. "You're not a member of the fourth estate."

"That being the case, I'll just deny I ever told you anything."

"You trust your tipster?"

"I think so. I didn't really trust Fred McMahan when he told me he didn't know who'd hired him, but he might be hard to squeeze. Angie isn't as tough as Fred. I think he can be talked into trading information for a walk."

"The weed of crime bears bitter fruit," said Olive. "When Dom gets back I'll mention our conversation."

22

I drove down into Edgartown and spent some time looking for a parking spot before finding one right on Main Street, of all places. Who can explain the whimsy of the gods?

I walked among the tourists who crowded the brick sidewalks, cameras around their necks, maps in hand, eyes flitting here and there, looking happy. Downtown Edgartown is lovely, so it's no wonder that visitors are impressed. However, some Edgartonians, including me, think it's too bad that the village's one-time pharmacies, grocery stores, and other shops selling useful things, have now become T-shirt shops, gift shops, and pricey clothing stores catering to tourists and the yachting crowd. On Martha's Vineyard these days, you have to go to Vineyard Haven if you want to buy anything you actually need.

Ah, the dreams of yesteryear.

Of course, in forty years, people will look back at this time as a golden age, when you could buy a house on the island for only a million dollars, and just fifteen thousand people lived here year-round.

I went into Gull Realty and found Jordan and Carole Cohen in their office. I thought Carole looked a little ragged. Jordan waved me to a chair.

"What brings you here?" he asked.

"The eternal quest for truth. What can you tell me about Alfred Cabot?"

He put his hands behind his neck. "He's rich. His principal home and his business offices are in Boston. He owns property in Aquinnah and a hotel in Oak Bluffs, and probably a lot of other properties in a lot of other places. He speaks only to God. Just kidding about that last part."

"I imagine Cabots have gotten used to the joke over the years."

"Why are you interested in Alfred Cabot?"

I looked at Carole. "Because I think he may be the guy behind the vandalism at your brother's place."

Her eyes widened then narrowed. "Alfred Cabot? Are you sure?"

I told them about Fred and Angie living at the Noepe, about their admission that they were the vandals, and about the report that Cabot had been seen entering their room. I didn't mention the incident at my house, but told her that Fred and Angie had left the island and probably wouldn't be back.

"They're the ones who did the actual vandalizing?" asked Jordan.

"Yes. But somebody hired them and Cabot looks like the someone. You're in the real estate business; do you know if Cabot wants to buy Roland's property?"

"If he does, he never told me." Carole tapped a pencil on her desk. "I think you should talk with cousin Sally. She's the one who's hot to sell the place. Cabot might have contacted her."

"Why would Cabot be interested in that piece of land? He's already got a hundred acres in Aquinnah."

"You can ask Sally. Maybe he told her." She leaned forward, frowning. "Have you heard anything about a connection between the killing and the vandalism? I'm worried that there might be one."

"A lot of people, including the cops, are probably wondering about that."

"What do you think?"

"I don't know."

"Well, I know my brother didn't kill her." Eve was probably just as sure that Cain hadn't killed Abel. "I don't believe he did," I said. "Melissa was a woman who liked men and made no bones about it. She and your brother were lovers."

She sat back. "Roland lives like a monk. Do monks have lovers?"

I thought of Abelard and Héloïse, and of Alexander X. "I imagine some do," I said.

"Melissa Carson was engaged to Alfred Cabot," said Jordan. "Doesn't that make him a suspect?"

"The jilted lover syndrome? He wouldn't be the first guy to murder a woman for stepping out on him. The cops probably have him on their list."

"If not him, then who?"

"It could have been a chance encounter. The killer just happened to be there as she walked out to the road. They call them murders of opportunity."

Carole looked wearier than when I'd come in. "I suppose. Do you really think that's what happened?"

"I think it's unlikely."

She frowned. "I know my brother didn't kill Melissa, but if they don't find out who did it pretty fast, I'm afraid that somebody will dig way back and discover that he deserted in Vietnam."

I got up and glanced at my watch. I had

about a half hour before the parking cops gave me a ticket. "I'll talk with Sally Oliver and see what she can tell me about Cabot." At the door I paused and looked back. "It might be best for everyone if Roland turned himself in. After all this time I don't think the army will be very interested in putting a decorated soldier like Roland Nunes in jail, especially after the life he's lived since then."

"I hope you're right." Carole smiled wanly. "Well, protect yourself at all times when you talk with Sally. She's got a bit of a temper and right now there's a lot of tension in the air."

"I'll keep my dukes up," I said.

I went directly to Prada Real Estate and was lucky again, because Sally Oliver was in her office. If it had had a back door, I think she'd have used it when she saw me come in the front one, but such was not the case. I walked past the receptionist and shut the lone door behind me.

Sally Oliver settled back behind her desk. "What can I do for you, Mr. Jackson?"

"Did Alfred Cabot ever try to buy Roland Nunes's land?"

A wary look appeared on her face. "What's Alfred Cabot to you?"

The wary look interested me. "I met him today," I said. "I've learned that he had some sort of relationship with the two guys who vandalized Nunes's property. If he was interested in buying that land, he might be the one who hired them. So, do you know if he ever tried to buy the land?"

She looked at me for what seemed a long time, and then she said, "A lot of people have expressed an interest in buying that land. He may have been one of them. I don't believe he ever made a formal offer. What makes you think he knows the vandals?"

"They were seen and overheard talking together."

"By whom?"

"Nobody you know. Someone with no interest in the vandalism. How well do you know Cabot?"

A small fire appeared in her eyes, and her cheeks reddened. "What's that supposed to mean?"

I said, "I mean just that. How well do you know him? Have you ever met socially? Have you ever talked with him? Do you have an opinion about what sort of person he is? Is he the sort of person who would hire vandals to frighten Nunes into selling to him?"

She seemed to withdraw into herself, and I had the sense of someone donning armor.

"I'm sure I wouldn't know. I've only met him casually." She looked at her watch. "I'm very busy, Mr. Jackson. I'm afraid I can't give you any more time right now. Perhaps you can come back later."

I looked at my own watch. I was about to become a target for the dreaded parking police.

"I have to go anyway," I said. "Thanks for seeing me."

I left and walked up the street to my truck. A half block behind me a young summer cop was cheerfully sticking tickets behind the wipers of cars parked overtime, and even though I'd escaped from her this time, I wondered once again about the wisdom of one-hour parking limits in the village during the summer. How could you ever go to a movie? How could a tourist enjoy a leisurely lunch? How could a visitor take a slow stroll through the shops and galleries? Of course I never did those things during the summer, but other people did. Where was the logic?

Maybe I should become a city planner.

I drove down Main and then took a left onto North Water Street, inching along to avoid hitting any of the tourists who habitually use Edgartown's streets as sidewalks and are sometimes actually offended when a car intrudes upon their sightseeing. I took another left onto Winter Street and creepy-crawled along while tourists reluctantly stepped up on the sidewalks as I approached them. I had paused to give a young man and woman time to move aside from in front of my truck when I saw Sally Oliver, driving a Mini Cooper, come out of the Prada Real Estate parking lot and turn onto Winter in front of me.

Hmmmm.

By the time I'd worked my way through the sightseers, the Mini was out of sight. I went on to Pease's Point Way and followed it to Main Street, but didn't see the car. I turned right and drove out of town. I saw another Mini, but it wasn't Sally's. There was no telling where Sally had gone, and, anyway, her trip probably had to do with business: a meeting with a client. A tour of a property.

Or maybe not.

I drove home and sat down in front of our computer, trying to remember how to make it do what I wanted it to do instead of what it wanted to do. My ignorance obliged me to keep it simple: I got online and typed in 'Mini Cooper photo.' Lo, another miracle in this best of all possible worlds: Up popped a photo of a Mini Cooper. I printed it out, admired my work and my genius, put my old Boston PD shield in my wallet, then got back into the truck and drove to Delia Sanchez's house.

When I knocked on the door, the man I'd seen earlier on the porch opened it. The top of his head was about even with my shoulder but he didn't look like he felt overmatched. He looked up at me with unfathomable eyes.

"I'd like to speak to Delia," I said.

He said something I didn't understand.

I shook my head. "I don't speak Portuguese."

Behind him I sensed the presence of many people listening. The man considered his words, then said, "She sleeps."

I dug out my wallet and flashed the shield. "I must ask her one or two questions."

He didn't like the shield but he was also afraid of it. I felt again like a bully, but stood my ground.

"You stay," he said and went away. I heard the murmur of voices; then he came back with Delia, whose face was full of worry.

"Don't be afraid," I said. I showed her the photo of the Mini Cooper. "Have you seen a car like this one in the hotel parking lot?"

She studied the photo and then nodded. "*Sim.* Yes, I have seen a car like that."

"Have you seen it often?"

She shrugged a small shrug. "Sometimes. I do not count the times."

"Two more questions, and I'll go. Was this car ever there when Senhor Cabot was not there?"

She took her lower lip in her teeth and flashed a look at the man. "I don't want trouble, *senhor.*"

"You're not in trouble."

"What do you want me to say?"

"Only the truth."

She pushed the photo at me. "O.K. I think this car comes only when Senhor Cabot was there."

"Did you ever see the driver of this car?"

She shook her dark-haired head. "No. I never see him. Never."

"Thank you," I said. "I won't bother you again. Go back to sleep."

I sat in the truck remembering seeing a Mini Cooper at Alfred Cabot's place in Aquinnah and was sure that Sally Oliver was lying about only having met Cabot casually. They were more than casual acquaintances; the question was, How much more? Were they lovers? Business partners? Both? Neither? A combination of the two? Who would know?

Martha's Vineyard Hospital is one of the island's major recyclers of gossip, but my main contact there, Zee, was out of town, so that source had to be scratched. I thought of everyone I'd encountered since I'd first become involved with Roland Nunes's problems and could think of no one who could tell me what I wanted to know, with the exceptions of Cabot and Sally Oliver themselves and, possibly, Fred McMahan and Angie Vinci, and none of them was going to talk to me.

I thought of Cabot's guard, who'd come up to the fence on his ATV. Maybe if I took his shotgun away from him and threatened to shoot him with it if he didn't talk, he could tell me something about Al and Sal. The servants always know the family secrets, it's said. If I was in a movie, I might be able to pull that off, but I was in real life, so I didn't pick up the option.

Who, then?

There were only a couple of people I could think of who might know: Babs Carson and Roland Nunes.

I drove to West Tisbury. I had done so much driving lately that I was single-handedly keeping the gasoline companies in business.

23

Robert Chadwick opened the door of Babs Carson's house and looked at me with tired eyes.

"You were here earlier. Must you bother her again?"

"Maybe not, if you can tell me something."

He stepped out and pulled the door mostly shut behind him. "I don't understand why you're doing this. Why don't you leave everything to the police? Why are you still at it?"

It was a fair question, but I ignored it. I was so involved now that I couldn't become uninvolved. "I want to know whether Sally Oliver and Alfred Cabot have more than a business relationship. Melissa mentioned Cabot having a mistress, but she didn't mention the woman's name. Do you know if it's Sally Oliver?"

His mouth hardened. "I don't like spreading gossip."

I said, "If you don't tell me, I'll have to ask Babs. If you try to prevent me from doing that, I'll go to the police and they'll ask the same question."

"Do you always deal in scandal?" He leaned toward me and his voice was angry and touched with contempt. "I thought more of you when we first met."

"I'm dealing with murder and vandalism," I said, "and crime is a dirty business. You're an educated man. You know that."

He hesitated, then sighed and straightened as the fire slowly went out of his eyes. "You're right about crime, of course. I apologize for my outburst. When I was teaching I prided myself on my objectivity. But this business has brought my emotions to the forefront."

I nodded. "Of course your feelings are powerful. It's because of your concern for Mrs. Carson. She's fortunate to have you for a friend."

"I wish I could do more for her."

"You may be doing something for her by telling me if Alfred Cabot and Sally Oliver are lovers. Do you know if they are?"

He still hedged, reluctant to be a rumor monger. "What difference could it make?"

"Sally Oliver told me she doesn't know

Cabot well. I think she was lying, but I'd like to know for sure."

He rubbed his bald head. "She told you that, did she? Well, I was once here when Melissa told her mother that Sally had been Cabot's mistress for some time. You know how Melissa talked about such things. She told Babs that it didn't make any difference to her if Cabot had a mistress because she didn't plan on giving up her own lovers just because she and Cabot were engaged and might even get married."

That sounded like Melissa to me. I said, "The only time I talked with Melissa, she seemed more interested in Roland Nunes than in Alfred Cabot."

He nodded. "Yes, life was like a game to her. Sex was fun and her rules allowed for a lot of it, with no hard feelings when the game pieces moved on. It's not the way I've lived or would want to live, but it was her way and I could never bring myself to condemn her for it. I liked her. She had more of the *élan vital* than most of us do."

I nodded agreement. "You've told me what I wanted to know. Go back and stay with Babs."

"What are you going to do now?"

"I have to talk with some people."

"Do you think they'll ever learn who killed

Melissa?"

Statistically, the odds of solving murders aren't too good, but I said, "I think so. I think the noose is tightening."

His smile was sardonic. "I hope that's an appropriate metaphor."

I drove back to the murder site and walked down to Roland Nunes's house. He wasn't home. The only indication that a woman had been in his house was that faint scent of perfume on the double cot. Back at the paved road I looked across at the narrow trace that was all that remained on that side of the road of the ancient way that led through Nunes's property.

I crossed and walked along that track between the oak brush and small pines that were crowding it from either side. It was about the same width as the path leading to Nunes's house. It ended, as Carole Cohen had told me, in a small clearing beyond which was another of those gates that increasingly cut off access to the ancient ways.

Bent grass showed where some sort of traffic — a motorcycle, perhaps? a small car? — had passed in and out again, and I wondered if this hidden spot was a place where teenaged lovers escaped from their parents' world while they tried to discover their own.

I walked back out to the truck and drove to the building site overlooking Menemsha Pond. Nunes was working there as calmly, it seemed, as if nothing unusual had happened in his entire life. When I reached him, though, I sensed that his face was bland through an act of will; that his eyes only appeared to be beatific; that his movements were under steely control.

He put down the air-powered nail gun he was using and pulled the hearing protectors from his ears.

"J.W. What brings you here?"

I sat on my heels beside him. "Did Melissa ever mention any enemies while she was with you?"

His voice was leaden. "Never."

"Did she ever talk about Alfred Cabot or Sally Oliver?"

"Yes."

"What did she say about them?

"She said they were lovers."

"She was engaged to Cabot. Did she tell you that?"

"Yes."

"Yet you were lovers. Did she plan to leave Cabot?"

"She never said so."

"What did you want her to do?"

"I wanted her to be happy." There was no expression in his face or voice.

"Do you think she was considering leaving Cabot?"

"What does a man know of a woman's thoughts?"

"What did you think?"

"I thought she was beautiful and desirable."

"Did she want to marry you?"

"I wanted to marry her."

"Did she accept your proposal?"

"No."

"Did she refuse you?"

"No." He paused. "She only laughed and kissed me."

"Did you believe that she would later say yes?"

"I neither believed nor disbelieved. I only cherished her."

I looked out over Menemsha Pond. There were boats, power and sail, crossing the water. To my right I could see Menemsha Bight, and beyond that, across Vineyard Sound, the small island of Cuttyhunk where thirty or so hardy souls lived year-round and were happy when the summer tourists went away in the fall.

"They call you the Monk," I said, "but

you've not lived a totally spiritual life, have you?"

"No. I've tried to live simply and so as not to injure others, but I've not managed that, and I've achieved no cessation of desire."

"Has your life been an atonement?"

"I wanted it to be. When I was a young man I did much harm. I didn't want to do more."

"Have you found peace?"

His answer came late. "No. I knew I would make a very poor monk. My best hope was to be a harmless man, but I'm not."

"Why do you say that?"

His eyes pulled at me. "I know that death means nothing and that we should accept it when others cause it or we cause it, but I can't." I saw one of his hands squeeze into a fist before he too noticed it and willed it back into a hand. He saw that I had seen the fist and nodded slightly. "My life has been a failure. I can't be what I know I should be."

"No one can be what he knows he should be," I said. "Would you have married her?"

He nodded slowly. "Oh yes, but I would have made a poor husband. My wife could never be sure that the police wouldn't come knocking at my door."

"Have you considered turning yourself in to the army? I'm sure you could survive any penalty they might impose, and then you'd be free."

"Perhaps I'd get out of jail, but Melissa is dead, and now I have to decide what to do with myself." His eyes were staring at nothing. "I'm hollow. I have a headpiece full of straw. My life is a whimper."

I looked into those eyes and saw emptiness. "You're not thinking of harming someone, are you?" I asked.

His face was unfathomable. "Who would I harm but myself, and what would be the harm in that?"

"You've spent your life atoning for the harm you did during war," I said.

"Do you know the story of the saint and the cobra?" he asked. "The cobra was trapped by rising floodwaters, and the saint took pity on him and carried him to safety. When they reached high ground, the cobra struck him fatally. The dying saint was astonished. 'Why have you killed me?' he asked. 'I just saved your life.' 'You cannot help being a saint,' said the cobra, 'and I cannot help being a cobra.' "

I'd heard variations of that tale before, but they had been told in tones unlike his. "I think you have a choice," I said. "Your life proves that you have."

He said nothing. I thought I saw a tear form, but he wiped it away. His despair was tangible. He had spent his life climbing out of the Void, but was now back in it. I was familiar with the place.

"I don't want to rehash Philosophy 101," I said, "but even if life has no meaning, you can create it. You can live and be happy."

He picked up the nail gun, pointed it at a beam, and pulled the trigger. The nail buried itself in the wood.

"I was happy a week ago," he said. He lifted the gun and nodded toward the embedded nail. "These are wonderful tools, but people get killed with them fairly often, usually because they're careless. Right now I have to concentrate all the time to avoid being careless. It takes all of my energy."

I tried to move us both away from his despair. "Melissa never mentioned anyone who was angry with her?"

"Only one. Alfred Cabot. She said he was unhappy when she told him she was seeing me. She thought it was comical. She thought a lot of things were comical." His eyes became hooded.

I had a sense of what he must have been like in Vietnam: tough, wary, centered, lonely.

"What did Melissa say about Sally Oliver?"

"She said Sally should get a life of her own and stop playing second fiddle in Cabot's. According to Melissa, Sally was his mistress during both of Cabot's marriages and still is."

"Did Melissa see her as a rival?"

"Melissa never worried about rivals. She laughed at them."

"What do you think of Sally?"

He shrugged. "She's my cousin. Like they say, you can choose your friends, but not your relatives. I know she wants me to agree to leave our land. Maybe I will, if I decide to turn myself in to the army. I won't need the land if I'm in jail."

"I don't think you'll be in jail very long, if at all. Why do you dislike your cousin?"

"She likes people too little and money too much. Like me, she has too much temper."

"She can be charming when she wants to be."

"Truly charming people don't turn their charm on and off. She does." He made a small gesture. "I shouldn't be criticizing her. I'm worse than she is."

"Is she cruel?"

"Everyone is cruel."

"Is she vindictive?"

He shrugged. "She's been spiteful to me ever since she learned that I planned to keep this land, but her spite just made me dig in my heels. Maybe if she'd been more loving, I'd have given in." He looked at me from the corner of his eye. "I'm a fool for love, after all."

"Don't berate yourself for being susceptible to love," I said. I was not good at giving love, but I knew its value. My wife and children were worth more to me than the universe.

I stood up. "Don't do anything rash. I'll see you later." I walked away and after a few moments I heard the sound of his nail gun as he went back to work.

24

I sat in the truck and thought back over what I'd seen and heard during the past six days. I felt tired but forced myself to regroup and drove to the Noepe Hotel. No Hummer or Mini Cooper was in the parking lot. I considered having another talk with the desk clerk, but had no reason to think she's be less close-lipped than before and I lacked the energy to assault her professional wall of silence about the hotel and its guests. Instead, I drove home.

The house seemed to echo with emptiness broken only by insistent meowed requests for their evening treats by Oliver Underfoot and Velcro. I fed them and poured myself a double vodka on the rocks adorned with two jalapeño-stuffed green olives. I took the glass and a tray of crackers and bluefish pâté up to the balcony, and sat and sipped and nibbled, looking out across the garden to Sengekontacket Pond, where a flotilla of swans was sailing by.

Tomorrow, almost exactly twenty-four hours from now, Zee and the kids would be home. To half of my psyche it seemed an eternity, and to the other half no time at all. I needed to finish preparations for their homecoming supper.

On the barrier beach between the pond and Nantucket Sound a few cars lingered so their occupants could enjoy the last warm rays of the evening sun, and out on the sound boats were moving toward harbor. At the horizon, the dark blue sea met the blue-white evening sky and between them I could just see the dancing line that was the south side of Cape Cod.

I wondered whether Alfred Cabot was besotted with Sally Oliver or she was besotted with him. Or were they besotted with each other? Or was their relationship only a comfortable habit, with neither of them motivated by passion?

Although they didn't seem the types to become infatuated, unexpected fervors often pop up where you least expect them. I recalled the eminently respectable professor in Boston whose bland public life included a wife and children and regular church attendance, but whose secret life eventually led him to murder the prostitute upon whom he had squandered his life savings in thousand-dollar increments he called "grand days."

I thought, too, of the cases of the powerful men, high in civic, financial, and governmental circles, who, when I was a Boston cop, had been discovered in diapers or less, having paid well to be whipped and humiliated by professionals in the sex trade.

As Fats said, "One never knows, do one?"

Whatever the quality of passion in their relationship, Cabot and Sally Oliver had presumably been man and mistress for a long time, so they were of value to one another. I wondered how much influence each held over the other. Clearly Sally didn't have enough to prevent Alfred from planning marriage with Melissa, but maybe Alfred's marriages made no difference to her; maybe she preferred her role as mistress and was indifferent to Alfred's wives. Clearly, too, Alfred had no intention of sacrificing marriage for Sally's sake or vice versa. Like many men, he apparently saw no need to choose between wife and girlfriend, since he probably thought of them as having little to do with one another.

Perhaps, however, his first two wives had disagreed with this generous view, since both had left him. Or maybe they had just been late in learning what Babs Carson and Melissa knew early: that Alfred was a blah.

The next morning dawned bright and sultry. No one would be up and around yet, so I filled the bird feeders, deadheaded some flowers, and prepared myself a full bloat breakfast: juice, coffee, bacon, eggs, and buttered toast. My arteries groaned but my taste buds danced a gleeful jig.

At nine o'clock I drove into Edgartown and, it being too early for most tourists to be abroad, immediately found a parking place not far from Prada Real Estate. I walked there and was gratified to see the Mini Cooper sitting in its accustomed place. I crossed the parking lot and examined it. Sally Oliver had a cute car but she didn't take very good care of it. There were small scratches in the paint on both sides. Nothing serious, but enough to make a true Mini Cooper fan wince.

I looked at the office windows and saw no one looking back. Sally was, I hoped, too busy at her work to notice me prowling around her car. I went back to the truck just as the chief of the Edgartown police came idling down the street in the department's newest cruiser. There being no traffic behind him, he paused. He was chewing on an empty pipe, wishing it was lit but unwilling to fill the car with smoke.

"A very handsome vehicle," I said, admiringly. "My tax dollars at work once again."

"Mine, too," said the chief. "You're hanging around town a lot more than usual since Zee and the kids went to America. It's not natural. I'll be glad when she gets back and you start living up there in the woods again where you belong."

"Tonight's the night," I said. "They'll be home before supper. I don't suppose you know who killed Melissa Carson."

He shook his head. "No, I don't. That's Dom Agganis's problem and West Tisbury's, not mine. She didn't die in Edgartown. I take it that you still have your nose in that mess. I thought you were supposed to be a fisherman."

A pickup driven by a young man and full of shovels, rakes, and lawn mowers came down the street and slowed behind the cruiser. More Brazilians going to work.

"I am a fisherman," I said. "I just haven't been fishing. So you don't know anything about the murder, eh? I thought you might be on the grapevine."

"I don't ask, and they don't tell," said the chief, glancing in his rearview mirror. "Well, *cherchez la femme,* or whatever. I gotta move before I get run over. See you later."

I got into the truck and followed the pickup down the street to the four corners, where it went right on South Water Street and I went left on North Water, then left again on Winter and on out of town to Oak Bluffs via the beach road where early birds were already setting up their umbrellas and spreading their beach blankets on the sand. It was going to be a hot one and they were making sure they had parking places along the road and had staked claims to some beach space. I could think of worse places to be.

I drove through downtown OB and on to the state police office. Dom Agganis was behind his desk and Olive Otero was behind hers.

Without waiting to be asked, I sat down on one of the hard chairs that were there for visitors.

"Now that you're comfortable, what can we do for you, J.W.?" asked Dom in a grumpy tone.

I got right to it. "Olive told you about Cabot knowing Fred McMahan but telling the OB police that he didn't?"

"I've seen the police report, but we don't know that he knew McMahan. Except for you saying it, of course, and I don't think the DA would think much of that evidence."

"I promised my snitch anonymity. The snitch can be squeezed, but I don't want that to happen."

"This is a murder case, so what you want doesn't mean much."

I said, "If we get to the point where a murder charge depends on me IDing the snitch, I'll do it, but not before. Humor me until then, because if Cabot does know Mc-Mahan, it means he's likely to be the guy who hired him. If you can catch up with McMahan or, better yet, his pal Angie, you may be able to put pressure on them to talk. I personally think Angie is the weak link."

"Yeah, Olive told me that idea of yours. Of course, we'd need a reason to grill Angie."

"Like I told you before, my sources tell me that he and McMahan went up to Boston to get charges of birdshot taken out of their fannies. Your colleagues up there might ask Angie about that. When you get shot, you're supposed to report it, but I doubt if he did."

Dom nodded. "That might serve as a reason to chat with him."

"I imagine you can find him at home in Charlestown. I think he lives with his mama."

"Yes, he does," said Olive. "I checked that

out last night. He wasn't home, though. Perhaps he was still having himself repaired. He may be home by now."

"If he doesn't want to talk," I said, "you might threaten to hang a murder charge on him. Tell him that he's a suspect in Melissa's killing. That might make him more malleable. Hell, he might even have done it."

"But you don't think so."

I looked at Dom. "There's another thing. Cabot and Sally Oliver are lovers. They have been for years, going back to when Cabot was married before."

Dom glanced at Olive, who spread her hands, palms up.

"Is that a fact?" he said, looking back at me.

"So I'm told."

"By the same high administrative source that told you about Cabot and McMahan?"

"No, by several people. Roland Nunes and Robert Chadwick are two of them. They both heard Melissa talk about it. I don't think you'll have any trouble verifying it."

Agganis rubbed his big chin. "The plot thickens."

"It thickens even more. I just took a peek at Sally Cabot's Mini Cooper. The sides are both scratched."

"So?"

"So, you remember telling me that nobody saw a car parked by the road the night Melissa was killed? Has anybody told you anything different since we talked?"

"No. But it's not a problem if Nunes killed her. He could have just followed her out and snuffed her."

"I think he loved her."

"You know what Wilde said about men and love. Maybe Nunes got the hots for her and she told him to forget the whole thing."

"Maybe. That morning, did anybody pay any attention to the trail across the road from the one that leads into Nunes's place? It's a continuation of the ancient way that crosses his land. I remember there were bumper to bumper cars parked in front of it when I got there. Maybe it got overlooked."

Dom looked at Olive, who shook her head.

"Maybe it's in somebody's report," said Dom. "If so, I don't remember it."

"The trail is about the width of the one leading into Nunes's place. Too narrow for a normal car and a lot too narrow for Cabot's Hummer, but about wide enough for a Mini Cooper if you don't mind scratching it up a little. You could park in there and nobody would see you."

"And Sally Oliver has a scratched-up

Mini. Are you saying Sally Oliver killed Melissa Carson?"

"You're the policeman. You don't need me to do your thinking. Did Robert Chadwick tell you about the voices he heard that night?"

"Yeah. We interviewed him. I remember he mentioned voices."

"He told me one of them was a man's voice. If he'd only heard a woman's voice, or women's voices, I'd say you should put Sally Oliver on the top of your suspects list, but he heard a man's voice, too. The voices stopped, then started again."

"Ergo . . . ?"

"Ergo, a man was there that night. The only man I know of who might have been in that car is Cabot, as either the driver or a passenger. If your lab gets its hands on Sally's car, can it tell if the scratches came from the bushes that line that trail across from Nunes's? If it can, you'll have a good reason to have Sally and Al come in the office for some serious conversation."

"And their lawyers will be right there with them, telling them to say nothing. Besides, Nunes might have been the man who was there."

"If Cabot hired McMahan and Angie, the DA may think he's got enough to go to a grand jury."

"We haven't proved that relationship yet."

"Sally is Cabot's longtime squeeze and she wants Nunes to sell."

"We'd have to prove that she talked Cabot into hiring McMahan."

"Melissa was cuddling up to Nunes and maybe telling Cabot that she had as much money as he did so he and his girlfriend could take a hike."

"Speculation."

"She told Cabot where she was going that night, and Chadwick heard a man's voice outside his wall."

"Like I say, it could have been Nunes's voice."

"Cabot knew where Melissa was and Sally's car was on the trail across the street."

"You don't know that. Besides, maybe she parked it there earlier in the week."

"Maybe Iraq really had WMDs. Either she was in the car or Cabot was in it or they both were in it."

"You have smoke but no fire."

"Sure. Maybe Jack the Ripper did it."

We sat in silence for a time, then Dom tapped a finger on his desk and said, "I don't think we have enough."

"We can call the lab about the scratches on the car," said Olive. "If they can do the job, we may be able to get a warrant for the Mini before she takes it to a car wash or paint shop, if she hasn't done that already."

"We can do that," said Dom.

"Maybe I can help," I said.

Dom looked at me and shook his head. "No."

"They'll be afraid of you if they see you coming," I said. "But they're not afraid of me. I may be able to learn something their lawyers won't let them tell you."

"No," said Dom. "Leave this to us. Go home and wait for your wife and kids to get back. I mean it."

I got up. "You're sure?" I asked.

"I'm sure." He frowned. "Don't interfere, J.W. Thanks for your help, but we can take it from here. Can I trust you on this?

"Is Benedict XVI Catholic?"

I went out and drove to Radio Shack in Vineyard Haven. There I bought a small tape recorder and mike.

25

Since the Noepe Hotel was closer, I drove there first, but saw no Hummer in the parking lot, so turned west and drove to Aquinnah.

When I got to Cabot's driveway, I was confronted once again by the guard at the electric gate. I gave him my name and said I'd like to talk to Alfred Cabot.

"You got an appointment?" He looked down at a clipboard he had in his hand. "What's your name, again?"

"J. W. Jackson."

"Sorry. There's no such name here. Say, weren't you here a couple of days ago?"

"That was me."

"Well, the boss didn't want to talk with you then, either."

"That was then, this is now. Tell Mr. Cabot it's about Fred McMahan."

The guard frowned at my old Toyota. It probably wasn't the sort of vehicle driven by acquaintances of Alfred Cabot. "What did you say your name was?"

"J. W. Jackson. Just tell your boss I'm here and that I want to talk with him about a guy named Fred McMahan."

The guard gave me a final frown and walked to the gatehouse. After a while the electric gate swung open and the guard walked back. "Go right up the driveway. Somebody will meet you at the house."

I drove up the narrow road, feeling like I was in one of those old black-and-white movies where some stranger drives through the trees up to some huge mansion while ominous or cheerful music plays, letting the audience know more than the stranger knows. Life would a lot simpler if we had background music we could hear, but such is not the case. More evidence that intelligent design is unlikely.

I came to the house, parked beside Cabot's forest-green Hummer, and got out. There was a man waiting for me. I recognized him as being the one who had driven the ATV up to the fence surrounding Cabot's land. He looked very fit in his summer clothes. His shirt was outside his pants, and there was a pistol-sized lump under it, on his hip.

"You're Mr. Jackson? Please come in." His

eyes flowed over me, checking for a similar lump, I guessed. Seeing none, he turned and led me into the house. We walked down a hall and into a central atrium topped two stories up with sliding glass panels and filled with exotic looking plants, including several varieties of orchids. The air was hot and moist. Was Nero Wolfe in residence?

Alfred Cabot was. He was on the far side of the room, watering a blue flower I didn't recognize. I'd never have guessed that Alfred Cabot was the sort of person who'd have an atrium full of flowers, but life is full of surprises. Often when I think I'm finally pretty much in touch with reality I discover that I still have a ways to go.

Seeing me, Cabot put down his watering can and came toward me. Beside me, the man asked, "Shall I stay, sir?"

Cabot waved a dismissive hand, and said, "No, that will be all, Elmer."

Elmer went away and Cabot pointed to a side door. "My office is in there. We can talk without being interrupted." Without waiting for my response, he led me into the office and shut the door behind us. He waved me into a comfortable leather chair and took another for himself. He gestured at a humidor. "Cigar, Mr. Jackson?"

"No thanks," I said, looking around. The

office was large and luxurious. Leather and carved wood were the materials of choice. The chairs were leather, the books on the bookshelves were leather-bound, and a couple of the small tables were covered with carved leather. The desk was large and heavy, and a credenza behind the desk held electronic devices. Among those I recognized were a computer, a fax machine, a scanner, and a printer, the accoutrements of modern business.

Cabot followed my gaze. "I can do most of my work from right here," he said. "It's very convenient, but I like city living, so this office is only used when I'm staying here on holiday. What can I do for you, Mr. Jackson?"

"I came to talk to you about Fred McMahan and Angie Vinci," I said, hoping that my tape recorder was working as it should.

"I can't imagine what I can tell you," he said smoothly. "I recall that you told me you had business dealings with them, but I don't even know them."

"Yes, you told me that. And you told the police the same thing. But the mention of McMahan's name got me in here to see you. Do you know what McMahan and Vinci were doing here on the Vineyard?"

"I have no idea."

"I think you do. They were vandalizing Roland Nunes's property. I was hired to find out who was doing the vandalizing, and I managed to catch them in the act. Later, I followed them to your hotel and had a chat with them."

His face was without expression. "What did you learn?"

"Enough to put together a scenario. Would you like to hear it?"

He glanced at a wristwatch that had probably cost him more than $9.99, then said, "I have some time. I can't imagine what your story has to do with me, but go ahead. I'll tell you if I get bored."

"All right," I said. "McMahan and Vinci are small-time hoods who hire themselves out to whoever will pay them to do illegal jobs. They advertise by word of mouth in some of the more expensive watering holes in Boston, the idea being to go where the money is. They were hired to come down here and give Roland Nunes enough grief to persuade him to sell his place. His land was cheap thirty years ago, when he first moved there, but it's worth a fortune now. A lot of people would like to have it, and his cousin Sally Oliver, who is in charge of the trust that owns it, would love to sell it. The problem is that he has a covenant that says the land can't be sold unless he agrees to move off it.

"So McMahan and Vinci came down here and took a room in your hotel and got to work. They did some damage, but Nunes is stubborn, and then Nunes's sister, Carole Cohen, decided to stop the crooks, so she hired me to catch them in the act and get photographs. I did that, and even though they'd gotten themselves rigged out in black suits and blackface, it didn't take long to ID them. Are you with me so far?"

"So far," said Cabot, "but so what?"

"As I said, I followed McMahan and Vinci back to their hotel room. I took their pistols and stun gun away from them and we had a talk. They were both hurting from shotgun pellets in their posteriors and weren't interested in going on with the job they'd been hired to do. They caught the first boat they could back to America and went home. The police are looking for them now and will probably find them. McMahan may be a tough nut for them to crack, but I don't think they'll have much trouble getting Angie to talk. He'll tell them everything he knows."

Cabot tapped a finger on the arm of his chair.

"And what might that be?"

"That you were the guy who hired them. You found out about the work they do in one of the bars you frequent near your office in Boston and hired them to run Nunes off his land."

Cabot leaned forward in his chair and gave me a look that was meant to cow. "That's slander. I never heard of them until yesterday. If you try to spread such lies, I'll have you in court so fast it will make your head spin."

"I won't be the one telling the tale," I said. "Angie will."

"A criminal's word against mine."

"There's more. You lied to the police about not knowing McMahan. You've been seen entering McMahan's room at the Noepe."

"Another lie!" His eyes flashed. "Was it that maid? If it was, she'll rue the day she was born!"

"It wasn't the maid," I lied. "The point is that the police may soon have plenty of reason to arrest you for hiring McMahan and Vinci. They may not know your motive yet, but it won't take them long to figure out that your girlfriend, Sally Oliver, is behind the whole affair. She wants to sell Nunes's land, and you have the money to buy it if she can get him to leave. It's a good deal for you, because even though you'll pay a lot for the land, your girlfriend will actually get half of the money you paid, so it'll still be more or less in the family. You'll make even more when you sell it to the next castle builder."

He looked at me with disdain, but I thought I saw worry behind the contempt. "My lawyers will make mincemeat out of the District Attorney."

"Maybe, maybe not," I said. "In any case, the vandalizing scheme is pretty insignificant compared to homicide. The DA is interested in the murder of Melissa Carson, and you're right on top of his suspect list. The cops already know about your involvement with Sally Oliver so you're an excellent suspect."

"Murder? I'm no murderer! That's nonsense! I loved Melissa!"

"Where were you when she was killed?"

"I was right here."

"Can you prove it? Jealousy is a classic motive for murder. Melissa Carson was romancing Roland Nunes. If she married him instead of you, he'd have plenty of money to build a better place on his land, and he might even produce an heir, so it's possible that the land couldn't be sold for at least another generation. She was killed as she was leaving his house." I gestured at his hands. "Her neck was broken, and you're a big, powerful man." I raised an eyebrow. "Do you really think that your man Elmer will risk a perjury charge by testifying under oath that you were here when Melissa died? Because I don't think you were here. I think you were there, with Sally Oliver, in her Mini Cooper, parked in the lane across the road, waiting for Melissa."

His eyes flared. Was fear the fuel? "You know a lot of liars! I was here. I don't have to prove I was!"

I leaned back in my chair. "Don't get worked up," I said. "Personally, I don't care where you were. I came here looking for work."

His hands were claws. "Work? What are you talking about?"

"Two things," I said. "First, I can finish the job McMahan started. Nunes and his sister trust me, but I don't owe them a thing and I don't care what happens to the land. I took her job because I needed the money. I think you might give me more to burn down his house and his outbuildings. The other thing I can do is give you an alibi for the night Melissa Carson was killed. The DA might not believe Elmer, but I'm not a friend or employee of yours, so if I testify that we were up here together that night, they'll believe me."

He studied me. "This is blackmail."

"I'm not threatening you," I said. "I'm looking for work. If you get caught, I get caught; we'll be in it together."

He put his fingers together. "You're proposing that I hire you to commit a crime. I can have you arrested."

I sat for a moment, then stood up. "There's a phone on your desk. Make your call to the cops. I'll let myself out."

I was halfway to the door when he said, "Don't be hasty, Mr. Jackson. Come back and sit down."

I went back to my chair.

"I'm going to make some inquiries about you," said Cabot. "Presuming that I find you to be a reliable person, what do you think your services are worth?"

I named a figure that was large to me.

He didn't seem to think it was worth a second thought. "You'll want that in cash, of course."

I nodded. "For both our sakes. Fifties and smaller. All old."

"When do you plan to do the work?"

"The sooner the better. Tomorrow morning, after Nunes goes to work. I think it was a mistake to try to do it at night while he was home. I can be in and out of there in a few minutes and no one will see me. I'll come in by the old path from the far woods. There won't be any walkers there that early."

"It will take me a while to collect your money in old bills."

"I'm in no rush. We have to trust one another."

His smile was ironic but real. "Yes. Trust is important among businessmen." He paused. "We must decide why you were here with me the night of Melissa's murder. As you say, we're not friends. What was your business?"

"I was trying to learn whether you knew McMahan and Vinci. You denied it. I was here for half an hour or so before you threw me out. Where was the guard at the gate that night? Where was Elmer? Why didn't they see me?"

Cabot thought for a moment, then said, "The guard doesn't work evenings, and it was Elmer's night off. I opened the gate from here, when you called on the speaker that's mounted on the gate post."

"Elmer will agree that it was his night off?"

"He'll be telling the truth. It actually was his night off. I think he went to a movie. I'll check and see what was playing that night." He was looking at me with interest. "You're not what you seem, are you? You look like an ordinary man with ordinary feelings, but you're not. You don't give a damn about anything, do you?"

"I give a damn about money," I said. "Not as much as you do, of course."

He nodded. "If this business works out, I might have more employment for you in the future."

"Somebody's going to have to take the fall for Melissa Carson's killing," I said. "Have you given that any thought?"

"Some."

"I think your girlfriend Sally Oliver would make a good patsy. She had plenty of motive and she was at the scene."

He didn't deny it. Instead, he said. "If she's charged, she'll say we were together or that I did it."

"And I'll say you didn't. Or maybe you can figure out a way to keep her from talking," I said. "Let me know if you think of anything."

I got up and went to the door. In the atrium, Elmer was sitting on a bench, sweating lightly in the tropic air. After I passed him, I clicked off the tape recorder in my pocket. He followed me out to the truck, and my rearview mirror told me that he watched me out of sight. Someone had called the gate guard, because the gate was swinging open as I approached it. I took a left and headed for Edgartown.

26

It was almost noon when I got to the village, and by the time I found a parking place on School Street, up beyond the historical society museum, I thought that Sally Oliver might have gone to lunch. But when I reached Prada Real Estate, Sally's Mini Cooper was still in its parking slot. I turned on the tape recorder and went inside. Industrious Sally was, according to her receptionist, in her office, busy with a customer.

"You're Mr. Jackson," she added, smiling a professional smile. "You were here a few days ago."

"Yes. Would you please tell Ms. Oliver that I'd like to talk with her about a property in West Tisbury? Another gentleman, a Mr. McMahan, has withdrawn his interest in the place, but I still am very interested."

I said I'd wait and she nodded and spoke into her phone. While I sat, I looked at the photos of Sally running, Sally swimming, Sally biking, and Sally holding trophies. She was very fit in every photo, and I remembered her firm handshake when first we'd met.

In time, her office door opened and a man came out, looking pleased at whatever he'd been told. Sally Oliver had a farewell smile for him but not a welcoming one for me. Still, she waved me into the office and shut the door behind us.

"What can I do for you today, Mr. Jackson?" She glanced down at a note on her desk. "Who's this Mr. McMahan you mentioned?"

"He's a very mysterious guy, apparently. You never heard of him, and Alfred Cabot never met him, but he's one of the two guys Cabot hired to trash Roland Nunes's property."

Her pretty face looked carved from ice. "I've never heard the name."

Clint Eastwood made several spaghetti westerns featuring a man with no name. Fred McMahan was a name with no man.

"Nobody's heard of him, lately," I said. "I just had a chat with your boyfriend and he and I have reached an agreement. I'm here to tell you about it."

"He's not my boyfriend. I told you I only

know him casually. And his business is his business, not mine."

"I think Cabot is your boyfriend and you should know about his business since you're the one who talked him into persuading Roland Nunes to sell his land. Fred McMahan, the guy Cabot hired — but you and he both claim you never heard of — has gone back to Boston with his partner, Angie Vinci, to have shotgun pellets removed from their backsides. They've gotten out of the vandalizing business on the Vineyard, but the police will be asking them some questions about who hired them, and there's a good chance Alfred's name will come up. If it does, yours probably will, too. Am I interesting you?"

"No."

"Part two of my speech is that Alfred and I have made a business deal. Since McMahan has quit the job, Alfred is going to give me some money to burn down Nunes's house and outbuildings tomorrow morning. That should encourage Nunes to sell. If you don't believe me, and you don't think your line's been tapped, call Cabot. He should still be at home."

She put her hand on her phone, but then hesitated. "Why would my line be tapped?"

I shrugged. "The police have been thinking serious thoughts about you and Alfred for several days now, but maybe they haven't tapped your line yet. Go ahead, call Cabot."

She took her hand away and brought her purse out of a desk drawer. "I'll call him on my cell phone."

"All right," I said, "but in case you didn't know, cell phones aren't secure at all. People can listen in without any problem, if they know what they're doing."

She seemed surprised and angry. "I use my cell phone all the time for my work!"

I nodded. "A lot of people do."

She glared at me. "Why are you trying to keep me from calling him?"

"I'm not. But I'm also not anxious to have the world know about the deal I've made with Cabot. If you want to talk with him, call him from some other phone. Better yet, talk to him face to face, because his line might be tapped, too." I pointed at her phone. "It's probably safe to call him and make arrangements to meet with him somewhere where you can talk."

She put her hand on the phone again, then studied me. "There's something else, isn't there? I can see it in your face."

I was pleased that she'd noticed my eager expression. "Yes, there is a third thing I wanted to talk about with you. It has to do with the murder of Melissa Carson."

Her hand lifted from the phone and strayed to her throat.

"I don't know anything about that," she said.

"If you say so. But the police know a good deal and they're digging deeper. You're Alfred Cabot's mistress, and Cabot hired McMahan to vandalize your cousin's property. You're the brains behind the scheme, and when the cops squeeze Cabot, he'll rat you out."

Her eyes narrowed. "He'll do no such thing. All right. I'll tell you the truth. We're going to be married!"

"My congratulations. Maybe you're correct. You know him better than I do. Maybe he's honest and true to the end." I leaned forward slightly. "Hiring vandals is one thing, but murder is quite another, and in this case the two crimes are linked. Cabot is a prime suspect in the killing, too, and he knows it, but he's not about to take the fall for that. Guess who he has in mind? You were at the scene when Melissa was murdered, so you're the one who's going to take the rap."

Her wide eyes grew wild. "What liar told you that?"

"Who do you think? Cabot can prove he

was somewhere else, but you can't. You had motive and opportunity and you're a strong, athletic woman, so Melissa was easy prey for you. I don't know if you intended to kill her when you met her, so the DA might not be able to stick you with murder in the first degree, but he won't have much trouble with second degree."

Those eyes blazed into mine. "I wasn't there. I was with Alfred. We were at his house."

"You were with Alfred, all right, but you weren't at his house. You were driving your Mini Cooper and Alfred was with you. But he'll deny it to the police and he'll have a witness to verify that he was at home with that witness that night. That leaves you alone in your Mini Cooper at the murder scene when Melissa was killed."

"I wasn't there and I wasn't alone!"

I leaned forward. "You parked in the lane across the road from the path leading to Nunes's house, and when Melissa came out you met her. A witness heard the two of you arguing. Melissa laughed at you and you killed her. A man was with you. I think it was Alfred Cabot, but, like I say, he has a credible witness who'll swear that he was in Chilmark at the time."

"Why would I have been there, waiting

for her? How would I have known that she'd be down there with Roland Nunes?"

"Because your sweetie, Alfred Cabot, told you. He knew because Melissa had told him earlier in the day. I was at her house just after they talked. She told him and he told you, and you were both waiting for her. Of course, he'll swear you were there alone and that he was at home."

"He can't testify that I was there without incriminating himself, the bastard!"

"He can testify that you confessed to him afterward, and he can have a witness to the call you made. He'll have to admit to initially withholding that evidence from the police, but he'll say it was because of the power of love."

"He's never loved anything but money in his life!" Her eyes flicked to the window. "My God! What the hell is going on out there?"

I followed her gaze and saw Dom Agganis standing beside the Mini Cooper while a hauler tow truck backed into the yard behind the car.

"That's my car they're towing!" She leaped to her feet and raced past me out of the office. I watched through the window as she reappeared and confronted Agganis. Her face was contorted and her mouth was moving but the office's soundproofing was good and I could barely hear her voice. Agganis produced a paper and gave it to her. A warrant, for sure. She looked at it and raged some more, but Agganis and the truck driver both ignored her as the Mini Cooper was winched onto the truck bed and driven away.

Sally was in a fury when she came back into the office, waving the paper. "This is a warrant! They're taking my car! Damn them! They can't do that! I'm calling my lawyer!" She slammed herself into her chair and snatched up her telephone.

"I think it's evidence in the murder case," I said, mildly.

She stared at me. "What do you mean?" For the first time I thought I detected an element of fear in her voice.

"I mean your car got scratched when you parked in the path across from the lane to Nunes's house that night. The police lab will verify that, and your story about being somewhere else will go up in smoke."

"How did they know about . . . ?" She put brakes on her mouth.

"How do you think?" I asked, with my best cynical smile. "Someone told them."

"Alfred!" Her anger made the name into a curse.

I looked at my nails. "You can't be sure. Maybe there's another witness. Some people like to walk at night. Maybe one of them came by and saw you and Alfred park there. Maybe it was a couple of kids planning to sneak in there to have some sex or to smoke some dope. Maybe when they heard about the murder they got nervous, so they called the cops."

"I'm being set up!"

"Could be," I said. "That's why I'm here."

"What do you mean?"

"I mean you need help, and I may be able to give it to you."

Her face became calculating. "How? Why?"

"For money. I don't have a regular job, so I have to find work where I can. Maybe I can find it with you." I met her gaze. "Alfred Cabot has hired me to give him an alibi for the night of the murder. I'm his witness. If they charge him with the crime, I'm to swear that I was with him at his house that night. That leaves you alone at the scene."

"But he was with me!"

"You know that and so do I, but you can't prove it. If they try to stick him with the killing, he'll swear that you confessed and offer me as his witness that he was home that night. You'll be the one who's nailed." I paused, then said, "Unless you and I can make a better deal."

Her eyes became thoughtful. "What sort of deal?"

"I think you probably killed the woman," I said. "Alfred doesn't strike me as the kind of guy who does his own dirty work. I think it was a spur of the moment thing. You meant to show your lover what a double dealer she was, but she went you one better and told him she'd decided to marry Nunes. You saw your hopes for the land disappearing and you lost your temper and killed her." She opened her mouth, but I held up my hand before she could speak. "I don't care who killed her. She meant nothing to me, and neither does Alfred Cabot. Neither do you, for that matter. I'm here because I can get you off the hook."

"How?"

"It's simple. You need an alibi that you don't have. I'll give it to you. It'll cost you your boyfriend and some money, but it'll keep you out of jail." I sat back. "Here's what I'll do. You'll swear in court that Cabot borrowed your car that night. Your lawyer will ask why and you can say that you guessed later that it was because his Hummer was too big to hide. His lawyer will object on grounds that that's speculation and the judge will sustain him, but the jury will remember. Cabot will deny that he borrowed the car and will offer me as a witness willing to swear he was at home when the killing took place. But when they put me on the stand I'll testify that I wasn't with him; I was with you at my house. I'll say that my wife was away and that we were alone. I'll say that we were there all night. It would be nice if you have a tattoo in some forbidden place that I would only know about if you were naked, but I suppose that's too much to hope for."

There was a silence in the room. Then she said, "What do you want in exchange for this little deception?"

I named my price. Because she had less money than Alfred, it was lower than the one I'd asked of him, but it was still substantial by my standards.

She thought awhile, then nodded, and said in an arctic voice, "I can manage that, but if you're willing to double-cross Alfred, why should I think you won't double-cross me?"

"Maybe I'm just sentimental about beautiful women in trouble."

"You don't have any more feelings than a worm."

"Such a cynic. How about this deal — you don't have to pay me until after the trial, if there is a trial. Maybe there won't be. In that case you won't owe me a thing. If there is, and if I testify, and if you get away with it, you'll owe me the money. Am I fair, or what?"

"The little bitch laughed at both of us," she said suddenly. "Then she threw her engagement ring into the bushes and stuck her face up into mine and said she was never going to marry Alfred. I hit her, but I don't remember much after that."

"You might make that story stick," I said. "Maybe you don't need my deal. It depends on how good your lawyer is. You'd better call him right now." I got up. "Let me know if we have a deal. I'm going to make some money out of this one way or another, either from you or from Cabot. I don't care which."

"You're scum," she said with contempt. "Scum."

As I went out the door, feeling that she might be right, I heard her phone ringing. On Martha's Vineyard, the real estate business never stops. I walked back to the truck, passing tourists who were enjoying Edgartown's lovely side streets, then drove to Dom Agganis's office.

Olive Otero was there, holding down the fort. I told her about the diamond ring and she said, "Ah, a broken engagement. Love doesn't seem to last too long these days. We'll get back up there and see what we can find."

Then I gave her the tape recorder and told her the tale that went with it.

She turned it in her hands. "You know we can't use this as evidence, don't you?"

"I know," I said, "but if you listen to it, you might find something that will help you. Cabot is very slick. He never really admits that he's involved in anything or says that he wants me to do anything illegal. He implies it, but he never says it. My impression of him is that he never says anything without a lawyer at his shoulder. The woman is a different matter. She admits that she hit Melissa Carson that night. Maybe you can use the tape to squeeze the truth out of her."

Olive nodded. "We'll listen to this, for what it's worth."

"If you can get Fred or Angie to talk, and if the lab can show that the Mini Cooper was scratched by the bushes across from the murder scene, and if you can spook an admission out of either Cabot or Sally Oliver, maybe you can get a conviction."

"That's a lot of *ifs* and a big *maybe*," said Olive.

I felt weary and hungry. I walked back to

the truck and drove home, wondering how long Alfred and Sally Oliver would wait before they contacted each other and began carefully trying to find out what I had said to each of them, and who was the greater liar, and who had the most to fear.

27

Oliver Underfoot wound around my ankles and Velcro lay in my arms and buzzed. I was wearing a loose summer shirt over the old .38 revolver I had stuck in my belt and was sitting in the rocking chair on the screened porch, waiting to see who would show up. The screened porch was often the most comfortable spot in the house during the summer, since the prevailing southwest winds kept it cool even on hot days such as this one. From my chair I could look up the sandy driveway and see arriving visitors long before they could see me.

Would there be one or two? Would the one feeling most threatened by me, or most anxious to do business with me, show up alone? Which would it be? Sally? Alfred?

Or would they arrive together, showing strength in numbers, to put me in my place by hanging together rather than hanging separately?

Or would anyone come at all?

I ran everything I knew and had heard through my mind, then looked at my suspicions. Some things I seemed to see face to face, others as through a glass darkly. The scheme to vandalize Roland Nunes's property had certainly been funded and planned by Sally and Alfred, and the DA could probably make a good case for that in court if Nunes decided to press charges. The murder was another matter.

Both Sally and Alfred had motives and opportunity. Sally had told me she hit Melissa but she couldn't remember what happened after that. Was she telling the truth? Each of them was physically larger and stronger than Melissa, and the DA could argue that each was jealous and fearful of financial loss, and had been at the murder scene that fatal night. The scratches on Sally's car might prove useful to him, and if he interviewed the two separately, as he certainly would do, he might get one of them to talk, or even agree to testify against the other.

But then again, the two of them might be made of sterner stuff. They might stick together like glue, defending themselves with the finest lawyers Alfred's money could buy, who would be very fine lawyers indeed, denying everything and laughing at the DA's evidence. All they had to do was create doubt in one member of the jury.

I put myself in the place of that juror and found that such doubt was already in my mind. Alfred and Sally might get nailed for vandalism, but they had a good chance of walking away from the murder rap. In fact, if Roland Nunes was the monk some took him to be, he might not even bring charges against Al and Sal for vandalism, and they might stay free as birds. Stranger things happen all the time, for justice has ever been elusive in this best of all possible worlds.

Alfred's Hummer came down my driveway.

It stopped beside my Land Cruiser. Beauty and the beast.

Alfred Cabot got out of the driver's side and Sally Oliver got out of the passenger door. Two men I'd never seen before emerged from the rear doors. The men were wearing neckties and carrying briefcases. Lawyers for sure, since, except for weddings and funerals, only lawyers and Mormon missionaries wear ties on Martha's Vineyard and these men were a lot older than the youngsters who were usually doing their two-year stints for the Latter Day Saints.

They all looked at the house, which long

ago had been a hunting and fishing camp but now had been roughly modernized into a home for the Jacksons. They exchanged words in low voices, then advanced. When they got near the porch door, I said, "Hello. Come right in."

Alfred Cabot led the way. Our porch is furnished with a couch and chairs, all padded with waterproof seats and pillows, and I waved a hand at them.

"Sit down," I said. "This is Velcro, and the guy at my ankles is Oliver Underfoot. What can I do for you?"

They sat. The three men had cool, hooded eyes, but Sally Oliver's were blazing

"It's not what you can do for us," said Cabot. "It's what we can do for you. This is Mr. Belltower and this is Mr. Webb. They're partners in Patt, Carlson, Church, and Connell. Are you familiar with the firm?"

I stroked Velcro, who was quite uninterested in my guests. "I've seen the name in the *Globe*. You got them down here in no time at all. It's only been two or three hours since we talked. A corporate jet, I presume. Now, what is it that you can do for me?"

Mr. Belltower had a gentle voice. "You've made an illegal proposition to our clients, and have threatened to involve Mr. Cabot in a murder investigation. You've also suggested that Mr. Cabot accuse Ms. Oliver of having committed that murder."

"And," said Mr. Webb, "you similarly threatened Ms. Oliver and suggested that she accuse Mr. Cabot of the crime. You've dug a deep hole for yourself, Mr. Jackson, and you're down in the bottom of it. We're here to help you out of it before you get buried alive."

"Accusations are easy to make," I said. "Proving them is something else. Do you have any evidence that what you just told me actually happened? Or are you just taking the word of these two possible suspects in vandalism and murder?"

Mr. Belltower said mildly, "If it comes to testimony, Mr. Jackson, we're confident that our clients' reputations will carry more weight than yours. However, we think it best if this matter never gets to court, so we're here to tell you that if you persist in involving yourself in our clients' lives and in making these outlandish accusations and propositions, we're prepared to use all of our firm's considerable resources to defend them."

"That's your job," I said. "It's why you get the big bucks."

"Part of that defense, of course, would include discrediting you, should you be involved in the proceedings. We hope you won't be, and that you'll not be tempted to pass your incredible accusations along to anyone else."

I had already passed them along to the police, so I said, "If you're through telling me what you'll do to me if I stay involved in this case, what is it that you came here to do for me if I don't?"

"Why," said Mr. Webb, spreading his very clean hands, "we will let you go on living your carefree life." He smiled a lawyer's smile.

"Nobody lives a carefree life," I said.

"Yours could become much more complicated," he said. "The law can be a heavy burden on an estate. Have you read *Bleak House?*"

"A long time ago, but I get your drift." I returned his smile. "Since we seem to be teetering on the brink of a relationship, may I have your card? And yours, too, if you please, Mr. Belltower."

"Of course."

I glanced at the cards and put them in my shirt pocket. Then I said, "I think you folks have me outgunned in matters of the law, and that it's likely that you can tie me up in lawsuits and other difficulties so badly that I could lose everything."

"Nothing illegal, of course," said Belltower in his gentle voice.

"Of course not," I said in a matching voice. "But like the song says, freedom's just another word for nothing left to lose. If you take everything I have, I'm free. Have you ever heard of a man named . . . well, never mind his name. Just take my word for it that he's real. He's an old guy who lives in Oak Bluffs." Omitting their names, I told them of the time Cousin Henry Bayles had confronted Ben Krane. When I was through with my little tale, they looked at me.

Webb frowned for the first time. "Are you threatening us, Mr. Jackson? Are you saying that if we take action against you, that you will kill us?"

I widened my eyes. "Of course not. What a thing to say. What gave you that idea? I assure you that I mean nothing of the kind. I'm shocked at the suggestion."

"You don't look shocked," said Mr. Belltower, thoughtfully.

"I repeat that I certainly am. What can I say that will make you believe me? Tell me, and I'll say it. Now, I admit that I know all of your names and your places of work, and I'm sure that I could find your residences and your family members if I was so inclined, which I assure you I am not because

I have no interest at all in using that information in any way at all." I petted Velcro and got a larger purr for my efforts, and then looked at Mr. Webb. "You seem to be a literary man. Have you read *The Brothers Karamazov?*"

"A long time ago," he said.

"You'll recall Ivan saying that if there is no God, all things are lawful, and Smerdyakov taking that as permission to murder his father."

"Yes, I remember something like that. What is your point?"

"It's a moral perspective different from that in *Bleak House.*"

"Not yours, I hope."

"No, but I don't believe in gods."

"You won't be very dangerous if you're in jail," said Cabot.

"I'm not dangerous," I said. "I've got too much to lose." I looked at Belltower. "Let me get us some lemonade. Then you four will want a few minutes alone, and I have to make a phone call. I'll join you again after you have your chat. How does that sound?"

"It's a warm day," said Belltower. "Thank you."

I put Velcro down and went into the house. There was lemonade in the fridge. I put the pitcher on a tray with four glasses, poured a glass for myself, and went out to the porch. I put the tray on a table, smiled a host's smile, and went back into the house, shutting the door behind me.

Using the bedroom phone, I called Brady Coyne's office in Boston, figuring I had a fifty-fifty chance of finding him there practicing law instead of being off casting flies into some trout stream. I was lucky. Julie, his secretary, said, "You aren't going to haul him down to the island for some fishing are you? He's got work to do." I assured her that I was not, and she put me through to his office. When we finished our opening hellos and how-are-things, I asked him what he knew about Belltower and Webb.

"Very smart, very tough guys. You don't want them mad at you."

"Are they honest?"

"What a question! Have you ever heard of a dishonest lawyer?"

"Well, are they?"

"Yes. Both of them. They look soft, but they're hard; but you can trust them if you can afford them. I don't think you can."

"Hell, I can't even afford you."

When we rang off, I took my glass of lemonade out to the porch.

"Hiring a killer?" asked Alfred Cabot.

"No," I said, sitting down. "Checking up

on your lawyers." I looked at them. "Do you really think your clients, here, are innocent as lambs?"

"I don't know much about lambs," said Webb, "but no charges have been brought against Mr. Cabot or Ms. Oliver, and if that should happen we will defend them against all accusations."

I said, "I think you'll have your work cut out for you if Roland Nunes decides to press charges. I'll probably be asked to testify for the prosecution because I saw Fred McMahan and Angie Vinci, a couple of small-time Charlestown hoods that Alfred may have failed to mention to you, at the scene of the vandalism. And I imagine that Angie or Fred or both will name Alfred, here, as the guy who hired them to do the dirty work. Whether Al, here, will testify that Sal, here, pushed him to hire them I don't know, although that's the way I think it worked."

"What you think doesn't make much difference," said Webb.

"What I saw does, and the photos I took will, too."

Belltower looked at me. "This is the first I've heard of photos. We'll want to see them, of course."

"Of course you will. I'd like to ask you a

353

question. Do you think Alfred, here, is capable of murder? Of breaking a woman's neck?"

Almost everyone is capable of murder, if the circumstances are right, but Belltower understood what I meant.

"I think not," he said. "Physical violence is not his line." Then he added, "Of course, none of our clients is capable of murder."

"How about Sally Oliver? She looks murderous enough right now."

Sally Oliver insulted my mother and suggested that I perform an impossible sexual act.

"Ms. Oliver is our newest client," said Belltower, "so, of course, she too is incapable of violence."

"She told me that she hit Melissa Carson and can't remember what happened next. That sounds like violence to me."

"Our position is that no blow was struck and nothing happened next. Ms. Oliver has told us that she and Ms. Carson argued, and that Ms. Carson slipped and fell. Mr. Cabot led Ms. Oliver away and they drove to her home. If need be, our clients will swear to that under oath."

"Leaving Melissa Carson unconscious on the ground with a bruise on her jaw."

"Perhaps she hit her head when she fell.

In any case, she was very much alive and conscious when our clients left. They murdered no one."

"Why were they there, if they meant no harm?"

"Mr. Cabot's fiancée was said to be involved with Roland Nunes. They were there to see if it was true. And it was. They exchanged words with her and left."

I thought Belltower seemed very good at his work. There was nothing bombastic about him. His mild voice was very persuasive. If he said his clients were innocent, a jury would be inclined to believe him.

As for me, I was more persuaded by the fact that neither Al nor Sal had been seriously tempted to toss the other to the wolves. I'd given them every chance, but instead they had formed a united front.

"Tell me," I said to Belltower, "after these supposed conversations I had with your clients, which of them phoned the other? Did he call her, or did she call him?"

Webb leaned forward. "Are you acknowledging that you encouraged each of them to accuse the other of murder and promised to provide each an alibi?"

"No. I'll admit I had a chat with each of them, but I'll swear on the Bible that I never encouraged them to do anything or promised that I'd do anything."

"That would be a lie."

"I don't think you can prove it. Who called who?"

"I believe that should be 'who called whom,' Mr. Jackson. In any case, Mr. Cabot called me, then called Ms. Oliver," said Belltower. "I believe you were just leaving her office at the time."

I remembered the phone ringing as I'd gone out the door.

"If your pure-as-driven-snow clients here didn't kill Melissa Carson," I said to Belltower, "who did?"

"I'm not a prosecuting attorney. Our concern is defending our clients."

I looked at Cabot. "Did you see anyone else there?"

"No."

I looked at Sally Oliver. "Did you?"

"No."

But if they were telling the truth someone else had been there.

"You can go home," I said to the lawyers. "I may be asked to testify about Fred and Angie if there's a trial, but otherwise your clients are safe from me."

"I'm gratified to hear it," said Webb, rising with the others. "But you'll understand if we keep you in our thoughts until this matter is concluded."

"I understand. Are you a churchgoing man, Mr. Webb?"

"Yes, I am."

"Just remember that I'm not."

He actually smiled. "I'll remember, Mr. Jackson."

I watched them drive away. It was past mid-afternoon. I got in the Land Cruiser and drove up-island, feeling bad.

28

The new house was crawling with workers. Roland Nunes was using his air-powered nail gun to build a railing on the wide deck that reached out toward Menemsha Pond from the living room. Beyond and below him, some small sailboats were racing between markers on the pond, their captains and crews paying no attention to the latest mansion being erected on the shoreline. Maybe they had seen photos of the stone cities of Malta, an island nation almost exactly the size of the Vineyard but having four hundred thousand permanent residents, and were not impressed by a single giant wooden house. As I watched, bright spinnakers flowered as the boats rounded a mark and fell away downwind.

Below the deck, the land dropped away fifty feet or so, in a sharp decline, to a beach covered with rocks that had once been in New Hampshire but had ended up here when the last glacier had stopped and then had begun its slow retreat to the north, leaving behind the mounds of stone and dirt that it had pushed south and that later, as the seas rose, became Nantucket, the Vineyard, Block Island, and the other islands on New England's south coast.

In my mind's eye, I could see the path and fieldstone steps that would later lead down to that beach and to the dock that would walk out into the pond on wooden pilings.

I had seen Nunes only the day before, but he now looked much older. His face was that of a saint who had sinned. When I crossed to him, he stopped his work and rubbed the sweat from his brow. The sound of hammer and saws and compressors seemed to grow faint in my ears, but I felt like I could hear his breathing.

"Have you confided in your lawyer?" I asked.

He glanced at the nail gun then brought his eyes up to mine. They were sad and tired. "I told him what he wanted to hear."

"I think you should tell him everything."

A look almost of relief appeared on his face. "You know, then." It wasn't a question; it was a statement.

"I think so." I shrugged. "I have no proof."

"The lawyer can only try to save me from others."

"You're worth saving."

"I thought that once. No more."

"Your sister loves you."

"She loves the person she thinks I am, not the person I am." He turned and looked down at the bright spinnakers. "I've spent the last thirty years of my life trying to live purely, but I'm no purer than when I came here. I'm the same person I was in Vietnam, the same one I've always been."

"I doubt it."

"Anger and lust, and maybe pride. Those are the three I could never overcome."

"I'm prone to all seven."

"I've broken all of the commandments."

"Me, too."

He turned back to me. "Have you murdered anyone?"

I shook my head. "I don't think so. I don't know for sure that what happens in war is really murder."

He looked at the gun. "To the dead it makes no difference. I'm not talking about war, though. I'm talking about Melissa."

"What happened?"

He cocked his head to one side in an odd movement, almost like a child might tip its head when pondering an issue. "She was at my house and when she left I asked when she was coming back. She laughed and touched my face with her hand, but said nothing and went away. I felt as though something important — some fundamental loss — had changed my life. I dressed and followed her. Ahead, I could see the light of her flashlight, and I heard voices arguing. I heard Melissa laugh and say she was never going to marry Cabot. Then the voices stopped and I heard a car drive away and I went on and found Melissa. Her flashlight had fallen, and I could see her on the ground, rubbing her head. I held her and touched her face and she struck at me and told me to go away, that she'd never marry me. She seemed dazed. Her voice was wild." His voice stopped, then started again. "I gave her a shake to quiet her and she was quiet. Then I saw that she was dead and realized that she'd called me Alfred as she struck at me." He paused, then held up the hand that didn't hold the nail gun, and looked at it. "I'd killed the only one I loved."

"It was an accident."

"Back in Vietnam I killed a lot of people. I had a talent for it."

"Yes. But you were a soldier and that was your job."

"Did you know that I joined the army

after a girl ditched me?"

"Jed Mullins told me that."

"Did he tell you that I felt like killing her and then myself?"

"No. He said he thought you might have become a sniper because of her."

"I think he was right."

"But you were a soldier then, and this death was an accident."

He shook his head. "It doesn't make any difference. She's dead and I killed her."

I didn't like that gun in his hand. "It does make a difference. Come with me. We'll go to your lawyer."

He put his free hand on my shoulder. "Did you ever think you've lived long enough?"

I felt both the strength of his hand and a charge of fear. "No. And I don't think you should think that, either."

The strong hand squeezed my shoulder. "Don't you sometimes think you've done enough damage? That it's time to stop, before you do more?"

"No." I looked into his weary eyes, trying to see his soul, then suddenly I felt the gun press against my belly.

"Back over to that wall, J.W."

He dropped his hand from my shoulder and pushed lightly on my chest. I wondered if I could knock the gun down before he could use it, but decided that I could not. I backed slowly to the wall. When I was there, he backed to the edge of the deck.

"The world has had enough of me," he said. "There are two documents in my house. One is for the police and one is for my sister. Will you make sure they get them?"

"Don't do this."

"Will you make sure?"

"Yes. But please don't do this."

He stood on his toes on the lip of the deck, his back to the pond. He put the gun in his mouth, and pulled the trigger. His body arched backward and fell out of my sight.

Behind me, some carpenter shouted in horror, and I heard the clatter of work boots running toward the deck. But by then Roland Nunes was in that far country from which no traveler returns.

I was making supper at home that evening when Zee's little Jeep pulled into the yard. As I went to the door, Zee stepped out, wearing her going-to-America summer shirt and shorts. The kids came running and I swept them up in my arms and got good kisses before I put them down and exchanged some better ones with Zee. It seemed like she'd been gone for a year, and I didn't want to let go of her.

But we did unwind our arms, finally, and she smiled up at me, with her great, dark eyes shining, and said, "Gee, maybe I'll go away more often."

"I hope not," I said. "How was your trip?"

"It was fine, but I'm glad to be home. How was bachelor life?"

"I have nothing good to say for it. I'll tell you about it later."

"Shall we unload the car? I did some heavy-duty shopping on the way here."

Whenever an islander takes a car to the mainland, the car returns stuffed with paper towels, toilet paper, food, drink, other supplies, and a full tank of gas, all purchased at mainland prices.

"We can unpack later," I said. "Right now, supper is about to be served."

"Perfect timing."

We all went inside. Joshua and Diana ran around as though they'd never been there before. Then we sat at the table and ate flounder, rice, and peas, and talked.

"Pa, you know what I liked best in America?"

"What, Diana?"

"The Whaling museum in New Bedford.

We went there and they have a real whaling ship only it's only half size!"

"I like that museum, too," I said.

"And we went to see baseball teams play."

"We saw the Pawtucket Red Sox," explained her big brother. "And we went up to Boston, too, and saw the Boston Red Sox play. We saw Trot Nixon. He almost ran into us catching a ball!"

"We were over in the right-field grandstands," said Zee. "About three seats in. Trot Nixon had to reach right into the stands to catch a foul ball. I thought he was going to land in my lap."

"Trot has good instincts."

"And, Pa?"

"What, Joshua?"

"We went and saw some humongous houses! Even bigger than the ones they're building here! Where was that, Ma?"

"Newport," said Zee. She looked at me over her wineglass. "The Breakers. We took the tour."

"It always reminds me of this place," I said. "Don't you agree?"

"No, it doesn't!" said Diana. "It's lots bigger!"

"Well, maybe a little bigger."

"Lots bigger!"

"But it doesn't have a tree house."

"Can we play there after supper, Pa?"

"Why not? It's summertime and there's plenty of light. You can play in the tree house, and after your mother and I unload the car we'll have a cognac on the balcony so we can see each other."

The children said that was an excellent idea, so that's what we did.

When the car was unpacked, Zee and I went to the balcony, where we sat close together and watched Joshua and Diana scrambling around the big beech tree in our backyard. The evening light slanted over our heads and out over Sengekontacket Pond, making the far barrier beach glow like gold. Some cars were still parked beside the highway on the beach while their owners enjoyed a final swim or a picnic. Beyond them, on the dark water of Nantucket Sound, boats were headed for harbor. Paradise enow. I felt blessed.

That night, in bed, when Zee's body finally disentangled itself from mine, we lay close together and talked in quiet voices. I told her of my week and of its consequences.

"Nothing good came of it," I said, "and nothing good will."

"None of it was your fault."

"I shot two men."

"They deserved it."

"Probably. I haven't lost any sleep over them. But look at the rest of it. Two people dead. Both good people."

"Bad things happen."

"He spent most of his life atoning for the acts his government asked him to perform. That's more than most of us do."

"But he killed the woman."

"It was an accident. Manslaughter at the worst, I think. It didn't register with him until afterward that she thought she was fighting off Cabot."

"He killed her in anger."

"Maybe so. Jed Mullins thought Nunes became a sniper because he hated the girl who left him. Maybe he had some sort of flashback when he heard Melissa say she wasn't going to marry him. Maybe he was shaking that girl from his youth. Of course this is all just ten-cent psychology."

"You liked him." Her voice was sleepy.

"I barely knew him, but yes, I liked him. Until the very end, I never thought he'd killed her."

"You couldn't save him."

"No, and I couldn't save his land, either. Now Sally Oliver has it and she'll sell it to some castle builder and he'll close off the ancient way and all of this will have been for nothing."

She yawned and snuggled close. "Maybe the District Attorney can prove that she and Cabot were responsible for the vandalism. He seems to have a good case."

"He may have a good case, but who's going to bring charges? Roland Nunes is dead and Sally certainly isn't going to complain to the police. No charges, no trial, no jail, no fines. The bad guys walk away without a scratch."

"Maybe Carole Cohen can bring charges."

"Maybe."

A bit later she was asleep, her arm across my chest, her breathing soft and regular.

Our room was dimly lit by starlight, and as I stared at the ceiling I seemed to see a greater darkness, and thought of wise old Khayyam who wrote that life was but a Magic Shadow show, played in a box whose candle is the sun.

But then I looked down at Zee, her starlit face ringed with tumbled, blue-black hair that created an ebony halo against her pillow, and I felt her body against mine, and I thought of our children sleeping in their rooms, and I knew that there was light in my life in spite of the darkness, in spite of death, in spite of stupidity, in spite of madness and cruelty and injustice, in spite of the Void. And I felt blessed.

SHERRIED BLACK BEAN SOUP

This wonderful, hearty soup is a meal in itself. Delish!

1 tablespoon olive oil
1/2 cup thinly sliced carrots
1 small onion, chopped
2 stalks celery, thinly sliced
4 cloves garlic, minced
2 teaspoons ground cumin
4 cups water
Two 15-ounce cans black beans, rinsed and
   drained
1 cup sliced turkey kielbasa
1/4 cup dry sherry
1 teaspoon instant chicken bouillon granules
2 bay leaves
1 teaspoon dried oregano, crushed
1/8 teaspoon ground red pepper
1 cup frozen or canned corn kernels

1 to 2 cups cooked spiral pasta (optional)
1/4 cup sour cream for garnish

In a 3-quart Dutch oven, heat the oil. Sauté the carrots, onion, celery, and garlic in the hot oil over medium-low heat for about 3 minutes. Add the cumin and cook until the carrots are tender. Stir in the 4 cups water, beans, kielbasa, sherry, bouillon granules, bay leaves, oregano, and ground red pepper. Bring to a boil and reduce the heat.

Simmer, uncovered, for 15 minutes. Add the corn kernels and continue to cook for 10 minutes more. Remove and discard the bay leaves and add the cooked pasta (if using). Ladle into bowls and top each one with some of the sour cream.

Serves 4

Sweet Potato Soup

This is a winter solstice favorite at the Jackson house.

2 tablespoons butter
1 cup chopped onion
2 small stalks celery, chopped (reserve leaves for garnish or use dried sage leaves)
1 medium leek, sliced (white and light green parts)
1 large clove garlic, chopped

1/4 pounds red-skinned sweet potatoes (yams), peeled and cut into 1-inch cubes (about 5 cups)
4 cups chicken stock
1 cinnamon stick
1/4 teaspoon ground nutmeg
1 1/2 cups half and half
2 tablespoons pure maple syrup
Salt and pepper to taste

Melt the butter in a large heavy pot over medium-high heat. Sauté the onion in the butter for 5 minutes. Add the celery and leeks and sauté until the onion is translucent (about 5 minutes). Add the garlic and sauté 2 minutes. Add the potatoes, stock, and spices. Bring to a boil, reduce the heat, and simmer, uncovered, until the potatoes are tender (about 20 minutes). Remove the cinnamon stick. Puree the soup in a blender (in batches). Return the soup to the pot and add the half and half and maple syrup. Season with salt and pepper. Serve hot, sprinkled with chopped celery leaves or dried sage leaves.

Serves 6 as a first course

GAZPACHO

This refreshing vegetable soup is best served icy cold.

1 small onion
2 cloves garlic
3 green peppers, seeded
4 tomatoes, peeled and seeded
1 cucumber, peeled
1/2 teaspoon chili powder
1/3 cup olive oil
3 cups tomato juice
1/4 cup lemon juice
1/4 cup dry sherry
Salt and pepper to taste
1/2 cup sour cream for garnish

Chop the vegetables in a food processor until finely chopped. Mix in other ingredients and chill. Serve cold with a dollop of sour cream on each bowl for garnish.

Serves 4

ABOUT THE AUTHOR

Philip R. Craig grew up on a small cattle ranch southeast of Durango, Colorado. He earned his MFA at the University of Iowa Writers' Workshop and was for many years a professor of literature at Wheelock College in Boston. He and his wife live on Martha's Vineyard. His Web site is www.philip rcraig.com.

The employees of Thorndike Press hope you have enjoyed this Large Print book. All our Thorndike and Wheeler Large Print titles are designed for easy reading, and all our books are made to last. Other Thorndike Press Large Print books are available at your library, through selected bookstores, or directly from us.

For information about titles, please call:
  (800) 223-1244

or visit our Web site at:
  www.gale.com/thorndike
  www.gale.com/wheeler

To share your comments, please write:
  Publisher
  Thorndike Press
  295 Kennedy Memorial Drive
  Waterville, ME 04901